THE CORAL PALACE

M. K. HUTCHINS

Immortal Works LLC
1505 Glenrose Drive
Salt Lake City, Utah 84104
Tel: (385) 202-0116

Cover Art by Ashley Literski
http://strangedevotion.wixsite.com/strangedesigns

This book is a work of fiction. Names, characters, businesses, organizations, places, events and incidents either are the product of the author's imagination or are used fictitiously. Any resemblance to actual persons, living or dead, events, or locales is entirely coincidental.

ISBN 978-1-953491-23-7 (Paperback)
ASIN B095PTZ67Q (Kindle Edition)

For Emmeline

CHAPTER ONE

Cooking in a cramped safehouse was less than ideal, but at least our cellar was well stocked. I tasted a piece of the celery I'd brined overnight. It crunched, delightfully bright with vinegar and balanced with notes of salt, honey, and spicy garlic. Just what my patient needed.

I filled a bowl with steamed buckwheat and drizzled a bit of warm cherry jam on one side. Then I thin-sliced the pickled celery into beautiful, pale curls and mounded them opposite the jam.

I cracked the door to my sister's room quietly, in case she was asleep. Dami lay on her mattress, trailing her fingers across the rough wooden wall where the shaft of light from the ventilation window struck it.

"I brought breakfast," I said.

She propped herself up on an elbow, her midriff stiff with bandages from where the arrow had hit her. "Is it that healthy stuff again?"

"Of course. You need to heal."

Dami flopped back on the pillow, her cropped, black hair fanning around her face. "I'd settle for porridge. I swear you're trying to pickle my insides with that muck. Wood caulk tastes better."

I'd more than proved my cooking skills in the palace—there was nothing wrong with the food. I set the bowl firmly next to her.

"Celery targets your ribs. Cherries target muscles. Together, this dish will affect everything that hurts around your cracked ribs. The sour will grant you strength, deadening the pain, and the sweet will give you the endurance you need to recover."

"Porridge?" she pleaded, hands together like a condemned woman facing a noose.

"This is as good as what the king himself eats."

"I'm your sister. Not his," she mumbled.

"You can complain about pickled innards once you've recovered."

She shoved her spoon into the dish, then stirred it around, burying the curls of celery under the fluffy buckwheat. She set it back down. "I'd rather eat military rations than this. Not much of a chef, are you?"

Another morning full of Dami's standard insults. I'd expected both of our near-deaths would have made us close—that we'd be like real sisters again. "It will help you heal."

"Not if I don't eat it." She dangled a piece of celery between her thumb and forefinger, like she held a worm. "See? Useless. What about something like that elk-rib hotpot you made four days ago?"

"I can't buy elk ribs every day. Someone might notice and discover the safehouse. It's not cheap, either," I grumbled.

"Well, then cook up some duck ribs."

"They don't have enough meat on them to really be effective."

"Bah. You're making that up so you can continue your regimen of pickled celery torture. Aren't chefs supposed to help people, not attack them with food?"

I stiffened. "I'm not a traitor."

"Fine. Go poison some Shoreed soldiers, not me."

"I'm not a traitor *to my profession*," I replied tartly. "I'd never attack anyone through life-giving food."

"Lies!" Dami held up the bowl I'd brought. "Behold the pickled celery, instrument of pain and suffering! How I languish under its constant, vinegary barrage!"

What was she, seven years old again? "We can't dawdle in the safehouse forever. Lady Sulat has a mission for us. And you could get an infection if you don't take care of yourself."

"Ugh. Are you actually worried about me?"

"Of course I'm worried! If anyone discovered us right now, your injuries would give you no chance to run away."

Dami lied to the government during wartime, pretending to be a boy so she could join the army. It was a crime she could hang for. She likely would have hung already, if Lady Sulat wasn't hiding and protecting us.

Dami snorted. "If anyone brings me to trial, I'll either be condemned by a bunch of sorry knots of wood like you and hang—in which case my ribs don't matter—or I'll get acquitted for saving General Yuin's life, in which case I can dawdle all I like. Either way, you can bring something other than a bowl of rutting pickles."

"Celery propagates by seeds or cuttings, Dami."

"Gah! Just stop bringing them! I'm fine!"

"Says the woman wrapped in bandages. The whole point, Dami," I said, "is not to stand trial in the first place. I don't think you have any idea how terrifying that is."

When Dami ran off to join the army two and a half months ago, I assumed her identity and took her post at the palace, so no one would find out she'd disappeared. I was nearly executed for my efforts.

And I accidentally learned secrets that could get King Alder dethroned. Not that I'd actually challenge his reign. An upheaval like that in the middle of the war with the Shoreed would only help them conquer us. But King Alder wasn't a man who liked loose ends. If he had the barest hint about Dami's treason or where to find her, he'd name me complicit and see us both hanged.

Dami shrugged that familiar, unconcerned shrug. I should have been used to it, but I kept searching her face for some flicker of compassion, some sign she still cared about me.

"You know," she said, "I might prefer standing trial to this. You're a terrible sister."

If I stayed a moment longer, I'd either start shouting or break down crying. I didn't want to do either in front of Dami. I headed for the door.

"Are you going to fetch me some real food?" Dami asked.

I closed the door behind me without another word and smoothed my skirts to keep myself from clenching my hands. The main room of our underground safehouse wasn't large—a hearth, chimney, a few doors that led into rooms like Dami's, one to a cellar, and one trap door in the ceiling. The four guards nodded respectfully to me and returned to their game of stones. I began a rather ambitious dish for lunch. I started by chopping fresh coriander. Its clean fragrance left no doubt that summer had arrived.

The trapdoor opened, letting in the sound of hammerstone strikes and tinkling obsidian. Our safehouse was under a military weapons workshop, which made it easier to hide the comings and goings here. The guards watched the entrance, but it was just Moss coming down the ladder. He was an older military man, short with gray hair. His beloved bolas hung from his belt, clinking together as he moved.

"Enjoying yourself?" he asked.

"Immensely." Cooking was certainly better than yelling at Dami.

Moss gave me a knowing look. "Yet somehow you look tense."

"That's because I'm a fool." I couldn't even mend her ribs. Why did I hope I could mend our relationship?

"Ah, Plum." Moss sat next to the soldiers and scooped up a set of stones to join in their game. "You'll have to be more specific than that."

"Very funny, Moss." I kept whacking at the herbs with my favorite obsidian knife. I wanted my sister back—the one who tromped through the forest, laughing, as we collected mushrooms together. The one who begged me to make her sweets. The one that got ridiculously muddy with me, digging up river clams. That had been years ago, before she haunted the forests like a wild thing, refusing to help at home. Before she deserted her family to join the army.

"Lady Sulat wants to meet with you this morning."

My shoulders tightened. I chopped faster. "Is this the meeting where she tells me what she wants me and Dami to do?"

"I dunno. She didn't say." Lady Sulat tended to be cautious with information. "You're not worried about it, are you?"

Of course I was, but I tried to calm the emotions on my face. "I'm fine. Do I look nervous?"

"You look homicidal."

I stared down at the coriander, all shredded and bruised into messy confetti, and sighed. I hated it when I couldn't tell Moss he was wrong.

LADY SULAT'S sitting room was as immaculate as always. The polished redwood walls and floors smelled of herbed soap. A trio of vases held summer's first offerings of flowers—delicate white lady's slipper and brilliant pink fireweeds.

I sat on one of the finely carved chairs decorated with chickadees and pine boughs, fidgeting with my sleeves. The fabric still seemed too long, reaching down to my elbows—an indication of my advancement into the green rank.

Lady Sulat swept in from her bedroom, her infant asleep and wrapped snugly to her chest. Her acorn-colored dress draped gracefully down to her mid-forearms, indicating her blue rank—one step higher than mine, one step below the king's. I stood, but she immediately gestured for me to sit again.

I tried to radiate calm confidence, despite my clammy palms. Lady Sulat had, in many ways, saved my life. I didn't want to disappoint her.

She took the chair next to mine, her face as serene and unreadable as always. "I'm surprised to find the great hero of Rowak looking so uncomfortable."

So much for calm confidence.

No guards stood with us in the room, but I could see their

silhouettes outside the cloth-backed, lattice doors. I should have felt comfortable there, secluded and protected. I tried to bow from my chair, but of course that didn't work well.

"There's no shame in being nervous, but you should try to hide it." Lady Sulat studied me. She'd honed her ability to read people with the aid of her birthgift—perceptive-of-eye. I felt like a dozen eagles were picking me over. I straightened my posture and folded my hands neatly in my lap.

"Dami is not yet recovered, I hear."

I refrained from dropping a hundred apologies or vomiting up insults against my stubborn sister. "That's correct."

"Before I can send you out of the capital for this mission, she needs to be in excellent shape."

I knew Lady Sulat wasn't going to keep us in the palace—it wasn't safe for either of us to be so close to King Alder—but I hadn't realized we'd be leaving Askan-Wod. "How far away are we going?"

"It's for a task that you're uniquely suited to," she said, not answering my question at all.

"Someone's ill?" I asked.

Lady Sulat pursed her lips. "No. But you will almost certainly run into members of the Bloodmarrows."

Poisoners. Spies. Traitors. I'd uncovered their agent in the Redwood Palace, a young woman named Violet, who'd tried to kill Lady Sulat. "You've found another location where you think they're active?"

"Yes."

"Is it in one of our forts? In Napil?"

"Plum, I'm still working on the arrangements for your travel. I'll tell you more when it's settled and your sister is recovered."

Dami would be nearly better by now if I'd gotten her to listen to me. I bit the inside of my lip, my face burning with shame.

Lady Sulat noticed. "I've heard from Moss that Dami is being stubborn. If it's any consolation, you couldn't leave yet anyway. I've assigned two of my best soldiers in Napil to accompany you. There will be a fifth person as well, but arranging that is taking more time than expected."

Hope lurched through me. "Is Bane, perhaps, that fifth person?"

I didn't want to leave him behind. Bane had listened to me when I'd needed help. He'd ridden a Hungry Ghost with me. And he absolutely cared whether I lived or died, unlike my sister.

Lady Sulat gently shook her head. "I'm afraid it isn't him. Do you really want to pull Bane into danger with you?"

Guilt flooded in to replace my longing. "No. I suppose not."

"Moss already knows the details I've shared with you, and you may inform Dami. I realize it would probably be impossible to hide from Bane that you're leaving, but please refrain from informing anyone else."

I nodded. The fewer people who knew, the less chance King Alder had of learning about our plans—or about my technically-treasonous sister.

"I will pay the fine for you leaving your position as a palace servant early, so you need not worry about your parents," Lady Sulat continued. "When you leave, I'll spread quiet rumors that your sudden notoriety was too stressful, and you've left on a pilgrimage of family shrines. That way, there will be no single location you're supposed to be at."

"Thank you for caring for my family."

"Of course." She patted her infant's back, even though he hadn't stirred. "Since you have roughly two weeks to prepare, I want you to make the most of them. You need to study poisons."

My gut recoiled at the thought. Food was supposed to be wholesome and healing. Chefs were supposed to look to the health of those they served. But Lady Sulat was right: if I was familiar with Violet's poisons, I'd be able to spot them more easily. Perhaps I could even make a number of antidotes to have on hand in case the Bloodmarrows moved against us. I nodded.

"Now that Master Chef Hawak is back and tending to the kitchens, I've asked Green-ranked Sorrel of Westbank to catalogue all of Violet's poisons with their known effects and any noted treatments. He was eager to help. Over the past few days, he's become quite adept at translating her ciphers."

The only thing worse than studying poisons was studying *Sorrel's* notes on poisons. We'd been engaged, once, but I broke it off to cover for Dami at the Redwood Palace. Sorrel dealt with his heartbreak by marrying Violet, not knowing she was a Bloodmarrow. I'd gotten Violet arrested for poisoning and then she'd died in prison. Sorrel took his grief out on me. With his fists.

He knew, now, that Violet had actually been guilty. He'd even helped me escape prison after he learned the truth.

But I couldn't forget the way he'd looked at me when he thought I was a traitor. I couldn't forget the way he'd raised his hand to me, just because he could. Because he was angry. Because he hurt, and he wanted me to hurt, too.

My bruises had healed. I knew Sorrel didn't have any reason to want to hurt me now. But that didn't stop a cold unease from wriggling up my bones. I didn't want to spend hours reading his handwriting. I didn't want to be reminded, hour after hour, that he was in Askan-Wod with me.

"Sorrel's not the fifth person, is he?" This time, I didn't manage to stop my voice from quavering.

Lady Sulat peered at me. "No. But he has agreed to take you on as an assistant. You'll report to him every morning and work alongside him until it's time for you to leave."

"Report to him...in *person?*"

"Yes. Starting today. You should get moving. He's expecting you."

CHAPTER TWO

Moss escorted me out of Lady Sulat's apartments. I dragged my feet through the butterfly garden. All the sweetness of a dozen different blooming flowers didn't stop me from feeling like a limp bear carcass waiting for butchering. I wanted to sit down and refuse to work with Sorrel, but I couldn't bring myself to actually do it. My country needed me to learn poisons. I'd be safe; Moss was with me. Sorrel had even apologized for his actions.

But I still wanted to run the other way.

"After all that time you spent fawning over Sorrel like a drunken puppy, I thought you'd be excited about this," Moss remarked.

"Well, I'm not."

Moss shrugged and blessedly gave up on teasing me. He led me past a number of gardens to a guest house—a smaller building than Lady Sulat's with the same wooden shingles hanging over broad porches, supported by redwood pillars like most palace buildings.

"This is where Sorrel's staying. There are four living quarters in this guest house; his is the west door," Moss said.

I started up the porch. Each step groaned under my feet. The warming morning air stung my nose with the scent of weathered wood and old paint. Somewhere in a nearby garden, I caught a hint of self-heal and creeping mint. How I wished I could go sit among those plants instead of coming here. I raised my hand and knocked.

Sorrel immediately jerked the door open. "Plum! I'm so glad you came." He smiled magnanimously, like I was an honored guest instead of an assistant assigned by Lady Sulat. "I was beginning to worry."

Gingery perfume wafted from his neatly-groomed hair. A red tunic I'd never seen before draped over him, as richly colored and bright as a carnelian. Even his fingernails and hands were scrubbed to perfection, any hint of kitchen toils erased.

I stared at those perfectly clean hands. I'd felt those fists on my jaw. How could they look so innocent now?

"Plum?" Sorrel dipped his head, trying to catch my gaze. "Are you well? Shall I go fetch you some of Hawak's whole-duck stock?"

"No, I'm fine." This was an opportunity, I told myself, to practice schooling my face. I smiled. It made my teeth ache, like eating a fistful of snow in winter. "Let's begin."

"Yes, do come in. We shouldn't delay. Creating a reference of cures is important for military intelligence," Sorrel said, oblivious that I'd shortly be using that intelligence directly against the Bloodmarrows.

The furnishings inside weren't as grand as Lady Sulat's, but they were certainly as clean. Had he called for a servant, or had he polished everything himself? Somehow, he'd managed to make the room smell of forget-me-nots instead of wood cleaner. I doubted anyone who wasn't perceptive-of-taste-and-smell would have noticed.

Moss remained outside, his silhouette just visible through the cloth-backed lattice door.

"I'll show you what I've started," Sorrel said.

We knelt next to the same low desk. He opened a manuscript box, set the lid to one side, and began turning pages from the main box into the lid.

"I've given each poison its own page. Then, if future researchers come across new information, there's plenty of space to add it. The majority of her notes are on how to make concentrated forms of poison that could easily be slipped into food and drink. I've also gone through the letters she received from her father, but most of those are enigmatic and not particularly useful."

How carefully he avoided saying *Violet*, the name of his dead wife. It couldn't be easy, thinking about the Bloodmarrow poisoner who'd pretended to love him. Would the other Bloodmarrows I faced be as innocent-looking as Violet had been? I couldn't pay attention to the next page Sorrel summarized. Would I be clever enough to keep me and Dami safe from them, or would we die together, boiled from the inside out by some horrible concoction masquerading as breakfast?

"Ah, I'm boring you," Sorrel apologized. So solicitous. "Would you prefer to decipher directly from her notes?"

I needed to learn all I could about poisons and their effects before leaving. "No. I'm sorry. I was distracted. Please continue."

He shifted the manuscript box closer to me, bringing himself with it. Our elbows were almost touching. Sorrel continued reading it out for me. Maybe I was imagining it, but he seemed to get infinitesimally closer with every sentence.

"Would you prefer for me to read by myself?" I asked when I couldn't stand it any longer. "You could work on unraveling more of Violet's notes in the meantime. I'll join you when I've caught up on your progress so far."

His face drooped. "Oh. I mean, of course you don't need me to coddle you. I'm...sorry that things started so poorly with us. I've always admired your cooking skill."

Except when he'd thought I was using it to poison people. I politely inclined my head. "Thank you."

His smile returned. "I'm grateful we have this chance to work together. Lady Sulat truly is insightful when it comes to people."

The words left my insides cold. Why did he think she'd sent me?

As I studied the pages he'd decoded so far, I occasionally glanced up at him, working at the second desk. Most of the time, he was already staring back at me. My skin itched all over in the stifling summer heat. I flipped the pages over to the letters Sorrel had mentioned, the ones from Violet's father, Chef Palaw.

Dearest Daughter. I managed to delay the caravan back to the Coral Palace, forcing LOA to spend the night on the road. She continues to amaze me. She did not reappear in her bedroom in the morning.

"Strange, isn't it? Even decoded, it makes no sense," Sorrel said.

I jumped. I hadn't heard him walk up behind me. He laid a lingering hand on my shoulder. "I didn't mean to startle you."

"I'm fine." I smiled, even as my gut churned.

"You don't look fine. Shall I go fetch us lunch?"

"Yes, please."

He trailed his hand off my shoulder and down my arm before finally breaking contact. I smoothed my sleeves, swallowed the fear roiling up my throat, and told myself Sorrel wasn't important.

I reread the letter. It made perfect sense to me. A Hungry Ghost might look human during the day and only appear ghostly at night. Regardless, at sunrise or sunset, a Hungry Ghost returned to the place they died—involuntarily, and with an uncanny speed that Fulsaan had described as quite unpleasant.

Clearly, Chef Palaw suspected LOA was a ghost. For a moment, I thought maybe this would be my mission: exorcising LOA by cooking her the perfect meal. But the Coral Palace was Shoreed's capital, and Chef Palaw's test confirmed that this woman *wasn't* a Hungry Ghost.

Sorrel returned with skewers of roasted rabbit meat and buckwheat branches smothered in gravy. Apparently, the apprentice chefs still took kindly to him.

"Eat well." He dished me up first with those too-clean hands. When he set the bowl in front of me, I flinched. I didn't like him coming so close.

"Is something wrong?"

"No. Not at all." Had I really thought he was going to hit me again, just because we sat in the same room? The last time we'd spoken, he hadn't been angry. I shouldn't expect hatred now.

Moss was right outside. He might needle me now and again, but I'd seen him use those bolas. I was safe with him here. I started eating.

Sorrel lowered his voice. "I don't know that I ever properly apologized."

"A-apologized?" I wished there was no need for food. That we could work straight through the day, without this obvious lull for conversation.

"For my behavior. When I visited you during your incarceration, I thought you were a traitor. I'm sorry. Sorry beyond measure."

What prerogative did he have to beat traitors?

"I've been thinking about that often. How foolish I was. I should have seen who you were, Green-ranked Plum of Clamsriver."

"I..." I didn't want to talk about the past.

"Here. Eat." He piled my bowl with more of the rabbit. "The gravy's a touch over-salted, but the rabbit is perfect."

I nibbled. Swallowed. "You're right. The rabbit is exquisite."

Smoky and juicy from the coals, pleasantly spicy-sweet from a maple-hotradish glaze. My muscles relaxed as its effects coursed through me.

"Tanoak said he prepared the rabbit himself. He's budding into quite the chef," Sorrel said.

We made small talk about the kitchen staff. That seemed safe enough until Sorrel mentioned that one of the apprentices, Dewar, had just gotten engaged. "He's very happy," Sorrel remarked.

I thought his expression would fall, thinking of Violet, but he continued smiling softly at me.

"I shall have to offer him my congratulations, then," I said.

"I know all too well that a bad marriage can make a man miserable, but I still believe a good marriage brings exceeding joy."

"I suppose so," I replied blandly, stirring my last bits of buckwheat and gravy together. I wasn't hungry anymore.

"Here, I want to show you something." Sorrel moved Violet's things off his desk and fetched a different manuscript box. "This just arrived from my father's library. He imported it at great cost—before the war, of course."

Sorrel opened the box and began turning pages.

Illustrated recipes—beautifully illustrated recipes—filled each page. Some were for familiar ingredients, like celeriac. Others discussed the care of food not available in Rowak, like oysters and bittercress. Another displayed a technique I'd never seen—baking a whole duck in clay.

It felt like Sorrel had revealed a treasure trove and was letting me run my fingers through the sapphires.

"This...this is amazing!" I laughed out loud, marveling at the next page—a recipe for popping cattails. The pictures made the resulting kernels look like billowing clouds. I wondered if they tasted that way, too.

Sorrel turned another page. "That's the first time I've seen you really smile all day. I'm glad you like it."

"May I...may I read it occasionally? I know we have work to do, but..." But how could I *not* read it? I wanted to lose myself in those recipes, in descriptions of simmering seaweed, grilled mussels, and poached seagull eggs.

Sorrel squeezed my hand. I imagined him grinding my bones together and my breath caught in my throat. But he merely leaned closer and whispered, "It's yours."

I stared at him. He couldn't be giving me something this rare. "I don't understand."

"It's a gift. An apology. I was working up the courage to bring it to you myself, but then Lady Sulat sent you to me. I thank my Ancestors that, despite my blindness, I've been granted this second chance to be exceedingly happy with you."

Sorrel didn't want to hit me. He was courting me. The kindness, the food, this manuscript.

All my delight rotted in the pit of my stomach. I slowly pulled my hand away from his. I kept my eyes on the floor instead of on the lovely illustrations of those ethereal-looking crabs. "This is too great a gift. I can't accept."

My words came out half-strangled. I didn't want to turn away this treasure trove of knowledge.

"Can you...will you..." he fumbled, voice low. Not that keeping his voice down would stop Moss from hearing—but Sorrel probably didn't know that Moss was perceptive-of-ear. "Plum, forgive me. I beg you. I should have been more patient. I should have sought out the reason you broke off our engagement. I was hurt and I acted rashly. I was rash again after...after she died. But I don't want to be miserable for the rest of my life."

Wasn't he being rash now, rushing back to me?

I could still imagine the two of us, pouring over recipes and cooking together, laughing and throwing buckwheat flour at each other in the kitchen. But I also knew I'd always look at his hands with distrust. That just because I could marry a person didn't mean I should.

"Sorrel, I can forgive you. I can work with you on this project. I admire your forthright apology." I bit my lip. I hated that Moss was hearing any of this. "But the past is past. It's gone, like...like..."

I tried to remember some saying of Nana's that poetically involved water in a river and failed. "It's like a bowl of soggy buckwheat noodles. There's no way to fix it, to bring it back."

"So we start over," Sorrel whispered, hopeful.

Pain tinged the corners of his eyes. I don't know if it was pain over Violet or pain over me. I hated myself for empathizing, for wanting to reassure him. I understood him, I thought. He'd had a certain vision of the future—a vision of cooking with a skilled wife and being happy—and it had shattered around him. Just like my vision had.

But I couldn't have that quiet village life now, separated from politics. And I couldn't lie to myself that the bruises Sorrel left on me meant nothing.

"Marriage isn't the only road to happiness," I said. Dami's fondness for punching people jumped to mind. "And I wouldn't make you happy anyway."

"I think you would."

Fine. Marrying him would make *me* miserable. But it seemed cruel to say out loud. "Let's get back to work."

He reluctantly laid all those beautiful pages back in their box. "Even if you won't accept it, I'll leave this here so you can read it."

"Thank you." But I didn't read it. I returned to my desk and continued studying his notes. Poisons seemed so drab compared to all the graceful limbs of those crabs.

At last evening came. Moss knocked on the lattice door. I stood and bowed. "I'll return tomorrow to continue our work."

"I eagerly await your return, Plum."

He spoke my name softly and bowed almost reverently. It wasn't the demeanor of a man who'd accepted my rejection. It was the quiet perseverance of a man who knew he had plenty of time, day by day, to change my mind.

If I had to, I'd ram Dami's pickled celery down her throat tonight with my spoon. I wasn't going to spend weeks sitting in this room with Sorrel staring at me like that.

"THAT WAS MORE awkward than I'd anticipated." Moss's words lacked their usual teasing tone. We walked together on the gravel path, toward the palace gate. Lady Sulat was fairly certain King Alder wouldn't risk murdering me in the palace in broad daylight, but kidnapping me in the middle of the night and disposing of my corpse was another matter. It was time to get back to the safehouse.

"It went better than I'd hoped."

"Really?" Moss almost sounded concerned.

This conversation could only spiral into mocking and innuendo. I trailed my fingers along a rhododendron bush as we passed, pretending I hadn't heard the question.

We exited the palace and headed north, the opposite direction of the safehouse. Moss liked to be circuitous. We strolled through a residential neighborhood where most of the doors were marked with black ribbons, showing support for the prisoner exchange. I wished there were more. If the exchange had overwhelming popular support, King Alder would be cornered into trading the Shoreed soldiers we'd captured during the failed coup for Rowak prisoners of war.

By the time we reached the market, the early summer sun was low in the sky, lengthening the shadows and enriching colors everywhere. Grocers still displayed their crinkly beet greens and scarlet radishes while merchants crowed about having the best cloth, bricks of salt, or amber hair ornaments. Servants and housewives haggled over the price of buckwheat while their children ran beneath the thatched stall awnings in a never-ending mass game that I didn't know the rules to.

"I still have a hard time believing the market is open every day. It's like a perpetual fair."

"It is the capital," Moss said. We turned down another street, one with a few wayhouses as well as merchants.

"I wasn't complaining." I wondered if the place Lady Sulat was sending me to would have a market like this, or if it would be a smaller town, like the one I'd grown up in. Even the buildings here were taller, many of them boasting two stories.

On one such building, a figure suddenly stood up. He nocked an arrow—and aimed at me.

"Moss!"

I turned to run out of the way, but Moss's reflexes were faster than mine. He tackled me hard to the ground. An arrow thudded next to us in the dirt.

CHAPTER THREE

Someone screamed. Someone else shouted for the city watch. Moss ripped me to my feet and yanked me into an alley reeking of refuse and old soup. He gestured for me to stand with my back flat against the wall, in the shadows.

My hands shook against the cold wall and my heart raced madly, but I obeyed, remaining as still and silent as possible. Moss nodded slightly in approval.

I breathed shallowly through my mouth, eyes and ears open. There were three arrows in the street in front of us, clustered together. Moss already had his bolas in hand, gleaming dimly in the poor light of the alley. The shoulder of his black uniform was dark with blood. One of those arrows had grazed him, but not too badly, judging by the size of the stain. He'd need my help as soon as we were somewhere safe.

"I think the assassin's gone," Moss whispered as a pair of city watchmen ran our way. "I've got to get those arrows."

Moss sprinted into the middle of the road and scooped all three of them up. The watchmen stumbled to a stop just in front of him. They wore crisp blue and white uniforms—officers under the Minister of the Interior, not the military.

"I saw the assailant running that way." Moss waved behind us.

"Those arrows are evidence, and you'll hand them over *now*," the older of the two watchmen demanded.

Despite his bleeding shoulder, Moss acted nonchalant. He turned to show off his armband. "I'm military. Authorized."

"You don't have jurisdiction. This isn't a battlefield." The watchman laid a hand on the mace hanging from his sash.

Moss adjusted his grip on his bolas. "It *could* be a battlefield if you don't want to file your complaint peaceably with the Minister of Military Affairs."

"I can have you arrested for interfering with an investigation."

"And I can break both your ankles before you get a step closer," Moss responded.

Moss was in no condition to fight; I couldn't just stay in the alley and let things escalate. I rushed out onto the street and bowed politely to the officers. They startled at my appearance, shuffling a half-step back.

"What my bodyguard means to say is that we're very grateful for your help," I said in a smooth, calm voice. "He's being stubbornly loyal about protecting my identity. I apologize. I assure you that this *is* a military matter."

With an unarmed woman standing between him and Moss, the officer's hand dropped off the mace. "I'm afraid you're mistaken, miss. An attack in Askan-Wod falls under the Department of the Interior."

"Ah, it usually would." I stepped closer and lowered my voice. "Can I trust you?"

The two men looked at each other, then nodded with puzzled frowns.

"I don't want to alarm the city, but that was probably a Shoreed assassin, seeking vengeance."

The oldest pursed his lips. "What do you think you did that would merit Shoreed hunting for your head?"

I bowed again. "My name is Plum of Clamsriver."

Their eyes widened. They'd heard of me, then, and the role I'd played in foiling Shoreed's coup. I wanted to collapse with relief but put on a warm smile instead. "The military will, of course, investigate this matter fully, but in the meantime, we deeply appreciate the quick response of the Askan-Wod city watch."

"I will still report this to my superiors," the older said firmly. He leaned to the side to stare straight at Moss. "Your name?"

"Lieutenant Yellow-ranked Moss of Askan-Wod."

The watchman's mouth twitched, like he was contemplating further protest.

I wasn't going to wait around for any of that. "Thank you for your diligence."

I hooked my arm through Moss's and strode the other way at a brisk pace.

"I could have taken them," Moss grumbled.

"You *shouldn't* if you don't have to. Think of your injured shoulder."

Moss scowled. "If you'd gotten yourself hurt stepping out like that..."

We turned a corner. The watchmen weren't following. "Now is not the time to get sentimental on me. Where do we go from here?"

"This way."

Rushing through the streets with Moss made my head spin, and after talking to the watchmen, my mouth felt as dry as well-cured firewood. But I still noticed the white-knuckled way Moss clutched those arrows. He'd been ready to fight two men to keep them in his possession.

"Those aren't Shoreed arrows, are they?" I asked.

"That's what I intend to find out."

WE MADE it to the weapons workshop over the safehouse. Moss sent one of the flintknappers to fetch a man named Oshun. I tried to drag Moss down to the safehouse so I could properly see to his wound, but he didn't want to come and go that often, especially since the knappers knew we were here. Instead, I asked the knappers if they kept bandages handy in case of accidents. A helpful young man handed me a box.

Moss and I settled in the single office of the workshop on the first floor. Moss laid out the three arrows on the low desk and stared at them while I folded his sleeve over his shoulder and cleaned away the blood. At least the arrow had been obsidian—the cut was clean, though deeper than I'd expected. I bandaged it snugly.

"You'll need to keep this washed. As for food..." I pursed my lips, thinking of what was in season. "A salad of strawberries and grated parsnips, drizzled with blackberry molasses and a splash of vinegar would do you a world of good."

The top of the parsnip would target his shoulder; strawberries targeted blood. The sour vinegar, which gave strength, would relieve his immediate pain while the sweet would grant the endurance his flesh needed to knit back together.

"It's not that bad."

"Stop trying to act tough or I'll pour the vinegar *on* your wound. For all I know, those arrows were poisoned."

Moss paused. "I suppose it could have been Bloodmarrows." He motioned me to sit by him. "Do they look poisoned?"

I bent carefully over each arrow and smelled. Wood, sinew, stone, feathers—no whiff of anything strange. I picked one up and turned it by the shaft. Like its fellow, the tip had snapped off. I didn't see anything on it, but poison could have been swabbed onto the missing part. "They don't, but that's not proof of anything. We should have someone watch over you in your sleep, just in case."

Moss grunted. "Which means staying in the safehouse, so you can treat me if there is a problem. I was looking forward to going home tonight."

He had a granddaughter—his first—that he absolutely doted on.

"When we know you're well, we can ask Lady Sulat to give you an extra day off."

Moss shook his head. "After this? No. I'll stick to you until you're off on Lady Sulat's mission. That's my job, Plum. When you're gone, I'll take a whole week off."

I knew Moss wasn't coming on the mission. But hearing him say it aloud like that made me feel small and alone all over again. Moss had kept me safe for so long.

I set the arrows down. Arrows that had been meant for me. "I'm sorry you were hurt protecting me."

"That's my job, Plum. I'm supposed to catch arrows for you—with myself if I'm too daft to figure out any other way to do it."

Despite Lady Sulat's worry, I hadn't expected to need saving. Not like this.

"Don't look so morose," Moss huffed. "You think this is the first scar I've earned?"

Before I could think of what to say, the lattice door slid open. A man at least a decade Moss's senior entered, his hands and face a multitude of fine wrinkles. He headed straight to the arrowheads on the desk without asking for introductions. Carefully, he turned them over with long, scarred fingers. "These are flintknapped like military arrowheads."

"I knew that much, Oshun," Moss said.

Why would these be military arrowheads? I frowned. "They *shattered*. Doesn't the military make better weapons than that?"

"We make a variety of arrowheads." Oshun's voice was as worn as his hands. "These are difficult to make—just thick enough to puncture through skin, just thin enough to shatter when they hit bone."

I peered at him. "Why would you make arrowheads you can't reuse?"

"The shaft's the hard part to make and that, we could salvage. But think about an arrowhead, shattered inside your muscles. The more you move, the more the obsidian shards tear through your body. Even if you found a surgeon before you bled out, good luck removing all the pieces. Guards prefer to use barbed arrows; the injured usually live long enough to be interrogated."

"Barbed?"

"Prongs on the end. Rips you just as bad coming out as going in."

Who thought of these things? For a moment, I remembered that night on the Old Road, the Shoreed soldiers dead around me. Which kind of arrows had killed them? Shattering? Barbed? Did it matter? I leaned back from that desk. I wished we only needed obsidian for kitchen knives and hunting deer.

"Good thing you were just grazed," Oshun said. "You'd be dead by this time tomorrow with one of these in you."

I glanced between Oshun and Moss. "So, it was a Shoreed assassin?"

The Rowak military couldn't be behind it—Lady Sulat and her husband, General Yuin, practically *were* the military.

Oshun lifted up the shards. "Not Shoreed. Their obsidian is usually green-tinted or speckled with impurities. The Rowak military buys up the grayish stuff from Napil. This is true black—the kind of stuff merchants in Rowak sell to everyone else."

"You must be perceptive-of-eye," I mumbled, staring at the fragment. It just looked like obsidian to me.

"Agile-of-hand. I've been working with stone for more than sixty years. I don't need a birthgift to see what kind it is."

I apologetically bowed my head.

"Thank you, Oshun," Moss said. "You've confirmed what I suspected."

"Which is?" I asked.

"Someone commissioned these to be made in the style of military arrows. Either the flintknapper didn't know about the two different kinds of obsidian or, more likely, wasn't told that someone wanted to use them to frame the military."

I chewed my lip. "Can we try to find the flintknapper? Surely there aren't too many with this skill."

"Askad-Wod alone has twelve civilian workshops. You're looking at more than twice that if you include military knappers," Oshun said. "Plenty of them take extra work on the side, though they're not supposed to make arrows like this for anyone but the military. These dangerous beauties are only fit for tearing up Shoreed scum."

I shifted uncomfortably where I knelt. Scum or not, Shoreed soldiers bled, suffered, and died just like anyone else. "Did you see anything else when you picked up the arrows, Moss?"

"No. And I doubt we'll find anything else," he said. "I already know someone who thinks Lady Sulat and General Yuin have too much power and would love to slander them in a scandal like this. Someone who'd be happy to see you dead in the bargain. He's not usually sloppy—we're lucky he made one mistake. I doubt he made two."

He was right. Neither the Bloodmarrows nor the Shoreed would waste time trying to frame Lady Sulat. Purple King Alder, Sovereign of Rowak, was finally acting on his desire to have me removed as a threat to his reign.

"Well. I hope that means you don't have to worry about poison, Moss," I said as cheerfully as I could manage.

ONE OF THE SOLDIERS, Torsal, had already started dinner for the other guards when Moss and I finally descended into the safehouse. He'd done a fairly good job, but I adjusted the seasoning while Moss made arrangements for one of the other men to run a message about the assassination attempt to Lady Sulat. Then I took a bowl of pickled celery and cherries to my sister.

"Is that another serving of torture-in-a-bowl?" Dami asked.

I dropped it in her lap. "Yes, it is. Stop whining about it and eat it."

Dami set the bowl to the side of her mattress and peered curiously at me. "You're in a good mood."

"Someone tried to kill me today, thank-you-very-much."

For a moment, I thought Dami was going to look shocked. Or worried. Something, anything, to show she still cared about me.

Instead, she blinked twice, then looked me up and down. "Whoever it was, they didn't do a very good job, did they? Now," she nudged the bowl farther away. "What's everyone else eating outside?"

"Carrot hotpot." How could she have changed the conversation so quickly from assassination attempts to dinner?

"Carrots...those target the legs, right? So, if I break mine, you'll fetch me some hotpot instead?"

I couldn't tell if she was joking or not. I frowned. "The hotpot is a touch on the sweet side, so it grants endurance. It'll help the guards not get leg cramps, and while it would help with pain management, for a broken leg you'd really need—"

"Thanks! I'm not really going to break my leg, idiot."

I clenched my jaw. "I met with Lady Sulat today and learned a little more about our mission. Did you want to hear about it or not?"

Dami sat up straight. Except for her cropped hair, she was an ideal beauty—bright eyes, smooth nose, delicate mouth. She'd be an asset to any mission; no one would ever suspect her of having a mean punch.

"Thank you for being serious about this," I said, trying to pay her a compliment. I sat down on the rough floor, next to the food she wasn't eating.

"Of course I'm serious. Being trapped down here is almost more boring than living at home with our parents. I need *out*."

I managed not to flinch. "This isn't about foolishly dashing off to something 'exciting'. Lady Sulat is depending on us—"

"Are you *still* mad I ran away from home? Really, Plum, you should be thanking me."

"Excuse me?" How could she say that with a straight face?

"Ancestors, all of Rowak should thank me! Weren't you exactly what the palace needed? I couldn't have stopped that coup like you did. Maybe you were sent here by a higher purpose. You pray all the rutting time."

"I don't think you can call your recklessness a higher purpose."

Dami shrugged. "I must have been inspired. Are you feeling inspired to fetch me carrot hotpot yet?"

Nana, I prayed silently. *You watched us both when we were young. How did you not yell at her?*

Maybe I imagined it, but in the innermost chamber of my heart, I thought I heard, *Sometimes, I did.*

"I'm not fetching you anything."

"Oh! How I wish I could have some soup!" Dami wailed dramatically.

I scowled at her. "These walls are thick, but we're in a safehouse. Keep your voice—"

The door opened. Torsal stood there with a bowl of hotpot crammed with buckwheat branches. "You called?"

Dami didn't hold back on her smile, or her eyelashes. She even twirled her hair. "Aren't you the sweetest thing?"

I gave Torsal a rather different look. "She'll slow her recovery if she doesn't eat her medicine."

Torsal ignored me, handed Dami the bowl, and hurried out. Dami ate noisily, splattering bits of broth and buckwheat on her mattress. "I taught Torsal that trick during lunch, while you were gone. Useful, huh?"

Useful was not the word I'd use. "Do you *like* being in pain?"

Dami snorted. "Let's skip the nagging. What did Lady Sulat have to say?"

An attempt on my life couldn't make our conversations civil, let alone familial. We'd never be real sisters again. Flatly, I told her what I knew.

"Huh. Leaving the city is probably a good plan. I hope wherever we go, it's someplace fun."

"*Fun?* Was running away to join the army just a game to you, too?"

"You really won't let that go, will you?"

Just once, I wanted to hear her say she was *sorry* that I'd almost died because of her.

"You should have just married that chef guy. What was his name? Sorrel? It's what you wanted," Dami said.

I was so tired of hearing Sorrel's name. "My actions protected you as well as our parents. I don't want anything if I have to destroy my family to have it."

"Yeah. Should've married him." Dami wiped her hands on the blanket. "Gone and done your chef stuff. What you were *meant* to do. As for me, well, I take it you remember what my birthgift is?"

I didn't justify her with a reply. Strong-of-arm.

"I was born to fight. I *like* hitting things. So, yeah, I'm hoping I'll get a chance to do some of that on this mission. Can't you understand that?"

"I understand wanting to use your talents, but we all have choices in how we use our birthgifts. I could have been the master chef if I'd turned Rowak over to the Shoreed. I decided to be Lady Sulat's servant instead—and I'm proud of that."

She glared at me. "Do you have any idea how happy I was in the army? I got to punch guys every day. Well, at least training dummies."

A headache threatened between my eyes. How did all our conversations lead back to this argument?

"You're a war hero, Plum," Dami said. "You're alive to whine about it, so you don't have anything to whine about."

"I didn't *want* to be a hero. I *wanted* to be a chef in Westbank, taking care of villagers and enjoying a library of recipes."

"See? I got you something *better*. You're welcome."

CHAPTER FOUR

That night, I prayed that I'd get to talk to Bane again before I left on the mission. I wanted to look at someone and see warmth radiating back to me. Dami might use me for target practice if she got bored, and the other three people Lady Sulat was sending with us might be just as indifferent to me. I'd only seen Bane once since coming to care for my sister—he'd come on Lady Sulat's orders to get an order of groceries from me. I feel asleep thinking about him.

Sometime in the middle of the night, the man Moss had sent to the palace returned with instructions from Lady Sulat to be cautious and report to her in the morning. After breakfast, Moss and I left the safehouse, bringing along an extra pair of guards. When we reached Lady Sulat's apartments, though, a man in a black military uniform with green-ranked sleeves stood in front of her door.

"Lt. Norash?" Moss asked.

He bowed. "Lady Sulat wanted to be here personally, but another matter demanded her attention."

Respectfully, with two hands, he passed me a wax writing board. I tilted it to better catch the morning sun.

Plum. I hope you are well. I fear the debate over the prisoner exchange has pressed His Majesty into hasty action. The exchange

*has been gaining popularity, but that would all change if the
military were framed for your death.*

*Unfortunately for us, my brother likes to plan for victory
regardless of how his schemes play out. He's now plastered news
posters all over the city, decrying the Shoreed as the untrustworthy
cowards behind your attack. Without stating it outright, the posters
suggest that executing all our Shoreed prisoners would be fitting
retribution.*

I bit my lip. Killing those men could easily provoke the execution
of all the Rowak soldiers in Shoreed camps. So much death, just to
keep General Yuin and Lady Sulat from gaining further popularity.
That sounded like King Alder.

I continued reading:

*Given that you're at the center of this matter, I'd like you to speak at
a dinner at Minister Ashown's house in five days. A number of
other ministers and officials will be present. Please keep up your
good work with Sorrel. I don't believe you to be in any danger inside
the palace during the day, as any such incidents would reflect poorly
on my brother, but extra soldiers will guard you when you travel.
I've also arranged to move your safehouse to a new location, one that
I know has not been compromised and is also closer to the palace.*

I supposed it was too much to hope that an assassination attempt
would get me out of studying poisons with Sorrel. I let Moss read the
whole thing, then handed it back to Lt. Norash. The morning was
warm enough he didn't need to soften the wax—he just rubbed his
thumb over it, erasing the message and leaving the writing board
blank.

"I thought Minister Ashown of the Treasury didn't like Lady
Sulat," I said. I wasn't the savviest politician, but I did try to keep up
with what was happening in the palace.

Lt. Norash snorted. "He doesn't like *anyone*, but he has a better view than most of how expensive it is to keep all those prisoners. He'd probably be all for killing or maiming them if he didn't have a son in their prison camps. Lady Sulat's new informant in the treasury gave her a few numbers, and she's used that to put pressure on him."

"Wait—*maiming?*"

Moss nodded glumly. "The Shoreed have done it—rendering men unfit for battle, then dumping them all at once at the border with hopes to overwhelm our medical resources."

I shivered despite the warm morning. "Please tell Lady Sulat that I don't know how much good it will do, but I'd be happy to speak at the dinner."

THINKING about how using the wrong words could cause the deaths of hundreds of men should have been distracting enough to let me ignore Sorrel as we studied and worked. But it wasn't. In moments of quiet, I felt his gaze creeping up my neck. Whenever I glanced up, he'd be staring at me, smiling wistfully.

I threw myself into memorizing all the ways Violet knew how to murder someone, from the subtle and painless to the horrific, but that didn't help either. It only made me worry about the mission. If a Bloodmarrow poisoned me with red viper root, would Dami sit and watch me froth to death, or would she prop my convulsing body upright and feed me the antidote?

Speeches, Sorrel, poisons, Dami, King Alder's assassination attempt. I couldn't shove any of them to the back of my mind. I had no appetite at lunch. Sorrel became so solicitous and worried about me, he reached over and pressed his hand against my forehead, searching for a fever.

His hands should have been rough, monstrous things on my skin. Instead, they were soft and warm, smelling of lavender-infused soap.

Somehow that was worse: a reminder that I wasn't in danger, that I shouldn't be afraid, that I was overreacting to his presence.

"You're more clammy than anything," he said. "This soup should help with that."

His hand trailed down my face, across my shoulder, and brushed down my arm until those same, unnervingly gentle fingers landed on my wrist. "Hmm. And your pulse is fast. I thought you were pushing yourself too hard in our work, but this is proof, Plum. Gathering this information is important, but not as important as maintaining your precious health."

He didn't politely withdraw his hand but kept it there, lingering on my skin. I pulled away, resisting the urge to rub my wrist clean on my skirt. "You're right. I just need to eat a little."

He sighed. "You put on such a brave face, but you can be honest with me. I heard about the assassination attempt. I thought going about your day like normal would be easiest for you, but perhaps you'd rather lie down? I can roll out my mattress for you."

I would sooner lay on a pile of rocks than on his mattress. "I'm happier pretending everything's fine. Your first instinct was right."

I shifted away from him, picked up my bowl, and choked down one spoonful after another into my roiling stomach.

AFTER FINISHING MY STUDIES, I dearly wanted to stop by the kitchens and visit my friend Osem. I wasn't sure I could handle a whole day of Sorrel followed by an evening trapped with Dami. But Moss told me that we'd make the guards nervous if we didn't show up to the new safehouse on time, so we should plan a visit for the following day.

He was being perfectly reasonable, but I still felt like a prisoner as he escorted me to the palace gate. We met up with a pair of guards and took every precaution on our route through Askan-Wod.

The new safehouse was an actual house, not an underground

bunker. From the size of the front room, it probably belonged to a yellow-ranked family. A few handsome calligraphy scrolls hung on the wall and an equally pretty rug adorned the floor. The rest of the rooms were well-kept and utilitarian. After so much time in palaces and bunkers, it almost felt like home, despite its tragically tiny kitchen.

I ate the simple meal one of the soldiers had prepared, then headed into the room I would share with Dami. She was already asleep, the mattress unrolled haphazardly over the floor. I supposed we wouldn't fight again this evening. I hung up my black skirt, rebraided my hair, and curled up on the swath of mattress next to her.

Asleep, she looked happy, serene. I closed my eyes and pretended that my sister and I had enjoyed a lovely day together. I tried to imagine our parents were sleeping in the next room over and that our family shrine was ten steps away—that come morning, I could kneel there and inhale the aroma of fresh pine boughs and pray to the carefully preserved heads of my Ancestors. That the most interesting thing I'd be doing was checking villager's crocks for proper seasoning.

My old life seemed so far away that it was almost dream-like.

OUT OF HABIT, I woke early. I hadn't asked Moss if I was in charge of cooking here but headed to the kitchen anyway. A pair of guards nodded at me as I navigated the dark hallway.

The brick hearth was cold. I started up a fire, then asked one of the guards where I could fetch water from. He got it himself, under orders not to let me wander outside.

Soon I had two crocks of buckwheat steaming away. Then I quick-pickled some celery for Dami. A small basket of early strawberries sat on the counter. I sliced those and drizzled them in blackberry molasses to garnish everyone else's breakfast.

"Got anything good to eat?" Dami leaned against the doorframe, arms folded. She'd loosely tied on her skirt, giving her broken ribs plenty of room.

"You're up."

"Surprised that I'm able to walk around, or surprised that I can get up before the sun?"

"The latter."

She smirked. "I can't sleep in the mornings anymore. That was my shift for guard duty."

"Oh." We always talked about her present injury, not the time she'd spent training or fighting. Maybe I should have asked. We'd had a hard time understanding each other before she left, and a lot had happened since then. "How about you sit? I'll make a ginger infusion. I think everything else just needs time."

She peered around me, spotted the celery, and wrinkled her nose. But she did sit on the rush rug next to the well-worn table. I filled another clay crock with water and tossed in some slices of ginger and dried blueberries.

"So. Umm. How was serving in the army?" I sat down across from her.

"Not quite what I'd thought. But not bad, either."

I ran my finger over the nicks and scrapes in the table. Maybe I didn't want to ask more questions. If she was happy, I'd resent the way she'd hurt everyone else to get what she wanted. If she was miserable, I'd itch to lecture her on how she'd been selfish to go.

Dami didn't want another lecture. And I didn't really want to hear, once more, how little my life meant to her.

"I like this place better than the last safehouse. More room," Dami said, changing the subject for me.

"Does it belong to one of Lady Sulat's officers?"

"He's not an officer, and it's his father's home." Again, the careless shrug. "The rest of the family left on a pilgrimage to their oldest ancestral shrine. This home just has plaques. Supposedly, we're travelers renting the house while they're gone."

I nodded. "A good story."

"And nice accommodations. The soldier gave us his parents' room and their mattress."

Generous, indeed. I hadn't realized when I'd fallen asleep that we'd been given the best room in the house.

"I think you'll get along with him. You're both kinda stuffy and uptight. His name's Bane."

CHAPTER FIVE

"Bane?" I choked.

Dami peered at me. "Yeah. I can't tell if you're terrified or excited. Do you owe him money or is something else going on between you two?"

Why hadn't Moss said anything? No, that was a stupid question —Moss would *enjoy* watching me find out at some awkward moment.

Did Bane resent me being here? Was I invading his privacy?

And was he here? Would I get to see him?

"Your tea is boiling over," Dami said.

I swore. My infusion of ginger and blueberries was spluttering all over the coals. I grabbed a towel and eased the crock onto a cooler part of the hearth.

Dami peered at me like a cougar with a kill in sight. "So. You and Bane."

I opened my mouth to tell her she was imagining things, that we were simply friends. My life would be easier if she believed it. But I spotted Bane, coming down the hallway toward the kitchen.

The moment he saw me, concern tightened every inch of his face. He ran to me and didn't stop until he'd pulled me tight against him. He smelled like smoke and juniper and summer rain, like always.

I breathed deeply. For the first time in days, I felt calm.

"You're here," he whispered, pulling back. He studied me like he hadn't seen me in years. "I heard about yesterday. The assassination attempt. Are you all right?"

I wasn't sure how to make my mouth work while he was looking at me like that, his messy black hair hanging low over his warm, brown eyes.

Dami laughed.

I jumped away from Bane, leaving a proper amount of cold air between us. My cheeks burned like I'd spent all day close to the coals, grilling skewers. I pressed the backs of my cold hands against them.

"Well, I judged you wrong," Dami said, eyeing Bane. "I thought you were all formality! And here you are, so melodramatic. Of course Plum's fine. That's why we're here. You can tell there's been no lasting harm because she's up and cooking at an accursed hour when even the off-duty military's still asleep."

Bane coughed awkwardly and hid his left arm, the one that had been amputated at the elbow, behind his back, like he sometimes did when he was nervous. "Well. I'm glad everyone is...well."

Dami grinned, all teeth. "So, what are your intentions toward my sister?"

"I apologize if I seemed improper. I was rather worried."

"Oh, I think Plum needs a great deal *more* impropriety. Would it help if I threatened her life several times a week?"

"Do you think I'm so bad a soldier I'd let you threaten her more than once?" Bane retorted.

"Oooh! Delightful! Are you going to imprison me or just stab me in a dark alley?" Dami asked.

I couldn't let this go on. I spoke in as calm and dignified a tone as I could manage. "Thank you for letting us stay here, Bane. I feel like I've invaded your home."

Bane nodded graciously. "It's no difficulty. My family has wanted to travel to our ancestral shrine for some time. Lady Sulat's offer to rent the house made it easy for them to afford the trip."

Dami rolled her eyes dramatically. "I thought there was some hope for both of you."

I wasn't going to let Dami ruin my opportunity to talk to Bane. How many more chances would I have before Lady Sulat sent us out of Askan-Wod? I glanced at Dami, but she showed no signs of leaving. "I'm sorry you didn't get to go with your family," I said.

Bane cleared his throat. "So, how do you find our kitchen? I know it's not the palace."

The kitchen was cramped. The cutting boards needed to be oiled and the crocks were of sub-standard clay. I couldn't insult him, but lying to Bane felt wrong—I'd done far too much of it in the months when I'd pretended to be Dami.

"That bad?" he asked.

The kitchen might not be luxurious, but it came with the best landlord I could dream of. "I'm happy to have it."

Dami snort-giggled into her elbow. "You two need me to leave so you can moon over each other properly?"

Yes. Yes, we did.

But Bane was all good manners. He bowed toward Dami. "We've been rude to leave you out of the conversation. My apologies."

"Ancestors, you're impossible," Dami swore. "Can't you two talk like normal people?"

Not with her here.

I pursed my lips. I couldn't have a personal conversation with Bane right now, but perhaps with a third person in the room, Dami and I could talk like sisters without fighting. "Bane's quite good at springball, Dami." It was her favorite sport. "We should find you a partner and play together in proper pairs."

"You're letting me out of my prison?" Dami raised an eyebrow. "I can't believe you're that eager to take advantage of my bruised torso. You've never been a competitive player before."

Oh. Right. Dami had to stay here.

Bane laughed. "Have you *played* springball with Plum? She's quite good. And she does seem to enjoy winning."

"Strange. Maybe she was trying to impress someone." Dami gave me her most-innocent smile.

"It's a pleasant diversion," I replied defensively. She was worse than Moss.

Dami giggled. Thankfully her bad ribs silenced her quickly; she grimaced and clutched them. I plopped her bowl of pickled celery in front of her. "Why don't you eat?"

"You know, yesterday I could *smell* a stand of buckwheat dumplings somewhere out on the street. Would it be so hard to send a soldier for some?"

"Pickled celery," I said sternly. "It's good for you."

Dami munched down a few with mock-meekness. "So. Bane. How often do you manage to drag Plum away from cooking to play springball?"

"On occasion," Bane replied, treading cautiously.

"I'm impressed. I didn't know Plum was capable of being content without a hearth in view. I'm half-convinced she's cold-blooded and the coals keep her from freezing and falling over. Did she feel cold to you, when you were clutching her?"

"I...I apologize for my behavior," Bane stammered as he glanced at me, a question in his eyes.

But I couldn't exactly admit in front of Dami that no, I wasn't the least offended that he'd held me.

"It's nice to have a change of pace and play springball now and again, thank you," I told Dami. I turned back to the crock, busying my hands with the familiar motions of meal creation, drawing some measure of calm from the smell of salt and herbs.

"And there she goes, proving my point and bustling about like a frantic mother duck," Dami said.

"I am not a duck!" I snapped.

Dami smirked. "I see you didn't deny the *frantic* part."

Bane glanced between us. "I think I've come at a bad time. And I do need to be getting to my post. I'm...I'm glad to see with my own eyes that you're well, Plum."

"Thank you. I'm glad you came." I wanted to apologize for all my sister's prodding, but I couldn't find the words.

He bowed to both of us and reluctantly left.

Before he was even down the hall and out of earshot, Dami chortled again. "That was rich! How is it that you didn't mention him before, Plum?"

"You were immensely rude."

"You were immensely entertaining." She propped her elbows on the table and rested her chin on her hands. "So. Are you going to tell me more about him? Have you two planned your formal engagement yet?"

I turned my back to her, ignored her snickering, and cooked. It was one thing to insult me, but she shouldn't have needled Bane like that.

Lt. NORASH MET Moss and me at the palace gate. Lady Sulat's officers had intercepted Chef Palaw's latest letter to his daughter, Violet. Given that all his other letters mentioned him being in the Coral Palace, he couldn't have heard the news of her death yet. Lady Sulat wanted me to use Violet's cipher to decode it.

I'd gotten the hang of deciphering Violet's letters working with Sorrel. While he fetched lunch, I transcribed Palaw's words:

> LOA says that you're dead. Murdered, actually, by General Behon to keep you quiet. I think it's low of her to lie just to upset me. She can't know any such thing—she has to be a living human like you and me. She slept all night on that road. Despite her recent churlish behavior, she continues to be a strong voice in supporting this war from inside the Coral Palace. Write me soon, Violet. I know you're completing your mission well. You're a talented Bloodmarrow. I'm proud of you.

Chef Palaw might be a traitorous Bloodmarrow, but part of me still felt sorry for him. By now, he probably had news that this LOA person was right. But how had she known? I chewed my lip. It took two weeks to travel from here to the Coral Palace, and it should have taken another two weeks for Palaw's reply to reach us. Violet had died three weeks ago.

Maybe LOA had an unusually fast messenger? Or maybe she was a ghost, just not of a kind that Palaw or I had any experience with. A ghost who looked human during the day and could move freely at night would be immensely powerful.

I rubbed the side of my head. LOA was for the war and had Palaw's attention. If she were a nigh-omnipotent ghost, she would have warned him to adjust the plans for the coup. An unusually fast messenger was a far better explanation. Just because I'd seen one ghost didn't mean that anyone else was likely to be secretly dead.

I endured another afternoon with Sorrel, then reported back to Lady Sulat. Her brow furrowed when I gave her the news. "More and more, you're the right person for this job, Plum."

"Anyone could have decoded that message." We sat across from each other on her fine chairs, her tall desk between us. I appreciated the desk; I didn't have to hold my hands perfectly still when she couldn't see them.

"But you're the only person I know who has any practical experience with ghosts." She left the implication hanging in the air.

My throat dried. She had said she was sending me to a place likely to host Bloodmarrows. And we already knew Palaw was at the Coral Palace.

Lady Sulat wasn't just sending me out of Askan-Wod. She was sending me out of Rowak altogether. "Lady Sulat...I'm not sure...I don't think I'm qualified..."

"I would have preferred to give you another week to grow in your confidence with poisons before telling you about your destination, but it seems you may need time to research ghosts as well."

A week, a month, a year—no amount of time would have prepared me to go to Shoreed.

"Perhaps you should spend tomorrow in the Royal Archives," she said.

I was tempted to agree, just to get away from Sorrel. "I've read everything in the Archives on ghosts already. But I don't know what you think I can accomplish in Shoreed. I'm no great spy."

Lady Sulat leaned back in her chair. "Do you know what Shoreed's greatest asset is in perpetuating this war?"

"Exiled Red Lord Ospren." He was Lady Sulat's oldest brother. If King Alder hadn't exiled him, the man would be ruling Rowak. He still had plenty of supporters in the country. With that support, Shoreed had nearly succeeded in a coup to place Ospren on the throne as their vassal. "You want me to spy on him?"

Lady Sulat didn't answer my question. "Plum, you're a highly talented chef. You'll have your sister with you as a discreet bodyguard, plus two actual guards."

"And this mysterious fifth person. I think it's time to give me those details as well."

Lady Sulat glumly nodded. "One of my lieutenants is interviewing candidates for that position out of the traitors who assisted in the coup. Several of them would like a way to regain their good name in Rowak, and many of them have Shoreed contacts that can help you get into the palace."

"There's no one more reliable?" I spluttered.

"Reliable Rowak citizens can't get themselves into the Coral Palace. I trust my lieutenant to do his job well. Every man in our military prison there is separated from his family and his home. That will be a powerful motivator for good behavior. The two soldiers accompanying you will take turns watching him as well. But I'm sure you see now why I want Dami with you. You need at least one person you can trust absolutely."

I did—and that person wasn't Dami. "You have to have better spies than me, even if I'm more familiar with ghosts."

Lady Sulat sighed. She maintained her posture, but she couldn't hide the heaviness in her eyes. "I'll give you the contact of a civilian messenger in Shoreed's capital that I trust, in case you uncover something remarkable. Knowledge is a powerful weapon. But I'm not sending you there to spy."

She waited, like she expected me to just *understand* what she wanted, but I could only frown. What good was I in Shoreed, if not to gather information? Lady Sulat certainly didn't expect me to throw the Bloodmarrows a dinner party.

"With so many factions pushing for this war, fighting will almost certainly break out again. Shoreed is still on our lands, eager for more territory, and the people of Rowak are hurt and angry," Lady Sulat said. "But I don't want to get reports that thousands more of our Rowak sons have died in battle."

"I don't, either."

"Good. Then you understand. You'll go to Shoreed. You'll position yourself. If somehow, miraculously, both our countries have decided to stop fighting by then, you can simply come *home*."

She said that word with such longing. I'd thought she'd merely been coy with where she was sending me, but I could see her reluctance now. She didn't want to send me on this mission. She didn't want it to be necessary.

"And if not?" I asked.

"Then I need you to end the war, Plum."

I was just a chef. Chefs healed people, not countries. But then I caught the sorrow in slope of her mouth, and I knew in a heartbeat that she hadn't assigned me to learn poisons so I'd be armed with protective antidotes.

Lady Sulat met my gaze and held it. "I'm sending you to Shoreed to kill my brother."

CHAPTER SIX

I didn't want to poison anyone. I didn't want to be anything *like* Violet. Poisoning was simply wrong. No one expected a noose to be kind. Everyone hoped their breakfast would be satisfying and safe.

Moss followed me, bolas clinking, as I left Lady Sulat's. Sweet salmonberry tea would settle my stomach. But I didn't want to be settled. No, I'd just have to make sure I found something besides Red Lord Ospren's death to stop this war. Me, the highly-reliable Dami, two guards, and a traitor. How promising.

I was headed for the gate when Moss reminded me that we'd set aside time this afternoon to see Osem and redirected me toward the kitchens. She was already out, fetching water from the well. "Plum!" Osem set down her buckets and jogged toward me. "You're hard to find these days. On purpose, I assume."

"Unfortunately, yes." Just seeing her made me nostalgic for the days when we scrubbed crocks together.

"I was getting ready to demand that Lady Sulat send you to me."

I raised my eyebrows. "Is something wrong? Or..."

Was she upset I hadn't come to see her more often? But she broke into an enormous grin. "I wanted to ask if you'd cook for my wedding."

I blinked. "You're betrothed?"

"Don't sound so surprised! You think I look like an old widow, don't you?"

She meant the words in jest, but I winced. She'd been widowed all too young. "No, Osem. Of course not. I just have no idea who the groom-to-be is. Wait—is it Dewar?" I asked, remembering my earlier conversation with Sorrel.

Osem wrinkled her nose and laughed. "Dewar? No. You remember how Lady Sulat arranged for me to learn reading and writing from an officer's wife in the city?"

"Yes."

"Well, my teacher has a younger brother. I saw him a few times, when his sister invited him over for meals, but then he kept coming for no particular reason—well, no particular reason that I knew of at the time." She laughed again. "I sound perfectly ridiculous, don't I?"

She sounded *happy*. Happier than I'd ever seen her. "Of course not."

"Since I have no family for him to ask, he asked me directly. I didn't dream he'd consider it—marrying a girl without relations. But apparently, my service in the palace has made me reputable enough for his parents to agree."

"Oh, Osem. I'm so happy for you. Does your betrothed have a name?"

"Yellow-ranked Sochen of Askan-Wod. He's a junior officer in the treasury."

I blinked. "In the...treasury?"

"Under Minister Ashown. Why? Is that not good enough for you?" Osem teased.

Lt. Norash had mentioned that Lady Sulat had a new informant from the treasury. I just hadn't expected it to be Osem, through a fiancé. Was I jumping to conclusions? I swallowed, throat dry. I didn't want to undermine Osem's joy, but I still found myself asking, "You said Lady Sulat arranged for this particular tutor, didn't you?"

Osem smiled. "You're quite a bit sharper than you used to be, Plum, and it's adorable that you're concerned. But Lady Sulat took me in when I had *nothing*. If she'd commanded me to marry a random stranger, I would have. Instead, she gave me an education and an opportunity to decide if I wanted Sochen or not."

"You *knew* she was using you?" It was a good trade for Lady Sulat, giving up ears in the kitchen for eyes in the treasury.

"My father chose my first husband to better our family's position," Osem said. "Women marry every day for status or for wealth. I'm marrying, in part, for information. It's not that odd. Honestly, the strange part is that I had a real choice. Sochen's wonderful. He offered to find a chef for our wedding, but I told him I already knew the best in Rowak. Can we hire you? Please?"

I tried to set aside my misgivings and simply be happy for her. "You don't have to hire me. I'd be honored. When's the wedding?"

"Two months. And I appreciate the sentiment, but knowing Sochen, he's going to insist on paying you anyway."

Two months. By then, I'd be in Shoreed, positioning myself to poison a traitor if I couldn't find a better way to end the war. But I couldn't tell Osem that. After I disappeared, she'd have plenty of time to find a new chef. "The end of summer is an excellent time for fresh produce. Your wedding will be as lovely as you deserve, Osem."

I just couldn't be part of it.

DAMI WAS RIGHT ABOUT one thing: I cooked when I was stressed. I blanched crinkly cabbage leaves, laid them in an overlapping mat, spread blanched spinach over that, and rolled the whole thing up into a tight log. When it cooled a little, I'd slice it into rounds. It would look marvelous in tonight's hotpot.

Footsteps approached me from behind. I didn't turn. Right now, if I argued with Dami, I'd scream at her. Then I caught a hint of soft smoke and juniper. Bane. I looked up just as he set a basket next to me, feathery carrot greens spilling out of the top.

"You weren't here to give me a list, so I did my best based on what you wanted last time I shopped for you." He pulled the vegetables out. "Carrots. More cabbage. We still had plenty of onions, so I didn't get any of those. Ah. Some blueberries I hadn't planned on but couldn't walk past. The beets. And finally, more baby celery. Bearak's stand was out, and the next one I tried had chopped off the leaves, like they were trying to hide the fact they were selling old produce—just like you warned me about. I found some at Grapeholly's. They didn't have much, but a little crisp produce seemed better than a basket of limp stalks."

The small bunch of celery was pale green and as smart and stiff as a soldier at attention. All the other produce was lovely, too—dark and fully ripe berries, pale white carrots shimmering like mother-of-pearl. It was all so beautiful, I wanted to cry. "Thank you."

Bane beamed proudly at me. "I did actually listen to your instructions. *All* of them."

My cheeks flushed. The first time he was tasked to get groceries for me, I'd talked for at least an hour about what I wanted. "The other person Lady Sulat had shop for us couldn't tell the difference between rhubarb and rutabagas. I...I didn't mean to lecture."

Bane's baritone laugh warmed me to the marrow. "You're a *chef.* You don't need to apologize for being particular. I'm glad my humble efforts are worthy."

"Are you teasing me?"

His grin made my gut wobble like an under-set custard. "Perhaps. But I did bring you blueberries. I remembered what you said about looking for produce so vibrant, it ought to be in a painting. I thought you'd like them."

"I love them."

We hadn't had any opportunities to talk alone like this, not since I started treating Dami. There was so much I ought to say before leaving for Shoreed.

Thank you for being such a loyal friend. Too cold and distant.

I think I want to be more than your friend. Too forward.

You smell amazing and I wish I could take something of yours, anything of yours, with me to Shoreed. Much, much too forward.

I'm sorry I didn't see how amazing you are the moment I first met you. True. But "sorry" didn't seem right. Bane didn't act like he needed an apology.

If I come back from Shoreed a poisoner, and you're too disgusted to be around me, I'll understand. Also true. Bane deserved better than a Bloodmarrow's mirror image.

"Is something wrong?" Bane asked, the smile slipping from his face.

"No, I...I just got more details from Lady Sulat. About the mission." I looked away from all the beautiful produce he'd brought me and met his gaze instead. "I'm going to be gone for a long time, Bane."

"I'll still be here when you return."

I reached forward, my fingers ghosting against his cheek as I tucked his hair behind his ear. Not the most proper thing to do, finding an excuse to touch him. He tilted his head toward my fingers, so I was suddenly cupping the side of his face in my hand. My palm burned, and my other hand suddenly felt icy-cold, desperate to soak up warmth from him. I wanted to put both of my hands on his face. I wanted to reach up on tip-toe and taste his mouth before I left.

But I'd spent the first months I'd known him lying to him about who I was. I'd broken his heart at least once. I hadn't found the right words to ask if he still wanted to trust me.

I hesitated. My hand wavered and fell to my side. We shouldn't be touching, anyway. We weren't engaged. Ancestors watch over me, I was leaving for Shoreed soon with orders to kill a man.

Bane's eyebrows drew together into a question.

"I, umm, sorry, your hair..." I stumbled.

He shifted back. "Ah, right. Of course. Yes. Thank you."

"Bane. You...I mean, we..." Why was this so hard? We could have talked about produce or springball or politics for hours. But talking about *us* made me feel like I was making forcemeat out of my insides.

"Yes?"

"Do you think a few of those carrots would go nicely in the hotpot tonight?"

"Plum, do what you think is best. I trust your judgment." He bowed politely to me. "I should probably go set the table."

I silently watched him leave.

LADY SULAT HAD authority as the Minister of Military affairs to order Red Lord Ospren's death. The man was a traitor who'd fled his exile residence and rallied the Shoreed against his own country. I could grasp that, in an abstract sort of way. But if I didn't have to desecrate his food to accomplish Lady Sulat's mission, I wouldn't.

I entered Dami's room, handed over her bowl of pickles, and cut her off before she could start complaining. "What's the quickest way to kill a man?"

Her usually surly glare of disdain sharpened into bright excitement. I'd never seen her sit up so quickly. "Did you and Bane *fight*? I didn't even hear screaming."

"No, we didn't." I sat down on the mattress next to Dami. "So. Slitting someone's throat—is that the fastest way to go?"

"It certainly isn't stabbing their hand. Am I going to wake up in the middle of the night tonight to see you kneeling over me with a knife?"

"Of course not!"

Dami shrugged. "Seemed like a fair question."

Though how I'd sneak up on Ospren in the first place, much less slit his throat, I had no idea. I tightened my hands in my skirts, a habit I thought I'd given up a long time ago. "Are you any good at archery?"

A few of those shattering arrows, like the ones King Alder had pointed toward me, would do it.

"Plum? I know you went and got yourself an advancement, but

I'm yellow-ranked. The military usually only trains green-ranked and above to be archers."

"Oh." It probably wasn't the best plan, anyway. It was a horrific way to die. "We're back to knives, then."

But I wasn't strong or skilled enough for a knife alone to be enough. I'd have to poison the blade. Violet probably had a recipe for something that cause a gentle, fast death in her box of tricks. I'd be a poisoner. But at least his death wouldn't come to him masquerading as a wholesome food.

Dami gave me the oddest look. "Plum. I hate to say it, but even when you're not rambling on and on about cooking, you're still the *weirdest* sister."

CHAPTER SEVEN

The gentlest poison I found in Violet's notes suitable for edging a knife was an extract made from bittersleep leaf. The same substance she'd tried to kill me with.

Maybe I could just ask nicely and Red Lord Ospren and Chef Palaw would end the war. A ludicrous thought. Ospren had ordered the death of his sister and her unborn child. He wasn't going to back down just because a girl from Rowak didn't want to hurt him.

I had to smile all day as I researched the best way to kill Red Lord Ospren, because at the first sign of melancholy, Sorrel would fawn all over me. By the time I left, my jaw hurt.

As Moss and I approached the gate, a palace guard wearing an armband embroidered with an amber bear stepped in front of us, blocking the way. Moss defensively pushed me behind himself. I stayed there, skin prickling with unease.

The man gave an elegant bow. "Green-ranked Plum of Clamsriver. I am Blue-ranked Lor of Salmonrun, the new captain of the Palace Guard. It is an honor to meet you."

I didn't recognize the name. He seemed young for such an important post—maybe twenty-five? The corners of his eyes were fashionably shadowed with umber and a wave of minty perfume rolled off him.

"Thank you." I bowed, not moving any closer.

Captain Lor whipped an envelope from his sleeves—purple, embroidered with amber thread. A royal envelope. He presented it respectfully to Moss, who handed it in turn to me.

I managed to open it calmly, like I was used to missives from monarchs who wanted me dead. The short note asked me to join him on the porch of the House of Reflected Learning. That wasn't even his residence but that of his son, the Purple Heir.

What did King Alder have planned? A dozen guards and servants lingered around the gatehouse. If he was plotting to finish me off tonight, he would have invited me more discreetly.

"If you are not otherwise engaged, I am to escort you," Captain Lor said.

Was King Alder hoping I'd refuse, making me look disloyal to Rowak? Lady Sulat needed me to present a patriotic face at Minister Ashown's party. Or did His Majesty actually want me to attend?

My stomach churned. If I knew what Alder wanted me to do, I could simply choose the opposite. I rubbed my finger against the edge of the paper. I should go, not because I was scared of refusing, but because King Alder might reveal useful information about his plans for me or the prisoner exchange.

I glanced at Moss. He raised an eyebrow slightly, as if to say I could decide whether or not I was ready for this.

I needed all the practice I could get before I left for Shoreed. "Captain Lor. I would be honored if you'd lead the way."

Moss MANAGED to direct us past Lady Sulat's residence so he could snag two more guards for me. The House of Reflected Learning itself was a long, low building, near the Royal Bear House. A broad reflecting pool stretched across the back porch, showing clouds, maple trees, and a corner of the Royal Shrine, painted black and white. It was a lovely backdrop for whatever King Alder was plotting.

Captain Lor led us up the front stairs and around to the back porch. Purple Lord Heir Valerian looked far too solemn for his twelve years as he knelt at his desk, the whole of the reflecting pool spread before him. His father knelt next to him, listening as a tutor lectured on the moral qualities of a righteous leader.

As soon as he spotted me, Valerian's serious face broke into an unreserved grin. "You came!"

"Patience. I have not even introduced you," King Alder corrected him, tone almost teasing.

Alder turned toward me. His shimmering purple tunic draped richly around him, covering his arms down to the fingertips. He was as lovely as the scenery. Some parts of his face looked so much like Lady Sulat's, especially around the nose and mouth. But they hardly seemed like siblings. She masked her concern with a cool, schooled expression. He buried his cold hate with warm, sweet smiles. "How kind of you to join us on such short notice. Purple Lord Heir Valerian, I introduce to you Green-ranked Plum of Clamsriver, a hero of Rowak."

An outright attack would have been less unsettling than hearing flattery from his lips. I kept my face composed and bowed deeply, first to King Alder, then to Valerian.

"Come sit with me," Valerian said, the words more excitement than command.

I did so. I even managed not to glance at King Alder as I passed him. What was he playing at, bringing me here to meet with his son?

"Ever since the Old Road Ambush I've wanted to ask you for your version of events," Valerian said.

"Version," I echoed. He sounded more like a city watchman than a child.

"I mean no offense by that, but everyone tells a story differently."

"You're wise to learn that truth so young," I replied kindly. Whatever I felt toward his father, I had no qualm with Lord Valerian. Lady Sulat often tutored him and they both seemed to think highly of each other.

"Tell me?" he begged, a little too pleadingly for a Purple Heir.

I did. A warm breeze rippled off the reflecting pool, scattering the image of green maple leaves into thousands of shifting pieces. No one —not Valerian, or his tutors, or King Alder, or the guards— interrupted as I recounted what happened that day.

When I got to the part about Old King Fulsaan, I expected King Alder to glower at me. I knew his father had been a Hungry Ghost, after all. But Alder looked over the pond with a lazy, unconcerned expression on his face.

I shivered and repeated my usual story that Fulsaan had been murdered the night of the Old Road Ambush and, in his righteous anger, had turned into a Vengeful Ghost. When his son and grandson were safe, he left for a peaceful afterlife. Valerian didn't protest. Either he hadn't seen Fulsaan shamefully transform into a Hungry Ghost, or his father had convinced him otherwise.

When I finished, Valerian beamed. I had the feeling if he were an ordinary child in Clamsriver, he would have jumped up and down and cheered. "Has anyone preserved this story for the history of Rowak?"

I blinked. "Not that I know of."

"Father, this is a travesty!" Valerian cried. "Should not such a great deed be remembered?"

"It should," he mused, staring out over the subtly shifting waters.

"I admit, I didn't even think of asking you for this narrative. I do, after all, remember being rescued," Valerian said. "But when I heard my father speak so highly of you, and when he reminded me that I'd never thanked you for saving my life..."

"I am honored to serve Rowak," I replied humbly, bowing where I sat, unease aching in my bones. What good could it possibly do King Alder to have his son think well of me?

Valerian shook his head. "You've been honored with rank. But I would honor you with memory."

Valerian gave some orders, and soon three historians sat with low writing desks, ready with ink and paper. Valerian himself dictated an introduction. Then I told my story again, to the unnerving silent sway of their brushes.

Did King Alder hope to catch me in some contradiction? I weighed each word carefully, but speaking still felt like twisting rope for my own noose.

We didn't finish until the sun was low in the sky.

"You were a good friend to my grandfather," Valerian said.

"I hope so," I said.

"You saved his son and his grandson, which is what he wanted." Valerian fidgeted with his long sleeves. "Did you know it's his birthday in three days?"

"I didn't, I'm afraid." A breath of wind rippled over the pond, stirring the water and ruffling the maple leaves.

"After the ceremony in the Royal Shrine, there will be a banquet. Will you come as my guest? I think Grandfather would have liked that."

Purple Lord Valerian, Heir to the throne of Rowak, stared at me with nervous, hopeful eyes. The scribes and guards around us leaned a little closer, listening.

The shadow of a grin touched the corners of King Alder's mouth.

I wanted to say no, but I couldn't refuse such a request from the Purple Heir. "It would be my pleasure."

"The day is nearly over," King Alder said. "Come, Plum. I'll escort you myself to the palace gates. You've been very gracious to my son."

I gave him my deepest, most thankful bow, even though I didn't want to walk anywhere with him.

Moss and the Royal Bear Guards trailed us. King Alder set a slow, ponderous pace. The gravel crunched under our feet, leaves whispered above us, and the smell of rhododendrons and grass filled the air.

I was still trying to think of how I could use this moment to my advantage when King Alder spoke. "You've provided a great service to this country. I am truly grateful."

He sounded sincere. Maybe he was. But he could be grateful and still want me dead. "Thank you."

"I heard about the attempt on your life." He folded his hands inside his sleeves, looking immensely royal with the late evening light shining off him. "Do you require additional security? I'd be happy to provide it."

"That's most kind, but not necessary."

He gave me a crooked, knowing smile as we passed through the springball courts. "Did Sulat convince you I'm to blame? Someone attacked you, you came out unharmed, and now you're even more indebted to my sister. Who actually benefited from your ordeal?"

I couldn't believe he was audacious enough to try to heap blame on Lady Sulat. "It's my understanding that the assassination attempt has had some influence on the prisoner exchange, Your Majesty."

"You are delightfully direct, Plum. Yes, it has. I assume my sister has instilled in you how just and noble such an exchange would be?"

"It *is* just."

He gave me another wistful smile. "I like my servants to think a little more independently than that. They can't advise me or correct my errors if they only repeat my words. Did Lady Sulat tell you the conditions the Shoreed set for such an exchange?"

No. She hadn't. My jaw tightened.

"The Shoreed want to trade all of our prisoners for all of theirs. Five hundred fit, fighting Shoreed soldiers for three hundred Rowak men—most of whom have lived as mistreated, underfed prisoners for years and are not ready for combat."

I was no great strategist, but even I could tell that was a dangerous arrangement for Rowak.

King Alder stopped walking, some fifty yards from the gate. Our guards stayed a respectful distance away. "I want this accursed war to *end*, Plum."

His voice hung heavy with a weight that could not be feigned.

Maybe he didn't oppose the exchange just because it would reflect well on Lady Sulat and General Yuin. But that didn't mean he was right.

"We ought to honor our Rowak men and get them home as soon as we can," I replied.

"Do you think our honorable men *want* to be freed if it means unleashing Shoreed soldiers to attack their comrades and slaughter villages?"

Most of Osem's town had been slaughtered. Everyone in her family except for her. "None of us want more war."

King Alder raised an elegant eyebrow. "Not even a certain general or a Minister of Military Affairs? Neither of them has much opportunity to advance their political agendas in peacetime, Plum."

"It's not like that." What a stupid, feeble defense I was making.

"You should think carefully about who you serve. I know Lady Sulat has been welcoming to you. Every good master protects those under them. But not everyone has Rowak's best interests at heart. My son is impressed with you. And so am I. You don't have to leave the palace tonight. You can stay. Become my person, my ally. Help me protect Rowak."

Alder had let a dozen innocent apprentices hang to keep his ghostly father hidden. I would never trust him or his warm, inviting smile. Even though Lady Sulat had asked me to become a poisoner. Even though she'd arranged Osem's marriage for her own benefit.

There, in the warm evening with the sky turning pink, I considered a world where King Alder was telling the truth. Where Lady Sulat had arranged the "assassination" to make me more willing to flee to Shoreed and do as she'd asked. Where she'd carefully kept the details of the prisoner exchange from me, so I'd be more willing to speak at Minister's Ashown's upcoming banquet.

Ludicrous. But not impossible.

I bowed again. I didn't let my hands shake. "King Alder, I am honored by your generous offer—"

"But you're not going to accept, are you?"

I kept my head bowed, my gaze on his embroidered shoes. "No."

"I didn't think you would. But you did save my life and my son's life. You prevented this nation from falling into Shoreed's grasp. When your trust in my sister runs out, Plum, I want you to know that you have other places to turn for protection."

CHAPTER
EIGHT

T he next morning, for the fifth time, I stepped up onto Sorrel's porch. My arms felt stiff, like I'd spent the past day scrubbing crocks. Still, I raised my hand and knocked, the sound loud and hollow in my ears.

Sorrel whipped the door open. "Plum." His mouth lingered on my name, relishing it—like calling me by the wrong one for a few weeks made the right one delectable. "How good it is to see you."

"Good morning." I kept my eyes down. By now, I knew every gouge in the polished redwood floor.

He escorted me to the table. "Last night I stayed up late and finished transcribing the notes on paralyzing limbs. Would you like to see?"

"Yes. Thank you."

Sorrel opened the manuscript box and flipped pages until he came to one with especially striking calligraphy. He handed it to me, his fingertips brushing over mine.

I managed a polite smile and read over the page. Briefly, I wondered if Lady Sulat had assigned me to work with Sorrel just to put me on edge—if that would benefit her somehow.

I read over the paralysis poisoning, then filed it into my other notes. Violet hadn't organized her information in any particular way, but the poisons all seemed to fall into three categories. There were substances not meant for human consumption—like the bittersleep leaf. Then there were misapplied cures. Giving someone with constipation endurance-of-bowels, for example, or someone with the opposite issue strength-of-bowels. Lastly, there was ill-prepared food, like badly over-salting a dish with blueberries to blur someone's sight. But there weren't many examples of the final kind—usually people could tell if they were eating a mess.

Before, I'd focused on life-saving antidotes. Now, I memorized the preparation of the poisons as well. The first two categories came with plenty of cooking instructions—how to incorporate bittersleep to target the heart, or how to mix it with foods to make the poisoning look like the progression of a natural disease. With my culinary background, I absorbed the information with uncanny ease. If I had the chance to deliver a cup of tea to Red Lord Ospren, I already knew a half-dozen ways to kill him.

I hated that knowing how to help people also qualified me to hurt them.

At midday, Sorrel fetched lunch like always. He returned with two bowls of buckwheat porridge topped with chewy, gelatinous strips of braised venison ears and a scattering of green onions. The porridge had a vegetable sweetness to it. Endurance-of-ears. The kind of dish students ate before attending long lectures.

It was delicious, but I still frowned at it. Had Sorrel requested this on purpose? Or had it simply been on the menu? "Plummm." He said my name even slower than usual. "I've been worried about you."

"I'm fine." I shoveled some porridge in my mouth. The faster I finished eating, the sooner I could get back to work.

His face creased with tender lines of concern, his eyes shining like newly-struck obsidian. "Maybe I shouldn't bring it up. But ever since...ever since the assassination attack, you haven't seemed quite the same."

"I'm fine," I repeated. The assassin wasn't the one troubling me right now.

"Plum. Sometimes...sometimes I think it's hard to see the hurt in ourselves."

This coming from the new widower who thought another romance would bandage his pain and scrub away Violet's betrayal.

"I sent for something. To cheer you." He set down his porridge and retrieved a manuscript box. "It's from the Toksang Empire."

My fingers itched to open it, but I managed to only give a polite "Mm," as I chewed a strip of venison ear.

He opened the lid and turned pages. There were too many solid pages of text for this to just hold recipes, though I did spot a few ingredient lists.

"It's a treatise on the proper care of Ancestors by a philosopher named Sage Eelgrass. The original was written over two hundred years ago. It contains a large number of recipes and recommendations for what kind of food is best to offer the dead. The customs among the Toksang vary from ours, but I thought you'd enjoy it."

Sorrel set it right in front of me. How could I not look? It had prescriptions for the newly dead, the long dead, and for birthdays of the deceased and the living. It even had recommendations for certain prayers. Salted cress if praying for a pregnancy, to give the Ancestors agile fingers when weaving infant souls. Sweet blueberries to help the Ancestors watch diligently over the fields for a better harvest. Could foods designed to target living bodies affect the souls of the deceased in this fashion? Part of it even suggested times for offering food to the ocean. Strange. The ocean doesn't *eat*. Maybe that part was Toksang superstition, but I still wanted to memorize every page.

I needed to read it.

I glanced up at Sorrel. He beamed. He knew—he knew I couldn't resist this any more than a child could refrain from eating summer's first strawberries.

"Can I borrow it?" I asked. I had precious little time left in Rowak, but it didn't matter. If I had to leave in the morning, I'd stay up all night reading.

Sorrel walked around the desk and knelt next to me. His arm was a finger's breadth away from mine. Close enough for me to feel the warmth of him. My trepidation crackled in that tiny space. His scent filled the air—all ginger and herbs.

"It's yours. To keep. Forever."

My stomach roiled. "I can't..."

The words tangled in my throat. I *could* accept this. I'd just have to smile and pretend that the day he'd pummeled me meant nothing. He'd quickly forgiven me for lying to him about my name, hadn't he?

"But this manuscript must be priceless."

Sorrel trailed his finger along a page. "Your happiness is worth it, Plum."

He didn't think he was really giving it away—he thought it would return to him, that I'd return to him.

I wasn't here to heal him from Violet. I wasn't here for him at all. "Sorrel..."

When I said his name, he grinned and grabbed my hand. I pulled back, but he squeezed tighter.

And now he'd grind the little bones together. If I told him I wasn't his, he'd backhand me like before. He'd kick my ribs as I lay prone and helpless on the floor.

"There's no need to be afraid, Plum," he whispered, easing his grip. "Our path has been a tangled one, but I'm glad that the woman who drove us apart has brought us back together again."

My heart pounded like I'd just run from one side of Askan-Wod to the other. He'd meant that to be a reassuring squeeze. A comfort. Gently, he took my other hand in his.

My muscles stiffened as if his touch was poisonous. I couldn't keep doing this. I couldn't keep studying with Sorrel, whatever Lady Sulat wanted.

Sorrel leaned forward. He kissed me.

Disturbingly, my first thought was that he must have had ample practice with Violet. His lips were cool and smooth, moving gently but earnestly around mine. My second thought was to hold still, in case he decided to hurt me for pulling away.

My third thought was that I had an armed guard outside.

I shoved Sorrel back. He bumped against the desk, knocking his porridge over. Bits of it flecked his tunic and the manuscript page. He stared up at me, eyes wide with shock.

"Plum?" He still said my name like a caress. "Plum, what's wrong?"

He wasn't even looking at the priceless manuscript. Just me.

I fled. Out the front door. Down the steps. Across the gravel. My coiled muscles needed to run. My lungs heaved. Vaguely, I heard Moss's footfalls keeping pace behind me.

I was panicking. Hysterical? Showing my emotions all over my face and acting without thinking wouldn't keep me or Dami alive in Shoreed.

After another minute of running, I forced my feet to slow. I took steady breaths and redirected my course to the benches outside the Royal Shrine. I stared at its pillars, walls, and tiles, painted in striking black and white, representing life and death.

Somehow, the simplicity was comforting. Black and white. Life and death. Plum and Sorrel. Opposites. Things that didn't belong together.

I expected Moss to plunk down next to me with a half-dozen rude lines about how Bane would be disappointed or perhaps asking how widowers taste. Moss, though, clasped his hands behind his back and stood at attention behind me, like a faithful guard. For all his teasing I supposed he was that.

"If we're going to be here long, I should inform Lady Sulat that we've changed our location," he said. "You're not entirely safe on the palace grounds."

"I'm sorry. I'm being ridiculous, aren't I?" I smoothed my skirt with unsteady hands. "I keep thinking he'll beat me again, even though I know I'm safe."

Moss frowned. "When did Sorrel beat you?"

Didn't he know? I stared down at the grass, at the thousands of individual blades casting thousands of individual shadows under the bright sun. "When I was imprisoned."

"I thought your guards did that. Does Lady Sulat know?"

"Doesn't she know everything?"

"Not *everything*."

I bit my lip. I'd only actually told Osem. I'd assumed she'd reported it. "I know what happened to me wasn't that horrible. Osem got just as bad from her guards when she was locked up. Many soldiers come home with far worse, and plenty more don't come home at all. I should be able to keep my composure."

But my hands shook on my knees, remembering how I'd called out for help and no one had answered. How a face I'd once adored had been attached to the fist pummeling me.

I wiped my palms on my skirt. Why had I just sat there and let him kiss me? Like I had no more wits than a rabbit playing dead? "I just need a minute more. Then I can go back, apologize to Sorrel for leaving, and keep studying poisons."

I could—I would—remain calm this time.

"No. We need to explain the situation to Lady Sulat first. I'm sorry, Plum."

"Sorry that I'm horrible with politics and duplicity?" I laughed hoarsely at myself, kicking at the grass.

"I'd say the opposite, if you kept something like this from everyone for so long." He looked at me with fatherly pity. "Come on."

I followed him across the gravel paths to Lady Sulat's, imagining her eyebrows arched in utter disdain when she heard Moss's story.

CHAPTER NINE

The door guards in their black military tunics admitted Moss and me to Lady Sulat's sitting room. She sat, nursing her infant son while her almost four-year-old daughter, Azalea, stacked towers of wooden blocks on the floor. Lady Sulat's face held that peaceful, soft cast I so rarely saw. It disappeared as soon as she noticed us.

"Was there another attack?"

"Yes, but not today," Moss said, earning him a cool, quizzical stare.

I looked away, face burning. I should have been... I don't know. Calm. Able to handle this.

Moss sat next to Lady Sulat and began quietly explaining. I knelt on the floor next to Azalea and pretended I couldn't hear them talking about me.

"Do you like blocks?" I asked, stacking one on top of another.

"Not there." She shook her head, removed my block and stacked it on a different tower. Then she patted my hand. "I teach you."

I tried a second block, but I'd apparently placed that one wrong, too. It didn't matter if I matched or mismatched the colors—she rearranged anything I set down. Moss and Lady Sulat continued talking, but their words mercifully faded to a background murmur as I played with little Azalea.

"How am I supposed to do it?" I asked her.

She smiled at me. "Do it better!"

That was all the instruction she gave, but I didn't mind. I watched her small, chubby hands rearrange and create, always so meticulous to place them just so and not let her long, blue-ranked sleeves touch anything.

"Plum," Lady Sulat said. I jerked upright, accidentally knocking over a tower.

Azalea sighed and patted my hand again.

"I'd like for you to finish your work, though obviously the current arrangements are insufficient. Would it be better if Moss were in the room with you? I can post another guard outside the door."

I swallowed back the fear clawing up my throat. I had nothing to be afraid of with Moss there. "Yes. I can do that."

"Thank you," Lady Sulat said softly. "I wish you had informed me of the full situation earlier. Don't assume I know everything—I'd rather hear something twice than not at all."

I nodded, insides cold. How could she protect me and Dami if she wasn't always one step ahead of everyone?

"Are you learning well?" she asked.

"I'm picking it up quickly. Back at the safehouse, I've made some of my own notes for reference, as well."

"Good. Make note-taking your main focus. As soon as the fifth member of your party can be made ready, I'm sending you out of Rowak, whether Dami's healed or not. Between Alder's attack and now Sorrel, I've already been too slow in sending you."

Soon, there'd be no more Sorrel.

Soon, there'd be no more Bane.

MINISTER ASHOWN's dinner party was that evening. Rather than have me return to my studies, Lady Sulat coached me on the guests and their political leanings. Then she turned me over to Poppy, one of her servants. After dousing me with pine soap in the bathhouse, Poppy brought me back to Lady Sulat's porch to tease my hair into a net of braids. I thought it would hurt, but Poppy was agile-of-hand and did her work expertly.

Lady Sulat had a beautiful peach-colored dress for me to wear, the skirt embroidered with white starflowers. We left together for Minister Ashown's home, the summer sun low in the sky. Four guards carried Lady Sulat in an elegantly lacquered sedan chair decorated with carvings of ferns. I walked alongside, flanked by two guards, Resin and Suruc. Moss had the evening off.

An eight-foot wall of river stones and mortar encompassed Minister Ashown's compound. Glossy cherry trees, their blossoms long since gone, stood sentry around a garden with banks of lacey flowers and ornamental shrubs. Across the greenery stood the main house, a broad building with wooden shingles and log pillars to support the eaves over the immense front porch. Handsome tables sat there in full view of the garden.

Lady Sulat exited her sedan. Together, we walked to the porch where Minister Ashown stood. The last time I'd seen him, he'd been another face in the wash of Purple-Blue council members acquitting me of treason. His expression was as severe as ever, with deep-set eyes and thin lips, but he greeted us both graciously and showed us to our seats.

I sat like a doll, not fidgeting, always smiling politely as other guests arrived. I actually remembered most of their names, their political affiliations, and their family connections.

Minister Grayfox of External Affairs, an older man who fit his name, sat next to me with his daughter, Advisor Orchid. We made pleasant small talk about our hometowns and the weather until Minister Ashown ordered the first course delivered: chanterelles in a rich sauce made from duck fat, flour, and stock.

I dipped my spoon in the sauce. Reasonably balanced but leaning sweet with a note of maple syrup in the background. Endurance-of-ear. So similar to what Sorrel had fed me for lunch. I shifted uneasily on my knees.

"What does the chef have to say about the meal?" Advisor Orchid asked me.

The flavors weren't as developed as they could be. The chef had used the richness of the sauce to hide the merely satisfactory seasoning. "We've had good rain for chanterelles this season," I said.

Advisor Orchid wrinkled her nose, but Minister Grayfox chortled. "You must be quite the connoisseur. It tastes marvelous to this old man."

"It is good," I mumbled, embarrassed. Just not excellent.

Lady Sulat caught our conversation. "She *is* a remarkably accomplished chef, Minister Grayfox. Do allow her some snobbery."

"And a hero," Minister Ashown cut in. "Can we entreat you to tell us about the night your cooking saved the king? It would be something to hear it from your own mouth."

Six ministers and another half-dozen guests stared expectantly at me. This is why I was here, wasn't it? To impress them and bend their opinion toward a prisoner exchange that might only lengthen this war?

I'd had plenty of practice telling my story with Purple Lord Valerian. My words started softly, hesitantly, but soon they flowed freely. The story almost felt like a folk tale instead of a part of my life. All the messy bits, all the bits that didn't belong in the public's ear, were carefully excised.

My audience listened intently, eyes widening at the dramatic parts. When I finished, Orchid set her spoon in her empty bowl. "You must be eager to have all our Shoreed captives executed. You saw their treachery firsthand."

"I also saw the bravery of our men," I said. "If we kill our Shoreed prisoners, they will kill their Rowak prisoners." These words I hadn't rehearsed, but they came easily anyway. I didn't want more death.

Minister Grayfox frowned. "You're not concerned about giving them back nearly twice as many men? Relatively fresh, fighting men, not beat down by long captivity? I can't help but think this will prolong the war—or even cause us to lose it."

He echoed King Alder's sentiments perfectly. I had no argument to give against him.

Advisor Orchid waved an elegant, dismissive hand in the air. "It's not a real exchange if they're keeping everyone from the Azure Flint Estate."

I had no idea what she was talking about.

Lady Sulat gracefully cut in. "True, the Shoreed insist that any men captured in the Azure Flint area are not Rowak prisoners of war, but Shoreed traitors. After all, the Shoreed went to war on the grounds that we've wrongfully held those lands for the past hundred years."

I silently thanked her for passing me that helpful summary—but couldn't she have explained earlier?

"A ludicrous claim," Minister Grayfox muttered. "Letting them keep those men is tantamount to admitting they've a right to the Azure Flint Estate."

Lady Sulat nodded. "Perhaps. But the ministers vote this week not to determine if we *agree* to the terms Shoreed has presented, but whether or not we are willing to open *negotiations*. The Shoreed have made an offer; we should make a counter-offer and at least try to rescue our soldiers."

I bit the inside of my lip. King Alder had omitted that detail.

Minister Duwill of the Interior cut in. "There are what? Perhaps fifty prisoners from Azure Flint? Even if we win them through negotiation, the numbers still don't add up."

Lady Sulat politely inclined her head. "You sit in council under the king of Rowak, the father of our nation. Would you advise a father to cast off his sons? Rowak is not merely a place. Rowak is her people. If we abandon those soldiers, we have shrunk Rowak's borders as surely as ceding the Azure Flint lands would. How can we expect our Ancestors to remember us if we forget and forsake the sons of Rowak?"

The speech warmed my blood, but my thoughts cooled it again. Were those her true feelings, or pretty words to shame these people into voting for the exchange?

"Your best argument is that we can't win without our Ancestors' blessing?" Advisor Orchid sneered. "Absurd. Sharp obsidian and strong arms win wars."

Lady Sulat didn't flinch. "You're being incredibly short-sighted."

Advisor Orchid shook her head at Lady Sulat like she was a naughty child. "None of you seem to think our soldiers are willing to sacrifice themselves. The solution is easy."

Nothing about this situation was easy.

"We can't afford to keep so many prisoners, so we should follow Shoreed's example in this matter," Orchid continued. "We maim our prisoners in any quick, efficient way that won't kill them within a week. Then we abandon them at the border."

How could anyone be that calloused? "That's what you really want?" I asked. "That's your grand vision?"

"I'd rather execute them all, but I'm under the impression that none of you have the stomach for that," Advisor Orchid replied dryly.

Lady Sulat folded her hands in her lap. "And you lack the foresight to create peace. Discussing a prisoner exchange is the first step in negotiating a *treaty*. If we refuse to talk to Shoreed, fighting is inevitable. But I firmly believe that the Old Road Ambush can—and should—be remembered as the last battle of this war."

Peace. It sounded too lovely to be real. I knew Lady Sulat didn't think it likely, but she was arguing for it—for a way to end this war without poisoning anyone.

"If we can secure a treaty," Lady Sulat continued, "then I am happy to trade all of our prisoners for all of theirs."

That caught Minister Grayfox's ear. "Interesting, interesting. Who did you have in mind to lead these negotiations?"

They continued talking for some time, but as far as I could gather, Minister Grayfox was willing to vote for a prisoner exchange if Lady Sulat nominated him as ambassador. Minister Duwill and the rest wrung other concessions out of her—a promotion for a son, a vote on another issue.

I didn't have much appetite for the noodles in the second course. It felt so mercenary. My earlier speech about how I'd saved the king seemed frivolous now, just a bit of entertainment before the real business began.

After the party, Lady Sulat invited me inside her sedan chair. Two of us made a tight fit, and the guards grunted as they lifted us up. Starlight and scant city torches gave us precious little light.

"I wanted a chance to talk to you privately," she said, voice low. "You did well."

"Well?" I felt like a child and a fraud. Could Lady Sulat really forge a lasting peace from a prisoner exchange or had she told us what we wanted to hear?

"You spoke quickly. You gave beautiful answers."

"Answers that didn't matter," I replied. "All those ministers still had to be bought."

Lady Sulat shook her head, her amber hair ornaments tinkling. "They needed a vision of patriotism. They needed to believe that negotiations could succeed. I just provided extra motivation to follow through."

They shouldn't need extra motivation to do the right thing for Rowak. My mouth tasted oily. "But you're not sure it will work. You're still sending me to the Coral Palace, in case eliminating Red Lord Ospren is the fastest way to end this war."

"I'd be an optimistic fool to set only one plan in motion. You're uncomfortable with all this," she said. It wasn't a question.

I glanced down, even though my eyes couldn't betray me in this near-darkness. I could smell Lady Sulat—a perfume of peonies—better than I could see her. I almost told her about my fears and King Alder's accusations.

But if King Alder was right, that would be an incredibly foolish thing to do. If I was going to survive in a world of politicians, I needed to be more guarded than that.

CHAPTER
TEN

Moss knocked on Sorrel's door for me. It flung open, if possible, even faster than usual. Sorrel stared straight past Moss and my extra guard, Resin. His shoulders sagged in relief.

"Plum." Sorrel made my name sound like a prayer of thanks. "I'm so glad you're here."

I pursed my lips. "I have work to do. That's why I came."

He held the door open and gestured for me to come inside. Confusion flickered in his eyes when Moss entered first. For a while, Sorrel said nothing as we poured over Violet's papers, he just kept glancing at me, the worry lines in his face deepening every time.

Eventually, he broke the silence. "Plum...are you upset? About yesterday?" he asked softly, as if he could pretend Moss wasn't here. "You left. Without your present."

My fingers froze on the brush I held.

"Can I deliver it somewhere for you, if it's inconvenient for you to carry?" he asked, a cautious hope spreading across his face. He still didn't understand. Not even after I'd run away.

Moss sat in the corner polishing his bolas. The familiar, rhythmic clinking helped me breathe. "I'm not upset about yesterday."

Sorrel beamed and moved as if to grab my hand.

"I'm upset about what happened while I was in prison."

His hand fell limp. "Plum..."

How I hated, hated the way my name sounded on his lips.

"I know we've had a bad start," he said. "But we should put it all behind us. You've always wanted to marry a chef, someone as passionate about food as yourself. Someone you could discuss braising and grilling with. I want that, too. Our Ancestors smile on us. We have a second chance at that bright future."

My throat felt like it was squeezing shut. I focused on the soft sound of Moss's polishing, eternally grateful for his presence. "You think rushing into another wedding will make either of us happy?"

"Oh." His shoulders relaxed and he smiled. "This is about my first wedding, isn't it? About me choosing that woman? It was a mistake, Plum. There's no need to be jealous. I was heartbroken over your rejection."

"And you thought marrying Violet would fix it. Now you think marrying me will fix the pain of her betrayal."

Sorrel inched closer, something pleading in his eyes. "You make me happy, Plum. I cherish our time together."

Time spent studying poisons. It seemed oddly appropriate.

"You beat me."

He stilled, then flicked a glance at Moss. His voice lowered further. "I was drunk. I was upset. I thought you were a traitor, Plum."

He hadn't been drunk the second time he hurt me.

"I thought you were my enemy," he pleaded. "Forgive me."

He bowed his head low, repentant.

"Forgiving you and marrying you aren't the same thing, Sorrel. I accept your apology."

He glared at me for the first time since we'd started work together. An angry, tight line ran between his brows. "How is that forgiveness? You wanted to marry me, Plum. You practically sabotaged my wedding to that traitor."

"I did not!" At least, not on purpose.

"And you lied to me. You can't pretend it's my fault everything went so wrong."

Why was I debating with him as if my refusal required justification? Arguing only gave him more chances to convince me that the foreboding in my gut meant nothing. Even if he never hit me again, I'd always know he was capable of it.

"It's over, Sorrel," I said simply, firmly.

He shook his head. "You're merely upset by the assassination attempt. In a week or two, you'll calm down. Can I deliver the manuscript somewhere for you?"

Merely upset? Could he not hear anything I'd said?

"It's normal to be irrational after something like this happens," he assured me.

Irrational. The squeamish part of me that still itched for the antique Toksang Empire manuscript shrank into a small, hard lump in my gut.

"I can be patient, Plum. We don't have to get married next month, or even this summer."

I coldly turned back to the paper in front of me.

"Why aren't you saying anything?" he demanded. "You're pouting like a child. None of this would have happened if I'd known who you were. And now I know!"

I breathed slowly, in rhythm with Moss's polishing. I knew if I looked at Moss, he'd jump in to defend me. But I didn't need his words. I didn't want to drag out this argument. I just needed him here, in this room, quietly anchoring me.

Sorrel's shoulders slumped, his anger sloughing off with it. "Plum. Plum...I don't know why you won't talk to me. Why you've changed your opinion of me so stubbornly. I misjudged you when I didn't know you. Don't you think there's a chance you're misjudging me?"

"I'm not sure why you're being so persistent," I said, my voice as smooth and calm as Lady Sulat's. "Why are you set on marrying an irrational, childish, stubborn woman? Surely finding someone else is better than having a wife you find distasteful."

"Plum—"

"I've made up my mind. I'll say no more on the matter."

Sorrel wheedled and chastised me in turn, straight through lunch and into the afternoon. It was nearly time for me to go before he stopped. I couldn't tell if he was plotting his next speech or if he'd given up.

I knew I'd never see those beautiful recipes from the Toksang Empire again. But a calm washed over me. I whispered a prayer of thanks to my Ancestors. I could, and had, chosen my dignity over my professional advancement as a chef.

If Lady Sulat did turn out to be everything King Alder claimed— a warmongering, self-glorifying politician—I hoped I'd have the same fortitude to walk away from her.

I left Dami snoring on the mattress early the next morning and slipped into the kitchen. I'd barely gotten the first crock of buckwheat on the coals when Bane strode in, black hair sweeping low over his worried eyes.

"Moss told me. Yesterday. He thought he ought to. I hope you're not upset at him."

I stared at Bane, mind churning. Told him about what? The dinner? Leaving Rowak?

Bane sighed. "I'm not sure why you thought you needed to hide what Sorrel did."

"Oh." I awkwardly rubbed the back of my neck. "Osem knew...so I thought Lady Sulat knew."

"I should have asked you about your injuries."

"It...it really wasn't that important," I said self-consciously, painfully aware of the air under his left elbow. I sounded whiny to myself, making a fuss over mere *bruises*. I scrubbed the baby celery stalks, making them shine like pale peridots.

"After the coup, you seemed happy to avoid Sorrel. I didn't want to question that. I was selfish for not wanting to question it."

I turned. "Bane. You're one of the least selfish people I know. Why are you apologizing to me?"

"I wish I could help stand guard duty over you." He added more wood to the hearth fire. "Is the extra guard making it...more comfortable?"

"For me? Yes. Sorrel doesn't seem to feel the same." I gave him a tiny, joking smile.

Bane didn't laugh. "I hope you're done with this project soon."

I chopped the celery with the best obsidian knife in the house. Bane didn't know what my next assignment was. My life would be at risk, I'd have to leave him behind, and I wasn't even sure if I trusted the woman sending me.

Bane would listen to me if I voiced my doubts about Lady Sulat. But I couldn't bring myself to do it. Saying it out loud would make it too real.

Cynically, I wondered if Bane would report such words to Lady Sulat if I *did* speak.

Bane's frown deepened. "You're terribly quiet. Did Sorrel hurt you again? Yesterday?"

"No, no. It's not that." I swallowed. Maybe we could discuss Lady Sulat in a round-about fashion. I set the knife down and turned my back to the hearth. "You know all about the prisoner exchange and how Lady Sulat supports it?"

Bane nodded.

"I'm not sure if it's the right thing." *I'm not sure if I can trust her.*

Bane jerked back. "What do you mean?"

"What if it just prolongs the war?"

Bane stilled. His brown eyes looked like cold, solemn agate. "We should try to free our men."

"Wouldn't they rather wait if it meant less fighting? Less death?"

He exhaled slowly, looking at the ceiling like he was praying to his Ancestors. Then he looked at me. "I was in a prisoner camp. That's why I lost my arm."

I peered at him. "I thought...I thought that happened in one of the first battles of the war."

"It's easier to say. Battle sounds daring. Getting captured doesn't." Guilt and shame thickened his words to a slow-molasses trickle, as if he might not actually continue. I laid a hand on his shoulder. I wanted to listen.

"I held my post like I was supposed to. I followed all my orders. Even during battle, with all that horrible chaos of..." He paused and glanced down. "Sorry. You probably don't want to hear about my friends dying."

Friends. Somehow it hadn't occurred to me that Bane wasn't just one known face among a sea of unnamed soldiers. "I want to hear whatever you want to tell me."

He shook his head and skipped that part, anyway. "I was injured. A slash across my left forearm. Even after we were captured, I was sure we'd be rescued right away. That everything would be fine. For a day or two, I could do the labor our taskmasters set us in the camp. Being strong-of-arm certainly helped. We dug latrines. Hauled rocks. We were making our own prison—one big enough to hold many more prisoners to do more work.

"But my wound festered. I couldn't move my fingers. The Shoreed had no desire to waste their chefs or their bandages on a Rowak soldier. They carted me up with some others who were in rough shape and dumped us near the Rowak border to fend for ourselves. One man tried to hobble back into the cart. They shot him through the throat three times."

I stared, wide-eyed, then curled back from him, embarrassed. Had I expected this to be a happy story?

Bane shrugged—not Dami's careless shrug, but a gesture that seemed to say the weight of the memory would never quite be gone. "We ended up separated, the dozen or so of us remaining. I couldn't find food or clean water for days. I drank out of mud puddles and vomited it all back up." He gave me a self-deprecating smile. "You're a far better survivalist than I am."

When I'd first arrived at the palace, he'd been so impressed that I'd managed to forage my way safely to the city. "You were injured."

"And I lacked your skills. I was burning with fever by the time some poor farm girl found me. Her family cared for me while they sent for the military. But it was too late to save my arm. A surgeon came. Nice, clean cut at the elbow joint," he whispered, as if he didn't quite trust his full voice.

Words failed me. They all would have been inadequate anyway.

"We can't afford to keep all the Shoreed prisoners we've taken," Bane continued. "Either we have to trade them, maim them, or kill them. I know some people like the maiming option. No one dies. They can't fight. But I'm hardly allowed to hold any other posts. I want to stand guard with Moss today and I can't."

"Because you have important work as a messenger," I reassured him, looking with pride at the slightly crooked armband he wore, decorated with a stylized switchback road climbing a mountain.

He shook his head. "No. I *can't*. I'm not considered fit for guard duty. I'm *lucky* to be a messenger. Strangers on the street, my family..." his voice cracked at the last word. "Prisoner camps kill people and they maim people, and they steal beautifully planned futures, Plum. With a few bandages, I could have kept my arm. I was going to have a grand career. Be an officer. Marry and have a family. And now..."

"And now you're still one of the best men in Rowak. And a hero," I said firmly.

His expression softened. He reached out and tucked my hair behind my ear, his fingers cool and dry on my cheek. "I came here to see how you were, Plum, and now I've talked too long about something else entirely."

I wanted to turn my head and kiss those fingers, as if kisses could heal what he'd been through. Instead, I reached out and laid my hand on top of his before it drifted from my face, surrounding his fingers with all the warmth I had to offer. "You talked for just the right amount."

Regardless of whether or not I could trust Lady Sulat, I no longer had any doubt that I'd done the right thing at the dinner last night, advocating for the exchange.

"Thank you, Bane," I said, "for telling me."

MY STOMACH SQUIRMED the next morning as I climbed the steps of Sorrel's porch. I paused at the top, leaning against one of those massive redwood pillars, and tried to summon my cool resolve from the day before. I was safe. And Sorrel couldn't budge me.

I knocked. And then knocked again.

The door opened a fraction. "You can come in," Sorrel muttered.

Inside, a few crumbs lay on the floor. Papers sat askew on the desk. It wasn't exactly messy, but it wasn't the pristine glow Sorrel usually presented.

I exhaled. I'd never be at peace in this room, but this was the prettiest I'd ever seen it. Sorrel didn't talk to me all morning. I worked in silence, taking meticulous notes of things I might need in Shoreed. I tried hard not to think about what that need was, exactly.

Moss, myself, and my second guard left the palace without incident, taking a new route back to Bane's house. Before we even reached the porch, a guard ran out to me. "We were just about to send someone to look for you. Dami's been poisoned."

CHAPTER
ELEVEN

I raced to our room. Some part of me expected to see her lying pale and dead on the floor with a cackling Bloodmarrow leering over her. But she was wheezing on all fours, red hives running down her neck.

"I'm...fine," she managed.

I'd seen her like this twice before. But each of those times, my father had been there. By the time she'd looked this bad, he'd already had the proper food for her. I ran back into the hallway.

"You!" I pointed at a guard. "Go sit with her! If she starts vomiting, make sure she doesn't drown in it!"

I turned toward the kitchen, but Moss was already blocking my way, his arms full of my notes on poisons. "Which of these do you need?"

I shoved past him. Papers scattered to the floor. "None of them!"

Strength-of-neck, to keep her throat open. That's what she needed first. I grabbed the beets Bane had so graciously bought and chopped off the greens and the roots. Beet stems targeted the neck. I crushed them in a mortar and pestle with a spoonful of pickle juice. Sour brought strength.

The stems mercifully gave up their liquid. Soon there was a purple puddle in the bottom of the mortar. I poured it into a cup, grabbed a spoon, and ran back to Dami. Bits of yellow-orange, bile-filled vomit stained the floor.

"Sit back on your knees."

The soldier helped her. Her hands were shaking now, her face clammy. I dribbled a bit of the concoction into her mouth.

"Even if you can't swallow, it'll seep in. You," I turned to the soldier, "As soon as she can handle it, give her another drip. Understood?"

"Yes."

I liked him. He didn't seem to care that he had vomit on his tunic. He held my sister and waited, ready to help.

I rushed back to the kitchen. Endurance of blood. Sweet bone marrow soup would be the most potent, but we didn't have fresh bones, and there was no time to go shopping for them. I rummaged in the cupboards for something else that would do, shoving aside bags of beans and jars of oil. Everywhere I turned, I seemed to run into another guard. There had to be at least five of them in here now, including Moss.

"Get out!" I shouted.

"If there are Bloodmarrows around, we can't risk—" Moss began.

"She wasn't poisoned! She's allergic to catfish! Out!"

This time, they listened. Finally, I found some coriander seeds and yarrow. I simmered a quick tea out of them and sweetened it with maple syrup. Endurance-of-blood would help calm her body's reaction to what she'd eaten.

The tea needed to steep longer, but I still rushed a cup of the weak stuff to Dami. She'd vomited again, right into the cup with her beet stem juice. I grabbed that cup and pressed the tea into the guard's hands. "This one now."

I ran back to the kitchen. I left the rest of the tea to steep and made Dami more of the beet step mixture.

It took an hour of dripping concoctions in her mouth before she was breathing easily. I helped her clean up and change into fresh clothes in the kitchen while soldiers swabbed her room. Then I got her safely tucked in under a warm blanket. She still had hives, but she was breathing steadily now.

I fetched her another cup of yarrow-coriander tea and she sat up and downed it without complaint. Apparently, she cared a good deal more about breathing than she did about her ribs healing.

"I'm not sure how you got exposed to catfish," I said, "but I'll go through everything in the pantry tonight. Dried and powdered, it could have been added to stretch one spice or another."

Dami's voice came out a little hoarse. "Don't bother. It wasn't from here."

I narrowed my gaze. "Did you make Torsal go buy you some of those buckwheat dumplings you kept going on about?"

"No. He refused. I snuck out and bought *myself* some dumplings."

"Dami!"

"She *said* they were duck dumplings, but she cut them half and half with fish, I'm sure of it now. That ought to be a crime." She itched her neck. "I *hate* hives."

"Dami..." How could she be so stupid? So selfish?

Why, why was I still surprised at her for being stupid and selfish?

"Before I started swelling up, Sergeant Farel lectured me on how bad it was to go outside and how we'll need to move the safehouse again, so you don't need to go to the trouble of scolding me yourself, all right?"

Move. I might not see Bane again before I left for Shoreed. "Do you not understand what *safehouse* means? All these soldiers are working to protect both of us."

Dami rolled her eyes. "Like anyone in Askan-Wod knows me. I'm not exactly conspicuous."

"Your short hair. That's not memorable?"

"I'll put a hat on next time. Thanks for the suggestion."

I stared. How could she joke about her own safety? "You're a brash fool."

Dami stopped scratching. "That's the best you have?"

"You could have been seen!"

"Oh, the tragedy. The neighbors can gossip about my bad hair. I'm sure they have nothing better to do."

"This isn't—"

"—a joke or a game. Do you know you repeat yourself? You sound like Nana when she went senile."

Every muscle in my body stiffened. "Don't talk about Nana like that."

"What? It's true. As soon as she came down with that fever, it was like her memory turned to mush." Dami yawned and stretched. "Do you remember the day before she died, how she couldn't tell us apart?"

My eyes stung. "You don't talk about the dead like that! About our *Ancestor* like that."

"Ancestor." Dami rolled her eyes. How did she have the energy for that when she'd barely been breathing an hour ago? "I don't know why she'd care what we say about her. Isn't she supposed to be in some kind of wondrous place with all the other dead people?"

I choked. "You don't think she watches over us? That she's not busy weaving souls for her descendants?"

"You're not married. I'm not married. Unless you're a lot friendlier with Bane than I think you are, what baby is she weaving a soul for? Seems like she'd have a lot of time to just relax and enjoy herself. Especially if she left us well enough alone to live our own lives."

"Your actions almost left her to roam as a Hungry Ghost!" My nails bit into my palms.

"Nana could have taken care of herself." Dami picked up her cup and tried to drink again, but it was empty.

She could disregard my life—but Nana's afterlife?

I didn't swallow down the hurt. I didn't find something polite to say. And I didn't shout—Dami would enjoy that. I collected myself. And I dug up the most hurtful thing I could think of to say.

"I'm amazed you survived two days in the army."

Dami jerked back. "Excuse me?"

"With the way you whine? How didn't you get sent home? Or at least beaten to a pulp by the other recruits. I'm your own sister, and I hate listening to you."

Her face hardened. "I was a great soldier."

"Yes. Great at catching arrows in your ribs. I'm sure all soldiers aspire to that level of *skill*."

She clenched her hand around her teacup, shattering it. "I saved General Yuin's life!"

For once, I wasn't the one on the defensive. "I'm glad to see that there's at least one life that matters to you—even if it isn't your own family's."

Dami spluttered. For the first time I could remember, I'd won an argument with her.

I turned and strode out of the room.

I SLEPT that night in the kitchen by the hearth. None of the guards insisted on moving me, though Torsal did bring me a mattress and blanket, which I quietly thanked him for.

Why couldn't we just be normal sisters?

Every time the back of my mind began crafting an expert apology, I replayed Dami's cruel words about Nana. With those, I built a cold, hard pillar of anger inside me. I wouldn't apologize. I didn't want to. I'd tried to hurt her as badly as she'd hurt me, and maybe I'd even succeeded.

Perhaps we finally had a measure of sisterly solidarity through mutual hatred.

THE NEXT DAY was Former King Fulsaan's birthday banquet. Lady Sulat had no idea what King Alder was planning either, but she agreed it would be bad for the prisoner exchange if I refused to attend with Valerian. She headed off to the Royal Shrine for the morning ceremonies and left me with Poppy to get ready.

Perhaps King Alder would poison half the guests and blame me. Perhaps he had caught some contradiction in my story. Maybe he'd only spoken to me in an effort to dissuade me from supporting the exchange at Minister Ashown's party? The Purple-Blue Council was scheduled to vote on the matter tomorrow.

Poppy soon had me in that same peach-colored dress embroidered with starflowers. She worked something into my hair that smelled like honeysuckle and braided it neatly. I wondered if maids were ever asked to act as assassins. It would be easy for her to slip a garrote from her pocket while she was working on my hair and finish me off.

Lady Sulat returned mid-afternoon, still looking resplendent in a dress that pooled around her like liquid lapis lazuli. She looked me over in her slow, careful way. "I think you need one more thing before we go."

She pulled one of the ornaments from her own hair—a polished stick of redwood with three amber beads dangling from it. "Turn around."

Hesitantly, I did so. Lady Sulat slid the stick into my braid. "There. I can't give you wisdom against whatever Alder's planning, but I can arm you with a regal appearance."

I turned back to face her, stammering. I hadn't expected such a personal gesture from her. "Th-thank you. I'll make sure to return it safely."

"It's yours."

She was being too generous. Wariness crept over my awe. Was this a well-placed bribe, just like Sorrel's manuscripts?

Lady Sulat graced me with one of her rare smiles, and for a

moment, I didn't care if she was tricking me. I wanted to trust her. I wanted to believe this was real.

"Arrangements are finally in place. You and Dami leave tomorrow." Her smile didn't waver, but it somehow became mournful anyway. "There's so little I can do for you once you're in Shoreed. I hope this ornament reminds you of all the brave and amazing things you've already accomplished in the Redwood Palace."

KING ALDER CHOSE to hold the feast for his late father's birthday in the butterfly garden. An odd choice, given that butterflies represented new life and fertility. The lawn by the pond would have been more appropriate, with the water reflecting the heavens.

Tiny white blossoms blanketed the flower beds, making it look almost as if snow had managed to fall in summer. Amber-colored butterflies gathered on the garden's windbreak—a manzanita hedge with glorious crimson bark. Other butterflies, their wings a wash of parsley green and pale yellow, perched on blooming goldenrods. The heady perfume of so many flowers made me wobbly on my feet.

I was about to seat myself at a low, individual table with the less important guests when Purple Lord Heir Valerian enthusiastically waved me over. I knelt, instead, at the table next to his. Servants laid out the first course—pickled beets and radishes, topped with their own finely-shredded greens. This food had already been presented to Fulsaan in the Royal Shrine. It granted strength-of-soul, which would help Fulsaan visit his descendants in the land of the living. The dish would do nothing for us; we ate only to respect Fulsaan and show our yearning for his presence.

Lord Valerian and I waited in respectful silence until King Alder took the first bite. Then Valerian turned toward me. "I'm glad you came. I think Grandpa will like having you here."

"Grandpa. I suppose he was one of those."

"The best! When I visited, he let me hunt bugs and throw stones in the pond." Valerian cleared his throat. "Not that I'd enjoy frivolous things like that."

Fulsaan might have been a horrible king and a horrible father, but I was glad the lazy old man had earned the love of his grandson. Valerian probably needed someone in his life who didn't expect anything of him.

"That doesn't sound frivolous to me," I said, gathering a spoonful with a little bit of everything on it. "It takes a certain amount of wisdom to set aside never-ending tasks and enjoy the world around us."

In Fulsaan's case, it was probably an overabundance of slothfulness, but I wasn't going to say that here. Valerian smiled at me. "Thank you. This was his favorite dish, you know. Grandma liked it, too. My father once said it was about the only thing they had in common."

Knowing what I did of their family history, that could be true. "But strength-of-soul doesn't do anything for the living."

"I think he just liked the way it crunched. Don't you?"

"I've always enjoyed pickled radishes."

His smile faded as he stared down at the bright vegetables. "He ate a lot of this during the winter, when he first got sick. He told me that he wanted to enjoy his last meal, and he was sure each one would be his last. If he hadn't been kidnapped, maybe he would have recovered by now. And we'd all be eating together."

"I'm so sorry your grandfather is gone." And I meant it, even if Valerian was wrong about how his grandfather had died.

We talked pleasantly of Valerian's memories of the old man as we ate. I hadn't expected to actually enjoy attending the banquet; perhaps King Alder had only meant to sway me toward his view with the prisoner exchange, that day he called me to the House of Reflected Learning.

Soon servants brought the next course—salt-roasted hazelnuts. These were paraded through the gathering before being taken away. Agility-of-spirit helped the deceased make their way to the

Realm of the Ancestors, and such dishes were especially important to offer in the first year. But it might cause a living soul to prematurely jump from its body. Not even the Sages—who often ate dishes that targeted the soul in their rituals—would eat such a thing.

Spicy garlic-rubbed radishes came next—a dish to enhance perceptive-of-soul. This would help all who ate to feel the presence of the deceased. The radish skins were beautifully blistered, smoky and sharp. The warmth of them spread through me. For a moment, I thought of Fulsaan's doughy face. His tired, pleading brown eyes.

But my thoughts soon drifted to Nana. Her bark-rough hands, her honey-scented hair. I wondered if she was watching.

I wish you were still here. That you could have met Bane.

I could almost hear Nana whisper back, *I would have liked that, too.*

The spice of the dish burned back up my throat. I knew Nana was safe. I knew I'd see her again someday—hopefully decades from now. But sometimes it still seemed cosmically cruel that she wasn't here, now, living and breathing in this moment with me.

The next course was candied hazelnuts, dyed a summery pink by beet juice. Endurance of soul. This was the dish most beneficial to the living—it kept our souls rooted to our bodies and helped us persevere through grief and mourning. I chewed slowly, wanting to linger in my heartaches. It felt right to miss Nana.

King Alder leaned back on his cushion—he was the only one present afforded the luxury of a backrest. As soon as he opened his mouth, other conversations died.

"My father, Purple King Fulsaan, is sixty-eight today. For twenty-one years, he cared for Rowak as its father. Now, he cares for Rowak as one of its Ancestors."

He continued, telling stories about Fulsaan. They were nothing like my memories of the man or Heir Valerian's stories. He spoke of a firm, just king eagerly engaged in the welfare of his nation. Was that how King Alder actually saw him? I was nearly certain Fulsaan would rather be remembered with a stiff drink than a long, solemn speech.

When King Alder's talk shifted to how much he missed him, I knew those words were real. Bitterness tinged them. I couldn't tell if Alder was bitter at the inevitability of death or bitter at me for exorcising Fulsaan and depriving him of a father.

"In this time of loss, I think of others that I miss. Queen Tiraan has been gone from us for six years, now, since before this accursed war with the Shoreed even began."

Valerian sat up straighter upon hearing his mother's name. He blinked furiously and pressed his lips into a stoic line.

"Those were happier times. Prosperous times. I had a healthy father and my beloved wife next to me. The flowers of summer smelled sweeter. I realize that I will never again have a father upon this earth. He is gone to our Ancestors, and I pray that this birthday celebration will fill his soul with strength, agility, perception, and endurance."

A butterfly actually landed on King Alder, gently stretching her blue wings. It was like a piece of the heavens had descended to adorn him.

"But losing my father has given me plenty of time to reflect and realize that while I will never have a father again, I need not spend the rest of my days without a wife."

Alder turned toward me. Slowly. Deliberately. "Thinking on my father's dedication to Rowak, my heart has softened toward another who shares his love of our great nation. Green-ranked Plum of Clamsriver, hero and patriot of Rowak, I offer my proposal. Marry me."

Purple King Alder, ruler of Rowak, bowed to *me*.

The garden seemed to blur, like paints in the rain, even as the too-bright sun stung my eyes. Silent butterfly wings fluttered between us.

Valerian stared at me with wondering joy. He crossed the

distance between us, knelt next to me, clasped my hands, then bowed his head against them. "*Mother*."

All the ministers, all the important officials, stared at me. Me, with the Heir of Rowak squeezing my hands. This was the moment Alder had been plotting for. Bringing me in to tell Valerian the story. The invitation.

If I refused and crushed the spirit of the Purple Heir, I was no patriot of Rowak, and my support of the prisoner exchange was discredited. Minister Grayfox already frowned deeply at me, mouth twitching in concern. But if I agreed, King Alder would have me under his thumb. Either way, King Alder couldn't lose.

My heart pounded like it had on the day Moss saved me from the assassin. If those arrows had killed me, King Alder profited. If the military was framed, whether or not I died, he came out on top.

The shadow of a smile touched King Alder's face. He acted boldly when all possible outcomes lead to victory for him.

I turned to Lady Sulat. Her face showed no expression—not in her natural way, but frozen as if she was struggling to school her shock. She'd gone pale.

Absently, I was aware of patting Valerian's back. Of him sitting up and burbling happy words at me. He adored me. King Alder had seen to that.

How could I extricate myself from this proposal without damning hundreds of prisoners on both sides to mutilation, starvation, and death? My mouth felt tight, like I'd drunk vinegar.

King Alder smiled magnanimously. He'd had plenty of time to figure out what to say. "Servants have already prepared your new quarters. Perhaps you'd like to retire there now. You seem to be quite overcome, darling."

The word *darling* seemed to stretch out like a snake, a dangerous word coiling around my neck and threatening to strangle me, leaving nothing but blue bruises behind.

Servants helped me to my feet. Valerian beamed at me. I smiled weakly back.

"We will start preparations for the formal engagement ceremony at once," King Alder said.

As servants escorted me away, the gardens filled with a buzz of whispers, as if a thousand grasshoppers had usurped all the graceful butterflies.

CHAPTER
TWELVE

The servants didn't take me to the Royal Falcon House, where queens historically resided, but to the guest apartments nearest the Royal Bear House. Unlike the guesthouse Sorrel was staying in, the interior of this building was one large, interconnected suite—a sitting room, bedroom, storage room, and a small room for servants. It all smelled of fresh linens and old wood polish.

My guards were now the guards King Alder assigned. They refused to let me out, citing my frail health and imploring me to rest. When two servants arrived, I thought I might persuade one of them to help me. But Yellow-ranked Dalea was a nervous thing, eager to get in King Alder's good graces again after breaking his favorite vase. And the other, the matron of my household, turned out to be Alder's old nursemaid, Blue-ranked Rose of Thistle Hill. The proud old woman stood with her chest puffed up like a rooster and glared at me with unmasked disdain. She acted like my pending engagement to her dear Alder was a personal insult.

I spent a week like that—isolated, locked up. Alder had cleverly put me in a beautiful prison. I imagined Dami feasting on whatever she fancied and laughing merrily at my predicament. Lady Sulat wouldn't start a battle on the palace grounds to get me out. Not for one chef.

I wondered how the vote on the prisoner exchange had gone.

Had I accomplished at least that much? Rose wouldn't tell me, and Dalea didn't seem to know or care.

My only comfort was that it would make King Alder look utterly incompetent if I died as soon as I was placed under his protection. But that made me wonder what else he might be planning for me while I sat here, useless.

On the eighth evening, Rose left. Perhaps to report to King Alder. Perhaps on some other matter. She certainly didn't tell me. Dalea entered my room to clear away my supper dishes and lingered, pursing her lips as she searched for imaginary dust on the windowsill.

With Rose gone, perhaps I had a chance to make an ally out of Dalea. "Are you all right? Rose doesn't seem to treat you well."

"No, no. I'm still learning how to do my duties properly. She's right to scold me." Dalea worried her lip between her teeth. "But she is out..."

"Yes? You can talk to me, Dalea."

That was all the invitation she needed to kneel next to me. "Are the rumors true?" She dropped her voice to a whisper. "Are you expecting?"

I stared at her. I had to be misunderstanding her. If King Alder wanted to accuse me of infidelity, he'd need to start such rumors *after* I'd had time to cheat on him. "What?"

Dalea shuffled closer to me. "I mean, you were, umm, good friends with King Fulsaan, right? That always did seem odd. Did King Alder hand-pick you to keep his father company?"

"Of all the ridiculous—!" I spluttered. "Rose just hates me."

"Rose hasn't said anything about it. She's too proper to gossip." Dalea rocked back and forth on her heels. "So. Did Fulsaan pay you? Or was it pure patriotism? There's quite the debate raging right now."

"Raging *where*?" I demanded.

Dalea grinned. "It's all anyone in the kitchens can talk about. I'm quite popular there now, since I'm your maid. Dewar said he'd make me an extra-special treat if I asked you about it."

My stomach sloshed. I thought the apprentices *liked* me. I didn't think Tanoak or Hawak would let such slander circulate. If people in the kitchens were talking about it, it would spread all over the palace.

"Dalea," I said firmly. "You're not to speak a word about this."

She bit her lip, trying to contain a smile. "Yes, Green-ranked Plum. I'll tell everyone in the kitchens I'm under strict orders not to breathe a word of this to anyone."

I groaned. "Dalea. I was simply friends with King Fulsaan. He was very, very interested in food. Please do not fan the flames of this pernicious rumor."

"Food. Right." Dalea winked at me. "I won't press you for more details. I think it's good of King Alder to want to legitimize his half-sibling like this."

Dalea disappeared out the door. I couldn't follow her. I couldn't stop rumors from flying.

Soon Rose returned—with King Alder.

"I came to see how you fared." He wore something less formal than his royal regalia—brightly dyed lightweight cloth instead of heavily embroidered brocade. "Let's talk, you and I."

We sat in the front room, a rug as red as plum wine stretched between us. Rose acted as chaperone, kneeling in the corner and spinning.

"I'm sorry to hear you've taken ill," King Alder said. "And even sorrier that you didn't accept my earlier offers of friendship."

"You can't lock me up indefinitely. There will be a formal engagement ceremony and a wedding, at least. I'll be able to tell everyone that you imprisoned me."

I hoped I sounded as unruffled as Lady Sulat always did, but King Alder only smiled. There was a touch of King Fulsaan's shamelessness and a bit of Valerian's boyishness in it that made him charming and sickening all at once. "Please do go ahead and tell everyone how horrible I am."

My throat tightened. "Why?"

"Oh. I invited your parents. They'll be my guests at the palace until after the wedding."

"You wouldn't—"

"Oh, of course I wouldn't harm them! But I make no promises about what the guards might do to the parents of a traitorous woman who besmirches the king's name. The last thing we need right now is to slander Rowak's monarch and signal how weak we are to the Shoreed. Such claims might even cause more Rowak citizens to support Red Lord Ospren."

He was seven steps ahead of me, and given his smug tone, he knew it. I wanted nothing more than to ball my hands in my skirt and tell him what a horrible person he was, but I tried to keep my posture and my face statue-calm.

"Our engagement ceremony," Alder continued, "will take place in seven days—just enough time for your parents to arrive. I've moved the vote on the prisoner exchange back to the day after that."

Those words felt like a slap. He'd used his proposal not only to trap me, but to give himself more time to work against the exchange.

Rose showed no signs of agitation at any of this. She just kept spinning.

"I'm not sure why you're here if you're not worried about what I'll do."

"It's a courtesy, to help you understand what few choices you have right now. You *are* new to the palace," King Alder said. "No one is coming to rescue you. Lady Sulat's not daft enough to attack and remove you by force."

"I know."

"So, your first choice is to refuse my proposal. Ruin your reputation as a patriot. This one vote over the prisoner exchange becomes uncertain, but then you're free to live a life of peaceful obscurity."

The door opened. Dalea only made it half a step in before her eyes widened. Rose swept her back outside. Out on the porch, Rose gave her some errand to run. King Alder stared at me, silent. I felt like a mouse under the gaze of a viper.

Only after Rose returned and took her seat did he continue.

"Your only other choice is agreeing to marry me."

Alder might be a king, but all the greenhouses in the palace couldn't make him appealing.

"If you do," he said, "I'll continue the stories about your poor health. After the wedding, I'll install you on the third floor of my Royal Bear House, where my father used to live. You'll spend the rest of your days locked up there, unable to harm me or help my sister."

I wondered how long those days would even be. Murdering me inside his Royal Bear House would be simple, and no one would ask questions if I'd supposedly had some horrible illness for months on end.

"Don't you have more to say?" King Alder asked. A wrinkle marred his forehead.

Had he expected me to sob and wring my hands? To beg for him to play nice? I calmly folded my hands in my lap. "Thank you for your visit. It has proved most informative."

"Which option do you choose?" he demanded.

I smiled sweetly. "I will be sure to let you know during our engagement ceremony."

King Alder left scowling.

I spent hours tumbling his words over in my head. Even if it sounded like King Alder had come to gloat, I knew he wouldn't waste time on merely being petty. He wanted to influence me.

Hadn't he tried to make rejecting him sound like the best option? *A peaceful life of obscurity,* he'd said. Then he'd promised that if I agreed to this marriage, I'd spend a lifetime locked up in the Royal Bear House.

He preferred that I rejected him. He wanted a public debacle at the engagement ceremony that would discredit me—and by extension, Lady Sulat.

Say no, watch the vote crumble, and leave as a free woman.

Say yes, spend the rest of my short life as Alder's ghost in the attic.

Those were the two options he'd laid out. Now I just needed to find a third option—an option where King Alder lost regardless of whether he married me or not.

CHAPTER
THIRTEEN

D alea started bringing me food from the kitchens appropriate for an expecting mother, and I couldn't convince her to stop. Morosely, I drank my sweet cranberry tea. I wondered if Lady Sulat had already sent Dami off to Shoreed with some other chef. Or if someone else was training with Sorrel to take my place. At least King Alder hadn't mentioned Dami—that meant he didn't have her, and he probably didn't know she'd committed treason. But that wouldn't last long if Dami kept recklessly prancing around outside the safehouse.

As day after useless day passed, I felt like I was walking over my own thoughts, turning them into mush. I asked for paper and wrote a few letters, but I never received any replies. Rose was almost certainly collecting all my correspondence, both in and out. One tedious afternoon I wrote a letter of pure gibberish, then encoded it in a cipher. I took some comfort in imagining one of King Alder's men swearing profusely as he tried to make sense of it.

On the eleventh day since Fulsaan's birthday, Lady Egal, King Alder's aunt and the Matron of the Household for the entire palace, visited me.

We'd hit the full heat of summer, and her gray hair looked wilted. Still, she entered with swan-like poise and grace. She seated herself across the rug from me. Dalea left us each a personal table with tea and a bowl of honeyed nuts.

I waited for whatever acerbic thing Lady Egal had to say. She'd found me disdainful from the first day I arrived in the palace, bedraggled from my long trip. Thanks to the falsehoods of her grandson, Fir, she later loathed me as a no-good liar. I could only imagine what she thought of me now. Fir had been her beloved, dutiful grandson, even if he had been working with Violet. Would she blame me for his imprisonment, just like Sorrel once blamed me for Violet's arrest?

At least Lady Egal wouldn't beat me with her hands.

"I've been trying to visit you for a week to discuss your new position as the King's consort. I heard you've been ill," she said mildly.

Apparently, even King Alder couldn't keep Lady Egal from doing her duties. Half of me wanted to blubber about the guards, but I held it back. This woman wasn't my ally, and by now my parents were on their way to Askan-Wod. "I'm feeling better today."

Lady Egal's eyes had a half-distracted, watery look to them. "I'm glad. Healthy or not, you have the very important task of naming your engagement present."

"To name it?" I asked, confused. A man often gave his wife an engagement present, but I'd never heard of the woman demanding something particular before.

Lady Egal frowned, the tiny wrinkles around her mouth deepening. "You do realize you'll be his consort, not a queen?"

I had no idea what she meant, and I hated that I didn't know.

"Tsk. They should have let me in earlier, no matter how sick you were. Didn't you realize you're not in the traditional residence of the queen, the Royal Falcon House?"

"Of course," I said. I just hadn't thought much on it. *Where* I was being held as a prisoner seemed rather inconsequential.

Lady Egal smoothed the front of her skirt with her long, elegant fingers, not meeting my eye. "King Alder has not proposed adopting you into the blue rank. You can't hold the position of queen. Any children you have will be green-ranked lords or ladies."

Ancestors forgive, I hadn't even considered this union might produce children, or how it would affect them. "I'm...I'm afraid I don't understand the distinction between a queen and a consort."

"Queens have a large number of legal rights, like the right to have her own personal guard of a number equal to half of the King's Royal Bear Guards. You're only permitted to pick a singular bodyguard and must rely on the palace guards otherwise."

I sat up straighter. "I can choose a bodyguard?"

"Yes. You have someone in mind?"

I nodded. "Please, tell me about the other differences."

She spoke at some length about items that were, presently, of less interest. A queen could demand to speak at any Purple-Blue Council; I could not. A queen had access to the ledgers of the Treasury; I did not. The list went on.

"Perhaps most relevant for you, the King may divorce you to marry a woman of the blue rank—to marry a queen—without any obligations to you. If that happens, you and your children would simply be kicked out of the palace. Which is why picking your engagement present is so important," Lady Egal said. I'd expected her to be impatient with me, but she went over every detail with a warm professionalism that I envied.

I pursed my lips. "Why does that make the present so important?"

"Historically, most consorts have asked for a grant of land. If they are ever deposed, they can retire from the palace as the mistress of their own estate. I'll warn you that you won't be able to pick *which* estate. Usually consorts are given land as far away from Askan-Wod as possible, to prevent their continued influence in palace affairs."

I stared at her. A whole estate? I thought she'd been talking about clothes or cutting boards.

"Will you ask for an estate? I can have someone research an appropriate one for King Alder to grant to you."

I wasn't even sure if I was going to refuse or agree to this marriage. "I need some time to think about it."

"I understand." Her posture sank a hairsbreadth and she sighed. "You must be so overwhelmed by all of this, but in a way, I'm glad."

"Glad?" I wasn't sure what she was hinting at.

"For you. I misjudged you. I listened to my grandson"—her voice cracked on that word—"and treated you unkindly. You, in turn, saved my nephew and my great-nephew, then brought peace to my brother after his death. You deserve this high position."

I stared at her. I hadn't anticipated an apology. "Th-thank you."

"He was a good boy, you know. Fir was," Lady Egal said, her voice tight like she was trying not to cry.

Fir had robbed me, sent snakes after me, tried to get me executed, and then had casually tried to recruit me as his servant when none of that worked out. *Good* wasn't the word I'd use to describe him.

But I hadn't been his grandmother.

"He fetched me tea personally," Lady Egal continued. "He liked sitting with me, talking with me, running errands for me. All my other grandchildren were too self-important for that."

She blinked rapidly and gave me a self-deprecating smile. "I sound like a blabbering mess, don't I?"

"Not in the slightest." She sounded like a loving Ancestor.

"He's in a military prison, now. I've visited him twice. Brought him some real bedding to ease his confinement. But a prison is still a prison."

I knew that all too well. Lady Egal composed herself and stood. "I should let you get back to resting and recovering. You said you'd like to name a bodyguard?"

That I didn't have to think about twice. "Yes. Yellow-ranked Bane of Askan-Wod."

BANE ENTERED my quarters the next morning. I couldn't imagine a more welcome sight. I'd missed his ruffled hair. His off-kilter armband. His buckwheat warm eyes. Here was someone, finally, that I could trust unreservedly.

His armband now showed an embroidered deer—the sign of a royal consort, I presumed. My stomach twinged. I couldn't run to him or hold his hand in mine. I was about to be engaged.

"Thank you for agreeing to be my bodyguard."

"I am honored to be selected by the woman our illustrious king has chosen as his consort." Bane bowed formally. "Lady Egal has adjusted the registries in the Archives accordingly."

Rose sat in the corner, spinning, watching us with hawkish eyes. But Bane was better at schooling his face than me; he looked every inch the perfect guard.

"Thank you. Please take up your post at the door."

For days, Bane was half a room away but impossible to talk to. It wasn't until the eve of the engagement ceremony that Rose stepped out again, presenting me with an opportunity I quickly took advantage of.

I mussed my hair, flopped onto my mattress, and called Dalea. "Would you be so kind as to fetch me a sweet calendula infusion from the kitchens? The summer heat is bothering me."

A reasonable request; without the doors open, these quarters were quite stuffy.

Dalea frowned. "Given your condition, I'm not sure I should leave you alone. What if you need something?"

"I do need something. A drink."

Dalea shifted uncomfortably on her feet. "But if something happens to you or the child while I'm gone, I'll be blamed.

"Dalea. *If* I were pregnant, and *if* I came down with a fever because you refused to bring me relief from the heat, you'd also be blamed."

That got her out of the house.

Bane stepped inside as soon as she left. "We don't have long."

I crossed the front room and stopped just a step away from him. I wanted to brush the hair out of his eyes. Or touch his arm. Instead, I soaked up the warmth of his eyes.

"Are you well?" he asked.

"Truthfully, I've been better."

Bane nodded. "We tried to get word to you earlier. Lady Sulat is spreading rumors that you're pregnant with Fulsaan's child."

Those were not the words I'd expected to come out of his mouth. I stared at him. "She *what?*"

"King Alder can't attack you openly if you're carrying his half-brother," Bane said in a low voice. "Given his loyalty to his father, he might not *want* to hurt you if he believes it. And it gives you an excuse to refuse the betrothal. You say you don't want to pretend that Alder, not Fulsaan, is your child's father. Or that you feel Fulsaan wouldn't approve of the marriage. With such a story in place, the vote might still go through the next day. It's a brilliant plan."

I pressed the heel of my hand to my forehead, not sure if I should be thrilled or mortified. "Alder locking me up for a mysterious sickness only makes it sound more reasonable."

Bane nodded. "Exactly. Lady Sulat used what she'd been given. Plenty of people *already* believe it."

I felt like I'd eaten a basket of raw onions.

Bane reached to touch my shoulder, thought better of it, and let his hand fall to his side. "Isn't this better than marrying King Alder? Or scorning him outright and jeopardizing the prisoner exchange?"

Probably. That didn't mean I relished the idea of telling everyone I'd been King Fulsaan's mistress.

"Lady Sulat will arrange to move you to a country estate, under the argument that the clean mountain air would be better for your health than remaining down here in the palace. After an ill-fated miscarriage, she'll help you fade into obscurity. She'll keep you safe."

"Once I'm wholly under her power again," I mumbled.

"You don't think Lady Sulat can help you?" Bane asked, puzzled.

I sighed. "Lady Sulat takes care of her own. I don't know if I want to be her person, though."

Bane's face softened, but the smell of wood polish in the room still felt chokingly thick. I tried to swallow the lump in my throat and failed. "You must think I'm a fool for being wary of her help."

Bane wasn't sneering or laughing. "No, but I am curious."

It felt traitorous to say aloud. "Do I only admire her because she opposes King Alder? Would she be any different than him, if she sat on the throne?"

Bane tilted his head to the side, studying me. "Well, what are your goals?"

"My goals?" I blinked.

"You don't want to serve her out of loyalty or debt or for protection. You want to support her ideals, too. If you don't know what you want, you can't know if you should support her or not. Right now, you've chosen indecision."

I frowned. "Indecision is *not* making a choice."

Bane shook his head. "Indecision is choosing not to trust, and choosing not to cut ties, either. If you take no steps to learn her goals, you're deciding to live in wary loyalty forever."

He was right. Absolutely right. "You're disgustingly wise sometimes. Did you know that?"

"Not endearingly wise? Not delightfully wise?"

I laughed. "You're annoyingly charming, too."

He tilted his head to the side, as if I was cupping his face with my hand again. "Is everything I do repugnant to you?"

"Only a little bit. Like parsnips that have gone woody," I teased. "Not like a reeking Hungry Ghost."

"Well, I'm glad it's not that bad. Why is it, Plum, you find me irksome?"

Because his face was so sincere. Because I wanted too much to lean right against him, to laugh with his arm around me. I wanted my world to smell like juniper and smoke.

If he were less wise, less charming, less himself, I might not find myself wondering what it would be like to press my mouth against his. And then remembering I couldn't.

Footsteps on the stairs. I stepped back from Bane. "Thank you," I said formally, "for discussing my security with me. It's good to know someone is thinking these things through."

Dalea entered the room, holding a tray with a cup on it. I turned to her. "Ah, thank you. That's all for now, both of you."

I casually took the tray from her and disappeared into my bedroom.

Inside, I tightened my fingers around the tray and leaned my cheek against the wooden door. Bane's footsteps led him back to the porch, away from me.

After a long moment, I sat and sipped. The drink granted endurance-of-skin, easing the itchy heat of the room. Bane's words rolled through my mind. What did I want?

I couldn't forget the Old Road ambush. The dead men on the ground of that peaceful forest, their blood turning cold on the dirt. Yes, they'd been traitors, but I'd always be a chef first and a patriot second. They were people who'd needed nourishment and care. They were grandsons and sons and brothers and uncles, with someone like Lady Egal, perhaps, mourning them.

More than my own life, more than my own freedom, I wanted peace. I wanted this war to end.

And suddenly, I knew exactly what to say at the engagement ceremony. I'd found my third option.

CHAPTER
FOURTEEN

I wished I had one last chance to talk privately with Bane and explain what I was about to do and why—but fate did not grant me more time alone with him. The following evening, Rose and Bane escorted me out of my residence and down to the broad, sloping lawn next to the pond for the ceremony. The pond looked as lovely as always, its shores of white pebbles shining like pearls in the low summer sun. Verdant reeds and bushes tumbled artistically over the far bank. I'd first seen this place with Bane. He'd taught me how to skip rocks here on a quiet spring afternoon.

A circle of gauzy tents cast long shadows across the green. Their doors were tied back, showing the interior tables. Even though there was no need for torches yet, dozens of them burned. The decorations were all so similar to Sorrel's wedding—as if King Alder was trying to remind everyone that I was the witless girl who'd accidentally lit the tablecloths on fire.

He hoped our engagement would fail. He'd set the scene for disaster. If he wanted to paint a romantic narrative, we'd be having this event in the butterfly garden where he'd proposed. I'd read him right.

I caught sight of my parents. My chest ached and my throat burned. It had only been months since I saw them, but it felt like years. They stood on the edge of the lawn, fidgeting and watching for me. I didn't care about decorum. I ran to them. They ran to me. I was enveloped by arms, by familiar scents. Radishes and herbs and wood-oil for seasoning cutting boards from Father; earth and flowers and fragrant carrot tops from Mother.

"Plum," Father said, the word round and heavy.

"Plum," Mother echoed.

I hadn't realized how much I'd missed them until they were physically here, holding me. I didn't trust my voice, so I whispered. "It's good to see you."

"We wanted to come earlier, but..." my mother trailed off.

I nodded. It had been safer to have them stay put. Lady Sulat and I had both written and said as much.

Father squeezed my shoulder, beaming. "I always knew you weren't so dedicated and skilled for nothing. A national hero and now, a queen."

A consort, I mentally corrected. But I didn't say it out loud.

"You must be so pleased," Mother said. "I know you were enraptured by the idea of marrying that Green-ranked Sorrel, but now you have a purple-ranked king."

Nausea swam through my stomach. Why wouldn't they be proud? They didn't know that King Alder was a murderer, and they had no reason to think he'd trapped me with this engagement.

"Are the greenhouses here lovely?" Mother asked.

"They are." Not that I'd had much time to linger in them of late.

"Are you happy?" Father asked. Now that I'd stepped back, he looked older than I remembered. Fine wrinkles lined his eyes and mouth. "I'm sure the greenhouses are amazing, but you so dearly wanted to marry a chef, someone you could share your love of cooking with. Do you regret letting Sorrel go?"

I wasn't sure if I wanted to choke or laugh, but I managed to put on my best smile. "You worry too much. I'm marrying King Alder. Of course I'm happy."

And then the strangest thing happened. My father's shoulders relaxed. The tight wrinkles around his eyes eased, and he exhaled. "I'm so glad, Plum."

He believed me. Didn't he know me? Couldn't he look into my eyes and see how I felt? Hadn't we spent years working together, tending to the health of the Clamsriver villagers?

I glanced at my mother. She dabbed her eyes, beaming. She couldn't tell, either.

The calm, rational voice in my head—it sounded oddly like Lady Sulat—kneaded my lumps of pain into something smoother. I should be proud. Relieved. If my parents couldn't spot my lies, how would King Alder?

I was getting better at this.

"Shouldn't you be inside the main tent?" I asked. "You have no small role to play tonight."

Mother squeezed my shoulder. It was like she needed tactile assurance that I was alive and well. "King Alder hasn't arrived, yet. We're not being rude."

"Has anyone given you a tour of the palace grounds?" I asked.

Father shook his head. "All the servants have been quite busy preparing this." He waved at the beautiful tents. "Maybe you can show us about tomorrow, if you're feeling up to it. I heard you'd been quite ill lately."

"Just nervous, I suppose. I'm feeling much better." I glanced around the lawn again. "Is Dami with you?"

It would look odd for my sister not to attend, but it wasn't exactly safe to bring her, either.

"Ah. She's laid up with a nasty fever," Father said in a stiff, stilted voice that sounded rehearsed.

Mother leaned closer and whispered, "We saw her last night. She's a bit...excitable about the engagement ceremony. Your friend Moss didn't exactly trust her to behave, so that's what we're telling everyone."

Good thing Rose had kept her distance—Mother was hardly being discreet. I wanted to ask what *excitable* meant, but it didn't seem safe to continue on this subject in public. More likely than not, Dami was overly excited to be rid of me.

I escorted them both into the main tent, Rose and Bane trailing some distance behind us. I asked my parents all about home as we walked. How the garden fared this year. If Sandpiper was doing well. Had Amari's baby been a boy or a girl?

As we talked, it felt as if there was a film between us, like the scum that rises when boiling stock. They didn't understand my life anymore. They couldn't look at me and know my heart.

I'd learned how to lie, but I'd also lost the intimate language of sharing my soul in a single glance.

Two tables stood in the central tent, one for each set of parents. Father and Mother took their place behind the one on the left. I knelt before them on the other side.

My parents tried to compose themselves, but they smiled wide, nervous smiles. They'd brought their best clothes—Father even had a new tunic, embroidered with ginger blooms. Mother wore our most expensive family heirloom, a maple hairpin inlaid with amethyst.

Four months ago, I would have thought their apparel exquisite. As guests filled in behind us, I knew they'd all be eyeing my parent's short, yellow-ranked sleeves. They'd note that the dye of their clothes was not as rich and dark as anyone else's, nor the weave as fine. We must look like paupers to them. The luckiest paupers in the world. For all my parents knew, we were. They kept giving me looks of pure joy.

Sages from the Royal Shrine bore the plaques of both Old King Fulsaan and his wife, Queen Laurel. There'd been no body to recover from Fulsaan of course, and he'd told me himself that he didn't know if his wife was even dead. She disappeared when he'd sent his son, Red Lord Ospren, into exile. I wondered if that looked strange in the Royal Shrine, two plaques side-by-side. Usually the heads of Ancestors were reverently de-fleshed by the sages, then given clay faces and polished stone eyes to watch over their descendants.

After the plaques were set on the table, Lady Egal and a man I'd never seen entered. He was bald, with a white beard and pouchy eyes. Lady Egal's husband, perhaps? They were both dressed in funerary clothes—black and white, as stark as life and death. They knelt behind the table, silent and solemn. Lady Egal was the oldest member of the royal household; it made sense to have her stand in for Alder's mother.

By now, the tents brimmed with guests, a garden of butterfly-bright cloth and shimmering hair ornaments. In my peripheries, I glimpsed Lady Sulat and Heir Valerian. The latter beamed at me, like this was the best day in his twelve-year-old life.

At last, King Alder himself entered. The only loom in all Rowak wide enough to weave his garments was here in the palace. The hem of his tunic swished around his calves; his sleeves covered all but his fingertips. He was wrapped in a waterfall of fine, shimmering fabric, dyed midnight blue. That remarkable shade made his eyes harder, darker, his black beard more distinguished. He knelt before the plaques of his parents, the hues of his clothes more saturated than the rug under him. But he matched. He belonged here.

I wondered if Rose had commissioned a yellow dress for me on purpose to make me appear pale and out of place. Or perhaps to remind the guests that I was once nothing more than a yellow-ranked kitchen maid.

King Alder couldn't officiate, as he was part of the ceremony already. His younger brother, Blue-ranked Lord Torut, entered and stood between the tables. I'd never formally met him, though I had broken into his apartments once. The back of my neck itched, but his gaze passed over me with no recognition. Lord Torut was a young man—not much older than Bane, really—with the ruddy nose of a perpetual drunk.

He was surprisingly sober this evening. He gestured for the musicians to begin. They played turtle shells and sang, welcoming the Ancestors to witness these events. Trays of food piled with delicacies were laid out for our Ancestors on a table behind Lord Torut. Food for the guests waited on another table, along with the traditional pickled duck eggs covered in edible flowers that would only be served to Alder and myself.

I could avoid looking at the food, but I couldn't stop smelling it. The briny eggs seemed to cut through everything else, leaving a lump in my throat. They had to be fresh, but they stank of sulfur to me. Pickled duck eggs enhanced fertility.

King Alder didn't so much as glance at me the whole time. He stared straight ahead at Torut and the table, his hands folded calmly in his lap. He thought he had nothing to fear this evening.

Lady Sulat likewise watched, but she seemed stiffer. More anxious. She expected me to announce a false pregnancy and create an uproar, after all. It was a clever plan. A believable one.

"We have called our Ancestors to witness this engagement ceremony," Lord Torut began. "We now ask for the blessing of the parents. Do the father and mother of Green-ranked Plum of Clamsriver give their blessing?"

My parents stood. They bowed to the proxies for King Alder's parents, then bowed to Lord Torut. Their motions seemed shaky. Unschooled. Even though they had certainly practiced.

"Yes," my father answered. "We give this betrothal our blessing."

Torut bowed to them in turn and my parents knelt. He then turned to Lady Egal and her companion. "Do the father and mother of Purple-ranked King Alder of Rowak give their blessing?"

The two of them stood and repeated the bows. Lady Egal's companion repeated the same words. "Yes. We give this betrothal our blessing."

They knelt again.

My palms felt clammy. My throat burned. Was my plan foolish?

No. I wasn't going to doubt myself now. I knew what I wanted.

Usually, the families then negotiated over the betrothal contract, but there wasn't much to negotiate. The rights of a consort were already laid out by law. Lord Torut read them, droning on as the summer heat sent sweat trickling down my neck.

"The only unresolved matter," Torut finished, "is the engagement gift. Green-ranked Plum, what do you ask?"

I breathed in the smell of fabric and food, of human bodies and summer grass. I exhaled the panic in my lungs. A hundred eyes watched me. My parents, beaming. Lady Sulat, anticipating scandal. King Alder even turned, his eyes full of victorious laughter, waiting for me to choose failure or failure—the only options he thought he'd given me.

"I have but one humble request."

The air clung, hot and sticky to my exposed skin. My hair felt triple its real weight. My toes tingled, pins-and-needles, from kneeling.

"Speak it," Lord Torut commanded. He looked tired. Maybe even bored. He'd probably rather be gambling somewhere in Askan-Wod right now.

"I can't ask for lands, or wealth, or the promise of such. They won't set my heart at ease."

Lady Egal stared at me, eyes wide in panic. King Alder relaxed further. This was the moment he expected me to refuse our engagement, tarnishing my reputation and killing any chance of a prisoner exchange.

But what I wanted the most was for the fighting and bloodshed to stop.

"I cannot rest easy and accept my position of consort until all of Rowak may rest easy. For my engagement gift, I ask for a peace treaty with Shoreed."

If it brought peace to all of Rowak, I could and would marry a murderer.

Gasps and sudden bursts of conversations bubble in the crowd, whirling into a foaming mess of gossip. I felt like the eye of a storm—perfectly calm inside, creating chaos without.

CHAPTER
FIFTEEN

Apparently, no one had coached Lord Torut on what to do in these circumstances. "Umm. Can everyone quiet down?" But his words had no effect. He lowered his voice and leaned toward his brother. "Alder, I think you're going to have to say something."

I had created a situation where King Alder couldn't win. If he agreed, he'd have to push the prisoner exchange through and send ambassadors to seek a treaty. If he rejected me as his consort, I'd walk away free, a patriot of Rowak—and he'd be the warmonger whose love was as fleeting as spring blossoms. Either way, the Purple-Blue council would vote in favor of the prisoner exchange.

I prostrated myself on the blue-and-white mat. "I hope I have not offended His Majesty!"

Inside, I felt as bright and beautiful as pure honey.

"Won't you answer her?" Lady Egal asked. She phrased it politely, but impatience edged her voice. Had she been the actual mother, she might accept or reject the terms herself, but she was only here to stand in for the ceremony.

"I accept," King Alder said, his voice ringing stately through the air. "Raise your head, Plum of Clamsriver."

Accept. Slowly, I sat up as commanded. King Alder studied me, his eyes as cold and flinty as ever. But he seemed merely annoyed. I'd expected him to be furious.

"You are a true patriot," he said, projecting his voice for all to hear. "I nominate you as the Acting Ambassador to Shoreed."

My pulse throbbed in my throat. I knew nothing about being an ambassador. I hated that it had taken me days to figure out how to respond to King Alder, and he'd only needed moments to compose his counter-move.

"Everyone in the Purple-Blue council sits in attendance," Alder continued. "Let's not delay any longer, leaving my heart in suspense. All in favor of sending my beloved Plum as Acting Ambassador to the Shoreed to negotiate the prisoner exchange—and hopefully a treaty— please stand."

The ministers who supported Alder promptly stood. Lady Sulat and Minister Ashown rose more slowly. King Alder had cleverly bundled my appointment together with the vote on a prisoner exchange and given them no time to protest or form other proposals. The only minister who remained seated was Grayfox, who'd hoped to be appointed as ambassador himself.

A faint summer breeze trailed through the tent, bringing with it the scent of cattails. King Alder smiled wolfishly at me. He took my hand and kissed it, his teeth scraping over my knuckles as he pulled away, like he wanted to rend my flesh and grind my bones. He squeezed my fingers, as if to say that he'd have to suffice with letting Shoreed dispose of me.

I smiled back. I had an opportunity to create peace. This was still a victory for me.

My mother blinked back proud tears. My father put an arm around her, looking a bit nervous, but not alarmed. They couldn't see that these were fake smiles and fake proclamations of happiness.

"Thank you all for supporting the wishes of my beloved," King Alder said. "Lord Torut, let's continue with the ceremony, noting that the betrothal is conditional upon securing a treaty with Shoreed."

Torut wiped his clammy face down with a handkerchief, then announced that anyone with objections should make it known. That was the purpose of an engagement ceremony in the first place—it gave time for friends, neighbors, and family members to hear of the engagement and note any reasons why it shouldn't happen, like a pre-existing marriage, unresolved debts, or a falsification of rank on the part of the bride or groom.

No one said anything, of course. Did anyone ever speak against royal engagements? They'd all have months to raise objections, in any case, while I was gone.

I was headed to the Coral Palace after all.

THE NEXT MORNING, neither the palace guards nor Blue-ranked Rose tried to stop me when I walked out the front door of my apartments, Bane trailing me as my bodyguard. The Purple-Blue council was already in session, voting on various other issues—including matters pertaining to my trip. As a betrothed consort, I didn't have the right to attend.

I headed to the plum orchards to wait. Even this early in the morning, the air smelled like sun-dried grass. The plums were small and unripe, a glossy green that made them look like emeralds in a blue sky. Bane and I had walked here together under white blossoms on the day we met.

I sat on one of the stone benches. He remained standing. Alert. A model guard.

"I'm going to talk to Lady Sulat today," I said.

"About the council meeting?"

I had to tilt my head up to look at him. "Well, probably, yes. But I know my own goals now, and I'm going to ask about hers. A charmingly wise man convinced me that living in indecision is a poor choice."

Bane coughed awkwardly. Only then did I realize I'd said the *charming* part out loud, and that I probably shouldn't have.

"I meant, I want to thank you. For your advice," I said formally.

"You're welcome."

Robins called to each other. The orchard was empty besides us—just trees and dappled sunlight. "Do you want to sit down?" I asked. "It's awkward, looking up at you like this."

"I'm supposed to be protecting you."

"You are. Should I, umm, not distract you by talking?" Maybe after what I'd just done, he didn't want to talk.

"I'm always listening, Plum."

Somehow, the lighting here made him seem more real. Drenched in color. As if I'd been looking at a washed-out version of his face this whole time. He was like a painting I couldn't touch. "Bane, it's not fair for me to ask you to come with me to the Coral Palace."

"I'm not afraid. Not of King Alder, not for what waits for us in Shoreed."

"I meant the engagement," I whispered.

"Your welfare is the welfare of Rowak. Whatever happens, I won't abandon you."

He gazed at me like I was the only plum in this whole garden, swallowing up my image and leaving prickles on my skin.

King Alder would never look at me like that.

"Bane, you should know, I didn't choose the engagement because I don't...I mean, that we couldn't..." I swallowed, face hot. Now was not the right moment to profess my feelings. Unless I failed as an ambassador, it would never be the right moment.

Bane's expression remained intently calm—no sad smiles, no frowns, nothing. It was the kind of calm that required a great deal of effort. "You've always recklessly done whatever you thought was right. I know you think you have nothing in common with Dami, but you're even more headstrong than she is."

"I'm sorry," I whispered. I knew firsthand how frustrating it was to get blindsided by such actions.

"I'd be even more sorry if you stopped being Plum. This is who you are."

I didn't deserve this man or his loyalty. I didn't deserve his calmness, or the fervent way his eyes locked with mine. My stomach roiled. "The engagement. It was my best choice," I apologized, as if those words could bring back the calm certainty I'd felt during the ceremony.

A breeze rushed through the branches. Shadows and light flickered across his face. "It was," Bane echoed. "War always demands sacrifices from us in the ways we least expect."

WHEN I ENTERED the front room of her apartments, Lady Sulat wasn't at her desk or conferencing with an important officer. She knelt on the rug, gently combing her daughter's onyx hair.

"Do I look like Great-Grandma yet?" Azalea asked.

"Almost, my little flower."

Azalea grinned. "I want white hair, too, when my head goes on a shelf."

"I also hope your hair is white when that happens, sweetheart," Lady Sulat whispered. She turned to me, but her hands kept their rhythmic motion. "My father's birthday and the trip to the Royal Shrine has made quite the impression on Azalea. Welcome."

Azalea turned, ruining Lady Sulat's combing. "Auntie!"

Auntie? Azalea charged and nearly tackled me around the knees. "Did you bring me sweets?"

"S-sweets?" I stammered.

Azalea stepped back, her glossy hair swishing. "Aunts are supposed to bring sweets! Owl said so."

"Who's Owl?" I asked.

Azalea crossed her arms.

"Don't pout, sweetheart," Lady Sulat said, squeezing her shoulder. She looked up at me. "Owl is Azalea's playmate. He's wetnurse Rill's son."

"He has four aunts and they *all* bring him sweets!"

I crouched down close to her. "I'll bring you something nice next time."

Azalea gave me a cool, considering look that I think she learned from her mother. It was downright unnerving to see on such a young face. "I accept your terms."

Where had she learned those words?

Lady Sulat smiled and shook her head. "It's probably time for you to play with Owl. I'll bring you back when I'm done speaking with your new aunt."

She gestured for one of the guards to escort her small daughter. Azalea clambered into his arms. "This way!" she pointed. "Onward to Owl!"

Once they left, Lady Sulat stowed the jade comb in a brocade-lined drawer of her dresser. "I'm afraid King Alder outmaneuvered me in the Purple-Blue Council today."

She gestured for me to sit with her in her elegant chairs carved with chickadees and pine boughs, then continued. "Given your rank, you're only allowed the position of Acting Ambassador. I tried to get Minister Grayfox appointed as the full ambassador for this trip, but Alder blocked me. He also managed to staff your caravan with guards entirely loyal to him. You're to leave tomorrow morning, and you'll only be able to pick two maids and a personal bodyguard."

My stomach sank. "Do you think these guards will actively sabotage the negotiations, or that Alder trusts me to fail by myself?"

"Oh, I think his men will slit your throat as soon as you're over the border. He'll accuse the Shoreed of your murder and use that as justification to slaughter all our prisoners. Then he'll become the honorably tragic figure Rowak rallies around."

Maybe I was becoming desensitized to attempts on my life because I responded by calmly folding my hands in my lap. Lady Sulat was right. If Alder killed me, he controlled the situation.

I thought I'd played the engagement ceremony so well, but I hadn't puzzled out King Alder's next moves.

"I assume you'll take Bane as your bodyguard?"

"He doesn't want to be left behind."

She nodded. "Dami should go as one of your maids, of course. Having a second, secret guard is sure to be useful."

I managed not to flinch. For all I knew, Dami would run off as soon as we left Askan-Wod. It wasn't like we'd been on good terms last time we spoke.

"And for your remaining maid, I highly recommend you take Poppy."

"Poppy?" I blinked at her, startled. Why would Lady Sulat give up her own servant for me? Was she trying to spy on me?

"Dami didn't strike me as someone who can manage a household," Lady Sulat said. "Poppy is competent and trustworthy. She has asked to accompany you."

I had a hard time imagining the kind, mild-mannered Poppy volunteering for such a dangerous venture.

Lady Sulat must have read my face because she explained. "Poppy has four younger brothers. The oldest of them will be fourteen soon." Fourteen—recruitment age for the army. "She'd like to see this war ended before then. Do you have some personal reservation about her?"

"Not about Poppy." I kept my gaze on the face of this enigmatic woman. "I'm not sure I trust *you*."

Lady Sulat paused. I'd actually startled her. She kept her face composed and tilted her head to one side, considering me. "A bold thing to say in my own house."

Perhaps too bold, but I didn't have time for subtlety. "You used Osem. You arranged her whole marriage for your benefit."

"Do you have other grievances?" Lady Sulat asked, her face that unnerving, cold calm. "Because Osem is not upset about her marriage. Rather the opposite. I take care of those who serve me."

"On the road to Napil, Fir once offered to take care of me as well. He promised me the post of Master Chef of Rowak. I could have served him, become a traitor like him, and risen to great renown."

Lady Sulat nodded, severe expression softening. "Being taken care of is not enough for you."

"I don't know why you want political power. And that frightens me." There was something refreshing about saying it out loud. My throat no longer pinched; my tongue no longer dragged. "King Alder said you planned the attack on my life—then staged it to fail so I wouldn't trust him."

Lady Sulat leaned forward in her chair, considering me.

"Aren't you going to defend yourself?" I demanded.

"Either I am innocent, or I am not. I have no new proof to put before you. I won't grovel for your respect."

She was right. Gushing about her innocence wouldn't make me trust her.

"Then tell me your goals. What are you going to do with my service, if I continue to offer it? What are you doing with the loyalty that Bane, Osem, and uncounted others have given you?"

Lady Sulat nodded her approval at the question. "I'm going to put Heir Valerian on the throne one day. And I'm going to keep him there."

Was she planning to murder King Alder once the war ended? Maybe she was just as bloodthirsty as her brother. I chose my words carefully. "Purple Lord Valerian is already the heir."

"So was Red Lord Ospren." Melancholy bled through her words.

The room suddenly felt too warm and too dark with the windows closed. I'd missed something—something important.

Lady Sulat didn't make me pry for information. She spoke openly. "Ospren had such visionary plans for Rowak. In truth, I see much of him in Valerian. The compassion. The ingenuity."

I opened my mouth to protest—Ospren was a *traitor*—but Lady Sulat held up a hand. I remained silent. "Do you know why Alder and my father could remove him? Why their fabricated lies about stealing treasury funds stuck and ended with Ospren's exile?"

"Oh." Her meaning fell into place. "Ospren lacked the political power to stay. He lacked supporters. King Alder manipulated the Purple-Blue Council to his ends."

"Yes. It wasn't even particularly hard, despite the fact my mother opposed the exile. Lord Ospren's ideas weren't popular among the highly ranked. His goal, after all, was to prevent poor men from being overtaxed by embezzling province governors. And now he's gone, branded with the red rank of those he empathized with."

Gone? Now he was waging war on us. Part of me wanted to feel sorry for him, but I couldn't. Not for the man who was responsible for so much death and suffering.

"Heir Valerian has dreams for Rowak, too. Beautiful dreams to improve roads and reform taxes. I want him to see them come to fruition. I want to have the power to keep him on the throne when the time comes. Power that I didn't have eight years ago when Alder sent our oldest brother away."

Her eyes seemed too-bright, even in the dim light of the room. I had no doubt that Lady Sulat was being entirely, wholly truthful with me. The truth burns in ways that falsehoods never can.

"Lady Sulat...you had me study poisons to *kill* Red Lord Ospren and end this war."

"He left his place of exile. He is a traitor. According to our laws, he is already guilty and worthy of execution by any means." Her voice did not quaver. She kept my gaze the entire time she was speaking. And yet I could somehow feel that she was crumbling inside.

"You miss him, don't you?"

Her mouth quivered so briefly, I'm not sure I didn't imagine it. "Alder always had a cruel edge to him. Torut dreams of nothing more than drowning his sorrows in drink. But Ospren—quiet, clever, kind Ospren—was my brother in soul as well as blood."

"How..." I fumbled. She didn't make any sense. "You want him dead?"

Her posture and pronunciation, if anything, became more formal —as if formality was a thick wall that could protect her from her own emotions. "Should I let my family relations cloud my judgment? I dare not. I must make my commands harsher than my attachments demand to counteract my bias. I won't see Rowak fall because my heart fails me. He is guilty of death. If negotiations fail and you need to carry out that sentence to protect our country, you should feel no shame or remorse."

Could she not cry? I wanted to embrace her. She looked as frail as a doll of sun-dried clay, ready to crumble away. I had doubted her, and in turn, she ripped open her soul and let me prod what was inside.

I dropped my gaze. I'd double-guessed my best judgment to doubt her. Just like she was double-guessing her best judgment to order the death of her favorite brother. "I'll find another way to end this war, Lady Sulat."

"I pray to the Ancestors of Rowak that you can." The way she said it, it wasn't an abstract statement of hope. I had no doubt that since the day she'd told me to poison her brother, she'd pleaded often with her Ancestors for another way.

I stood, then bowed deeply, keeping my head down. "Forgive me for my harsh words."

She placed a hand on my shoulder, gently leading me to stand again. "I will, sister."

Sister. That's what I'd be to her, after I married King Alder. That simple title seemed more glorious than any other that had been granted me.

"I'll try to end this war without harming Ospren," I promised. "I wish I was leaving accompanied by your soldiers, with Moss at their head."

She smiled softly. "A nice sentiment, but I wouldn't send Moss. He's served his country well for decades. He has a granddaughter now. Pulling him away from her would be cruel."

I felt like a selfish twit. Moss wouldn't want to leave on a long, dangerous journey. But still, in the back of my mind, King Alder's words of doubt played. Was Lady Sulat only sending people she considered expendable with me?

No. I didn't believe that. Lady Sulat positioned her people not just to help herself, but to enable them to live better lives. Osem and

Bane had both ended up in good posts. I had a chance to stop this war. And ultimately, Lady Sulat had a chance to protect the heir of Rowak.

King Alder was wise to sow seeds of doubt in me. I didn't think I'd ever be able to rip up all the weeds. But that didn't mean I had to choose inaction. To choose against Lady Sulat. Moss wasn't coming, not because Lady Sulat was planning for me to fail, but because she cared about those who served her.

"So. What's the plan?" I asked.

CHAPTER SIXTEEN

The plan was simple. At Napil, before I even reached the border, Lady Sulat would arrange to have Governor Slate arrest my guards for public drunkenness. Then a dozen of her soldiers would volunteer to escort me on to Shoreed without delay.

I left Lady Sulat's residence and headed to the kitchens, Bane trailing me. I did want to find a treat for Azalea, but more importantly, I needed to say a proper farewell to Osem. Maybe I should have gone to see my parents first, but saying goodbye to them felt too real, too final.

Bane walked stoically behind me. I kept turning back to glance at him. Did he always look this stern on-duty? Should I insist he stay in Rowak? Would that be crueler? It would certainly be safer.

My foot caught on a tree root growing into the gravel path. In a heartbeat, Bane was there, arm extended to catch me, but I'd already righted myself. We stared at each other, his hand inches from my waist.

We stepped back at the same moment. My face burned. "I, umm, tripped."

"I noticed."

I glanced around, but it seemed that only Bane had watched me act so clumsily. I had to be more focused.

Bane stood stiffly now, back to being my serious guard.

"If you really are set on coming with me, this is your last day in Askan-Wod, too. I'll ask Lady Sulat to let me borrow another guard so you can see your family. Are they back yet from their pilgrimage?"

Bane looked away. "Yes."

"Then we're turning around. You'll miss them even more if you don't get a chance to talk to them."

I'd only managed two steps down the path when Bane's soft voice stopped me. "We're not asking for another guard."

I met his gaze and held it. "Don't give me some lecture about duty or whatnot right now. I know you're a soldier, but you're also a son, and I'm not dragging you out of the country without letting you see your family."

It was the only kind thing I could think of to do for him—and I was going to do it.

"They've been back for a week. And I don't need a fresh round of ridicule before we leave."

"Ridicule?" I pursed my lips, the heat of the late morning sun itching down my neck. "I don't understand."

"I love that you actually mean that." He waved his truncated arm at me. "Why would anyone pick someone like me as a bodyguard? My family thinks you suffer from an overabundance of charitable pity."

My mouth dried. The gravel suddenly seemed too loud under my feet. "Bane...that's not why..."

"I know," he assured me. "But they still think it's wrong that I accepted this position at all. If I go see them now, they'll tell me I'm not good enough to go to Shoreed, and they'll do everything they can to make me stay."

I pursed my lips, floundering for what to say. Should I be angry on his behalf? Enumerate his many virtues? "Do you want me to go talk to them? Tell them about everything you've done?"

"It won't help, Plum. They don't even care that I helped save Rowak. After all, it didn't get me a better post. Or a wife. Or an increase in rank."

Now that he mentioned it, people didn't treat Bane the way they treated me—even people who knew his role in stopping the coup. And I hadn't even noticed. "I'm so sorry. I should have said something, done something. You're in the official history, but—"

"It's a *good* thing. Lady Sulat had to heap glory on you to save your life at the trial. In doing so, she made you a target for King Alder. If he were constantly reminded that I, too, was close to everything happening, that I saw the Hungry Ghost and knew what it meant..."

Alder might send assassins after him as well. Lady Sulat was right to underplay his role. That didn't make it fair.

"Your family ought to understand, though. They ought to be proud of you."

He gave me his sad smile. "There are many things that ought to be and aren't."

And with the scent of honeysuckle floating between us, I thought that we ought to be walking hand in hand through the summer gardens. That we ought to be laughing and chatting. That this war ought never to have happened in the first place.

The two of us finished walking to the kitchens, Bane trailing loyally behind me instead of at my side.

As soon as I cracked the back door, Osem abandoned her pots, ran out, and hugged me tight. "Oh, Plum."

"I'll miss you, too. And I'll miss your wedding. I'm sorry, Osem."

She stepped back, both hands on my shoulders. "I'm not upset about that. You're marrying *King Alder*."

I exhaled, as if breathing could erase the image of his cruel face. This was what I wanted. "I'm going to save Rowak."

Osem sighed. "Plum, you're a dear, but sometimes I wish you had a better sense of self-preservation."

The door opened again. Master Chef Hawak—a broad, middle-aged man with a glow of good health—stepped out. "Osem! What are you..." he saw me and trailed off. Then he gave a quick bow toward me. "Consort Plum. My apologies. How may I help you?"

Master Chef Hawak, treating me like his superior. How strange. I supposed I was, now, but it turned my skin to gooseflesh. "Umm. If you have something, I'd like a treat. For little Azalea."

Without delay, Hawak bowed and swept back inside.

Osem glanced at the door. "Well, *that's* a nice trick. Wish I'd learned it on days when my neck was sore and my hands raw."

"You're almost done with scrubbing crocks now. I hope your marriage goes well." I tried to pour all the sincerity in my bones into those words.

Osem tightly squeezed both my hands. "I hope you survive yours."

HAWAK BROUGHT me a beautifully wrapped honey praline. I tucked it into my waistband for later. Then Bane and I stopped briefly at Lady Egal's to ask about which guest apartments my parents were lodged in. Thankfully, they weren't in the same building as Sorrel.

A pair of Royal Bear guards stood outside their lattice doors. Bane shifted in front of me and his hand drifted to the short spear on his back.

The guards bowed politely. One slid open the door and said, "They're waiting for you."

Hesitantly, steps squeaking under me, I climbed onto the porch and entered.

The windows were open, allowing a gentle, warm breeze through the room. The furnishings were handsome, though not overdone. There were four individual, sitting-height tables on the floor. My parents sat behind two of them, facing me. One table was empty. King Alder sat behind the other. His back was to me, but it was impossible to mistake him for anyone else with all that purple and gold fabric pooled around him.

I inhaled calmly, imagining myself as a river and my fear as nothing more than ripples washing past me. I straightened my posture, composed my face, and prepared for the verbal battle ahead. "I didn't know you were all here together."

"Ah, Plum!" Mother beamed. "Your betrothed honored us by coming for lunch. We sent a messenger for you, but you weren't at home."

I knelt at the remaining small table in the room, next to King Alder. Bane stepped back outside, taking a position by the door.

"I took a walk for my health," I said. "It's lovely outside today."

My father frowned. "We did hear you'd been sick." He turned to King Alder. "Are you worried about sending her to Shoreed so soon, when she's been unwell?"

Alder turned to me with an adoring smile. He laid his hand over my own. I pretended it was Bane's hand and curled my fingers around his—even though Bane didn't have a left hand, so the thumbs and fingers were all in the wrong places.

I could do this. If it saved thousands of lives, I could be Alder's betrothed for a day, and his wife when I returned.

Alder reeked of rosemary soap and expensive oils, without any hint of juniper.

"My dearest Plum has made it abundantly clear that this matter is of no small urgency to her. I defer to her wishes." King Alder squeezed my hand painfully hard. I squeezed back.

My parents didn't notice. Father was too busy studying my face, like sight alone could diagnose my every ailment.

Lunch arrived, a soup of oyster mushrooms garnished with green onions, chilled with snow from the mountains. Elegant, simple. I sipped the dark broth—it had lovely sweet overtones that complemented the earthiness of the mushrooms. This would grant endurance-of-skin and endurance-of-lungs—perfect for making hot weather more bearable. As I ate, my skin seemed to cool. The flavors were exquisite. Master Chef Hawak hadn't held back on this dish.

My father's eyes widened at the first bite. "This broth! Plum, do you think that's roasted onion in there? And parsnip. There's something else sweet, too, but I'm not sure—" he glanced at King Alder and trailed off. "Forgive me. I'm a chef by profession."

For a moment, eyes alight with excitement, he'd looked like the father I remembered. Now he was a courteous subject again. I managed not to glare at Alder for being here, for ruining our time to say goodbye.

"No need for an apology. I've always been impressed with your daughter's skills. I understand you taught her?"

My father melted under the praise and mumbled something incomprehensible.

I changed the subject. "I admit, my king, I'm surprised to see you here. I thought you'd be quite busy today, given that the ambassadorial party leaves tomorrow."

"I see you've already heard the news." His voice held an accusatory bent, and I silently cursed myself. I should have asked him about it, feigning ignorance. Now he knew I'd talked with Lady Sulat.

Though he'd probably already guessed as much.

"Of course." I refused to let him fluster me. "As you said, it's very important to me."

He smiled thinly. "There is much to do before tomorrow, but what kind of son-in-law would I be, to neglect my new mother and father the day after our engagement? They'll think me unable to treat you well if I cannot treat them well."

King Alder was the height of manners. My mother flushed deeply. Both my parents flattered all too easily. They hadn't been in the palace long enough to learn better.

He continued, "I've made all the arrangements for your envoy, except one. Selecting your maids falls on you. Who would you like besides Dalea?"

And now he'd put me in the awkward position of disavowing the maid he'd personally assigned to me. "I'm afraid I can't bring Dalea."

My parents' eyes widened in shock. Mother silently shook her head, as if trying to discreetly communicate that one did not contradict a king, even if he was your betrothed. Maybe especially if he was your betrothed.

"Is her work unsatisfactory?" Alder asked, nonchalantly taking another spoonful of soup.

"Oh! Of course not. But Green-ranked Poppy is a dear friend that I've already promised to bring with me. And I couldn't bear to leave Rowak without my sister as well. I know you'd happily send me with an extra maid, but there's no need to burden the Royal Treasury on my account."

King Alder laughed, as if he'd actually enjoyed that bit of sparring. My parents both exhaled audibly.

"Oh, my darling Plum. You're so very interesting." His smile seemed to say *it's almost a pity I have to dispose of you.*

King Alder was solicitous of my parents for the rest of the meal, leaving them entirely flustered as they answered questions about their home and health. Before he left, he placed a single kiss on the top of my head. It felt like the kind of kiss one laid on the head of a newly deceased relative before taking their remains to the sages.

As soon as the door closed behind him, Mother rushed to my side and squeezed my arm. "He's smitten with you! His every word is so kind, so considerate."

Father's brow furrowed. "I only wish you were staying safely next to him. I didn't know you cared about the war so much. You never seemed interested before."

I hadn't cared before I saw what this war had done to Osem and Bane. Before I stood on the Old Road surveying the aftermath of an ambush. "How long are you staying in the palace?"

"Not long," Father said. "Lady Sulat, the king's own sister, arranged for us to travel with a cloth merchant east all the way to Meadowind. We'll leave in two days."

I smiled at them. Lady Sulat was still one step ahead of me. "Will you get to see Dami again?"

"I don't think so. Safety issues. You know." Mother shook her head. "We're probably lucky we got to see her at all. I'm glad you're taking her with you—you can keep an eye on her."

It was supposed to be the other way around. Father frowned. I could tell he didn't like the idea of either of his daughters running off into enemy territory, let alone both of us.

Mother sighed wistfully. "I always worried about how we'd get Dami married. She's beautiful, but so...I don't know. Spontaneous. I don't think she'd settle down unless she got to choose. And now she'll have so many young men to choose from. Sister to the king's consort. Life is so surprising."

Father pulled me into a hug. "Your Ancestors must be proud of you, Plum. You've done—you keep doing—so much for your family."

I hugged him back fiercely. "The king's Ancestors must favor me for so much good fortune to find me."

Father didn't notice the desperation in my arms. He and Mother both smiled gratefully, believing me. We talked a little longer. I kept up the illusion that I was honored to be engaged.

I left their guestroom wondering if I'd ever see them again—wondering if the last words they heard from me would be lies.

THAT EVENING, I sat on Lady Sulat's porch. Bane stood behind me, next to one of those thick, redwood pillars. The sun was low in the west, casting long, rich shadows across the bleeding hearts and ferns in the flower beds. Still, I waited. Moss was due back here tonight.

Orange and pink streaked across the dying sky when he walked up the gravel path. I stood to greet him.

"Heard you're leaving tomorrow," Moss said.

"I am."

I thought he'd make some great final joke or toss out a last stinging bit of innuendo, but instead, he hugged me fiercely. The old man smelled like pine trees, dust, and aging paper. "Come back safe, Plum."

"That is my intent."

Moss' eyes were uncharacteristically bright. "Are you sure? With all the trouble you find, I thought you went looking for it on purpose."

CHAPTER SEVENTEEN

The next day dawned clear and bright—as beautiful a midsummer morning as one could hope for. A covered cart waited for me outside my apartments. Usually, carts had the bed open to the sky with two huge wheels in back and the cross-beam in front where the porters pulled or pushed. This one was built like a miniature house on four wheels, with a shingled roof, windows, and walls painted with vertical red stripes, mimicking the red pillars of the buildings in the palace.

Servants had already loaded a second, plain cart with provisions and goods. Poppy strode up to me with a satchel. "I have the Purple-Blue Council's official document of stipulations for negotiating a treaty, as well as some notes Lady Sulat wrote you."

I needed all the help I could get. "They're in that bag?"

"Ah, no. I put the notes with your clothes. But I thought you might want this on your person."

Frowning, I took the satchel from her and peered inside. All my encoded notes from my time studying with Sorrel and Violet's wooden box of poisons stared back at me.

Maybe I'd need the antidote notes, but I wasn't using those poisons. Especially not on Lady Sulat's favorite brother. I wanted no part in making her more like King Alder. I exhaled through my nose. "It can go with everything else in the supply cart."

"Are you sure?" Bane asked.

I jumped. I'd forgotten he was just behind me. "Of course!"

"I didn't mean to suggest you should..." he flustered. "I meant it would be more secure on your person."

He was right. I hated that he was right. "Never mind. I'll carry it. Thank you."

Poppy passed it over. The leather satchel handle felt slippery in my hand. I used one of the wheel spokes as a step up into the cart where I shoved the bag under my seat.

Nana, please help me find a way to avoid using those, I prayed. *Please let the negotiations go smoothly.*

Bane and Poppy followed. We'd discussed it earlier; if Bane rode with us, he could sleep while we traveled, then stand watch at night.

A dozen of King Alder's guards arrived. Their leader, a square-faced man named Sergeant Dun, introduced himself. Dami showed up last, glowering at everyone. She climbed into the cart and slouched in the corner, away from me.

The cart jerked forward. We were off.

"How are your ribs?" I asked.

Dami responded with a huff. How nice.

Poppy pulled out a skirt and began neatly embroidering it with tiny pink blossoms. Even though she was agile-of-hand, I didn't know how she managed to sew in a moving cart without pricking herself. Bane made himself as comfortable as he could and closed his eyes.

Through the streets of Askan-Wod, ribbon-dancers and flautists followed us. Children ran alongside the cart and whooped. Others, more solemn, took down the black ribbons they'd hung in support of the prisoner exchange and waved them at us.

I couldn't imagine King Alder or Lady Sulat leaning out the window to wave, so I sat with my hands in my lap and tried to look dignified. Soon, we left the city behind and all I could see were ferns and the massive trunks of redwood trees. That, and Alder's men. Everyone outside of this cart was my enemy.

By then, Bane was snoring softly. I'd heard it said that soldiers could sleep anywhere, but I wished I'd had the foresight to bring a pillow in here. I'd grab one for him when we stopped.

Poppy's whisper broke the silence. "I don't suppose you know what the fashion in Shoreed is?"

I thought back to the manuscript boxes of recipes Sorrel had shown me, but none of them depicted people. Violet would have known. "I'm afraid not."

Dami wrinkled her nose as if the mere mention of clothing was offensive to her.

"If we want people to treat your sister like an ambassador, she needs to look the part, despite her youth," Poppy said, as kind as always. "She's representing all of Rowak."

Dami snorted. Poppy politely ignored her and talked with me instead about colors and patterns she thought would complement my skin. Lady Sulat was right to send her with us. We needed someone as organized and detail-oriented as Poppy watching out for us.

WE STOPPED for the night at a carter station, halfway to Napil. Once the cart stopped, Bane stepped out to stand guard and Poppy hurried inside the building to make my room ready.

That left me alone with Dami. "We can't stay mad at each other for the rest of this trip," I said.

"You want to put a wager on that?" Dami raised an eyebrow. "Because *I* can do it. Don't know about you."

How her spine wasn't aching from her posture—slumped and wedged in the corner—I didn't know. She'd been like that for hours. My legs were sore, and I'd been sitting like a normal person. "I'm upset. About a lot of things," I admitted in my most-neutral voice. "But I'd like to be amiable anyway."

"Is that what you told King Alder? 'Oh, never mind that you tried to kill me, let's play nice and get married?' That's a crappy way to live, Plum."

I pursed my lips. "Our marriage isn't about him. It's about Rowak."

"Yeah. Exactly your problem. Guess what? It's not Rowak that'll be rutting you at night. Do you know how that works? Want me to explain? See—"

I cut her off. "I've *helped deliver babies*, thank you very much."

"You going to pop out a few of those for His Majesty, too?" Dami demanded. "However annoying your obsessive cooking was, I thought you wanted to be a chef. And now you've let that go, too."

I stretched my fingers so I wouldn't ball them in my skirts. "This isn't about me. It's about saving lives and ending a war."

"Yeah, yeah. I'm going to go help Poppy." Dami stomped out of the cart.

I leaned my head against the wall and closed my eyes, easing the pain throbbing between them. *Focus on the treaty,* I reminded myself, *not the marriage.*

I thought about how Bane had lost his arm. I hadn't been there for him—I hadn't been able to cook for him or clean his wound or save his limb.

But I would do that for countless soldiers, now. I'd see them returned home, to a country at peace.

Dami was wrong. I hadn't stopped being a chef. I'd found a place for myself where I could prevent more injuries than I could ever hope to cook remedies for.

BANE ESCORTED me from the cart to the station, yellow pine needles from last year snapping under our feet. The inside was low-roofed and only roughly finished—knots in the wood sticking out, rush mats thrown over the unpolished floor. The rotten-egg stench of overcooked cabbage mixed with the suffocating heat of summer.

How spoiled I'd become, living in the manicured palace. I almost laughed at myself, then noticed something odd. I didn't see a station steward or other guests. Just my own party.

My stomach tightened, but I found Sergeant Dun and kept my voice merely curious. "Why is the station empty?"

His mouth twitched. "Well. Considering that not long ago, Shoreed assassins attempted your life, we were worried about your security. We had everyone else here seek hospitality at the nearest village so we could properly secure the station."

Ice crept up my spine. Lady Sulat had assumed King Alder would order my murder over the border, where the Shoreed were easily blamed. But here, the guards wouldn't have to worry about getting back to Rowak territory—or about witnesses. They'd just spoon-fed the identity of the guilty party to the nearest village. No one would accuse my guards.

I smiled gratefully at Sergeant Dun. "I appreciate your diligence. Excellent work."

The guards planned to kill me tonight.

CHAPTER EIGHTEEN

Lady Sulat's soldiers were a full day away in Napil. Sergeant Dun and his men numbered twelve. I just had myself, Bane, Poppy, and Dami. And if it came to a fight, my sister might sit in the corner and laugh while soldiers slit my throat.

"Is something wrong?" Sergeant Dun asked.

"Oh, no. Nothing's wrong." How could we survive this?

His gaze turned flinty. "Nothing? You're making a face."

Protesting further wouldn't help. I wrinkled my nose. "It's the soup. I can tell it's not well-made. I'm sorry. I know that's snobbish of me."

He relaxed, letting a smile touch his blocky face. "Smells fine to me."

I shook my head and pulled him toward the three large crocks on the hearth. All of them had a sickly, brown-green cabbage stew in them. I snatched up an abandoned bowl, dipped it in, then sampled the soup. I didn't have to fake my grimace. "*Abominable.* Here, you try."

Sergeant Dun sipped, then shrugged. "I've had worse."

"And you ought to have better. I'll go get a few things and, hopefully, make this mess edible."

Dami rolled her eyes at me as I headed outside. I think that helped make my actions seem authentic. Bane and two of Dun's men followed me. I paused between the supply cart and the passenger cart. I could simply improve the soup and stall for time. Or I could go to the passenger cart and gather a few of Violet's things from where they were stowed under the seat.

Even if Dami and Bane had the advantage of a surprise attack, they couldn't take out a dozen men. This was a problem I had to cook myself out of. But giving these men a good meal to linger over would only delay the inevitable. Making them stronger and healthier didn't help us, either.

I had to hurt them. I had to turn their warm, soothing supper into a weapon. Or I had to accept that three people I cared about would probably die tonight, along with myself.

I still wasn't like Violet, I tried telling myself as I opened the box and tucked a vial of powdered bittersleep leaf into my waistband. I wasn't going to kill any of these men. Just knock them out so we could travel safely to Lady Sulat's soldiers in Napil.

But of course, there was always a chance that even well-intentioned poisons could turn deadly. A miscalculation. An unexpected reaction. An allergy.

I grabbed a benign piece of paper—a recipe for spring greens hot pot—and stepped back out of the cart. Bane's eyes widened, but he composed himself before the other guards noticed. He knew why I'd really entered that cart. I rummaged for a few carrots and parsnips in the supply cart to brighten and sweeten the soup, then strode anxiously back inside like there was nothing more on my mind than salvaging supper.

I hummed, hawed, and fussed over the crocks, carefully adding in bittersleep to the two largest when I dumped in the carrots. The smallest crock I left unadulterated. Then I dished up all the soldiers first.

Dun and two of his men waved their hands, refusing bowls.

"It's actually good now," I promised.

"I don't doubt it," Sergeant Dun replied. "But we're taking the first watch. Warm food will make us sleepy. We'll eat when our shift's almost over. Leave it on the hearth."

I wanted to swear, but I smiled sweetly instead. "That's very dutiful of you."

One of his men, a thin fellow with big eyes, coughed next to Sergeant Dun. In a tone that sounded rehearsed, he asked, "Sergeant, since it's our first night out, can we celebrate? I brought a jug of wine. I thought maybe the ambassador and her ladies would like to join us for a toast or two."

Get us all tipsy, then kill us. That would be the clean way to do it. In all honesty, it wasn't that different from my plan, except for the part where I was hoping to avoid fatalities.

"That's an excellent idea," I cut in. "I'll grab another jug from the supplies." If most of the soldiers were drinking, Sergeant Dun and the two men who hadn't had any doctored soup wouldn't think it was strange when their fellows started snoring. If I was lucky, those three men would join our celebration, overdo it, and fall asleep themselves.

Dami stared at me. "Are you feeling all right? You want to have *fun*?"

"It's been a long day. And I'm excited about the peace treaty. Why not?"

Sergeant Dun nodded. "I agree. I'll stand watch outside with Corinal and Flint, so we keep our wits about us."

I grinned through gritted teeth. Of course he wasn't about to get sloshed when he had a murder to perform. "Let's get the wine, then!"

THE ALCOHOL rather sped up the poison. After a cup or two, the men slouched to the ground, their bodies limp and lifeless. I checked their pulses. Alive.

But they still looked like the corpses that littered the ground during the Old Road Ambush.

And I'd still *poisoned* them.

Dami whistled low, surveying the room. "Well done, Plum. I didn't think you had it in you. Really, I assumed you were just so focused on the food you couldn't see what was going on. I was going to try to pick them off one by one whenever they went for a piss in the woods, but this is a *lot* neater."

Poppy swayed on her feet. "I...don't understand."

Apparently, two drinks were too many for her. "Poppy, can you sing drinking songs loudly while we talk? Keep up the ruse?"

She shrugged and bawled out a melody. In that moment, I could have sworn she was endurance-of-lungs.

"Do you think we can sneak out a window?" I asked.

"With three of them listening outside?" Bane morosely shook his head. "If there were actually a loud, drunken party going on in here, maybe. But they'll hear us."

Dami picked up two spears from the passed-out guards and handed one to Bane. "Surprise attack's our best bet. Open the door and stab them before they can turn to look at us. Three against two. You ready?"

I swallowed. I'd already hurt so many people with food. That ought to have been *enough*. Dami and Bane shouldn't need to put themselves in danger. "Maybe..."

But I couldn't think of anything else we could do. Stomach churning, I turned to my sister. "Dami, if you die, I won't forgive you."

She snorted. "What? And you'll forgive Bane?"

"I'm still trying to figure out how to ask for his forgiveness. Be safe."

They both nodded and turned toward the door. "You're taller," Dami said. "You strike high. I'll strike low. Then we won't get in each other's way."

"Agreed."

Before they could reach the door, though, it opened. Sergeant Dun, his men, Dami, and Bane stared at each other for a heartbeat, then charged.

CHAPTER NINETEEN

Poppy stopped singing and stumbled back toward a wall. One of the soldiers rushed at Dami. One ran at Bane. And Sergeant Dun sprinted toward me, spear low.

I did the only thing I could think of: I snatched one of those crocks off the hearth, singeing my hands, and flung the whole bubbling concoction in his face. Sergeant Dun howled and stopped to wipe cabbage out of his eyes. I snatched up a guard's spear and held it out, trembling, in front of me. I didn't know how to use this. I didn't know how to defend myself.

Behind Sergeant Dun, the man fighting Bane screamed. I knew Bane was strong-of-arm, but I'd never seen him use his birthgift for violence. One moment there was a man in front of him, and the next, he'd skewered him and ripped the spear back out, drawing out a stew of blood and viscera. The man slumped to the floor and didn't move again. His skin paled as his blood drained out.

Sergeant Dun turned sideways so he could see both Bane and me. Dami was still fighting her opponent, pushing him back toward the wall.

Bane shifted into a fighting stance, his left arm held behind him for leverage. "Get back, Plum," he shouted. "If I overreach—"

He didn't have to say more than that. I would be in the way if I tried to fight. A liability. I stepped away.

"Flint underestimated you, didn't he?" Dun asked.

Bane responded with a powerful lunge. But Dun moved like a dancer, side-stepping the attack and taking a swing at Dami. She was ready for it and dodged. But that gave the other man time to close in.

Bane struck again, forcing Dun to block him and leave Dami and the guard to their duel. She shouted a few obscenities and forced him back a step.

I tried to breathe normally, but my throat felt swollen shut. Lady Sulat always acted like depending on her supporters to do their jobs was a natural, easy thing. Letting Dami and Bane fight was anything but. I wanted to run in. I wanted to feel useful. I didn't want to let them carry this burden.

But the most helpful thing I could do was to stand back.

Dun lunged again. Bane blocked and counter-attacked, but Dun jumped away. Then he sprang back with a sudden lunge. Bane side-stepped, but the obsidian spearhead grazed his arm, drawing a bright line of blood.

I gagged on the aroma of death. *Nana help him!* I begged.

I can't, little blossom. He's not part of my family.

Bane felt like family. I cared about him like family. *Help Dami, then. She can help him. Please, please let them both live.*

I didn't feel anything in response, only my own churning fear.

Bane made a wild lunge that Dun easily dodged. Bane's spearhead shattered against the wall, sending obsidian shards skittering through the room. Dun grabbed the haft of Bane's spear in his other hand.

Just then, Dami skewered her opponent with the same, gory, strength-of-arm blow that Bane had dispatched the first man with. She whirled toward Dun and charged.

Sergeant Dun glanced at her. Bane didn't. He yanked his spear to the side, throwing Dun off-balance. Then he let go of his weapon and punched Dun in the face.

Bones crunched. Dun's nose disappeared in a smear of blood. The sergeant screamed, stumbling backward. Before Dami could reach him, Bane ripped his own spear back from Dun and lunged. The momentum carried him forward, Bane crashing on top of Dun, running him through with the broken obsidian point and pinning him like a bug to the floor.

Dun convulsed, then lay still.

Bane was alive. And because of me, three men were dead.

"Thank you," I whispered, not sure if I was talking to Bane or Dami or Nana. I didn't know what else to say. The air reeked of blood and wine. It was hard to breathe without gagging.

Dami glanced at the men Bane had killed. "Wow. I bet that first guy bled out in *seconds*."

Poppy stared blankly at everything. I couldn't tell if she was in shock or if she wasn't taking in the scene at all. I put an arm around her. "Let's get out of here."

She stumbled. We had to veer around all the prone bodies. Outside, under a clear black sky, I leaned us both against the nearest redwood and gulped in its clean, spicy smell. It still didn't cover the tang of blood in the air.

I'd become a poisoner, and Dami and Bane had still been forced to fight and kill to protect their lives and mine. I knew the poison had helped. Without it, we couldn't have won this fight.

But I still wanted to take Violet's box and all my notes and burn them. I rubbed my hands against my skirt, as if that could make them something other than the hands of a poisoner. I closed my eyes, like that could block out the death I'd seen.

And then I felt guilty. I'd only had to pour some powder into some crocks and witness the violence. Dami and Bane had actually had to *do* it. The wind blew toward us, bringing a fresh whiff of death, and I couldn't hold it in anymore. I pushed away from the tree and emptied my stomach onto the ground.

"Did you eat some of your own poison?" Dami asked.

I shook my head. "It's just...the blood. Those men are dead because of me."

Dami snorted. "First, don't take credit for other people's work.

Two of those men are dead because of *Bane*. And I got the other one."

Poppy hiccupped. And hiccupped again. "Are we going to just stay here next to the pretty tree?"

I hated that she was the one talking sense. "No. We ought to make it to Napil tonight. We're still not safe here."

"Unless we go slit all their throats in their sleep," Dami said.

I glared at her.

"Yeah, yeah. I wasn't *actually* suggesting it. But we could, you know."

I gathered the things we shouldn't leave behind—the amber for the trip, my notes, the poisons—and we started off down the dark road between the giant redwood trees. I didn't feel safe until we were too far for Dami to easily massacre all the sleeping guards. The smell of blood stayed with us, drying onto Dami and Bane's clothes.

I rubbed my arms against the chill of night. "When we get to Napil, we all need to tell the same story. We were ambushed in the carter station by some unknown group. King Alder chose his guards poorly and they scattered. We had to run. We don't know if the assassins are still tracking us."

Sergeant Dun had already planted the seeds of that story in the nearby village. And it gave us the perfect excuse to pick up our new military guards in Napil. Instead of dealing with the fall-out of the change, Lady Sulat would be able to reproach King Alder for his negligence in choosing such incompetent and unfaithful men.

"A good plan," Bane said.

Dami grunted her agreement.

Poppy paused on the road and threw up. "I've never had—" she vomited again, then wiped her mouth with the back of her hand. "Never had more than a sip before."

I walked next to her, helping her keep her balance. But soon she was stumbling. She went from singing bawdy songs to sobbing. When the two of us started to lag, Dami put an arm around Poppy, too, but it wasn't enough. Eventually, Dami and Bane took turns carrying Poppy. Dami spent hers swearing under her breath. Bane gritted his teeth through his. When they paused to trade off for the fourth time, I stepped forward.

"You're both strong-of-arm, not endurance-of-back. Let me take a turn." Aches bled through me from marching mile after mile under the dark redwood trees, ferns rustling at our ankles. They had to be feeling much worse.

Bane wouldn't hear of it. "You're the ambassador and you're not trained for this."

"For what?" I asked, eyes blurry. My thoughts swished around my skull like wash water in a crock.

"Marching," Dami said. "Some of us have a *military* background. Comes in useful, now and then. If you collapse, we'll just have two bodies to carry." She laughed at me as she picked up Poppy. Poppy promptly vomited for the sixteenth time, right down the front of Dami's dress. Dami swore. But she kept going. My sister was strong. Stubborn.

At sunrise, we reached the gates of Napil—sturdy gates surrounded by a palisade made from whole logs. The sun gleamed red and amber off the worn wood. The guards hadn't opened the gates for the day, so we had to call up to them.

I was the only one with a voice left. Bane and Dami collapsed against the wall with a passed-out Poppy. I wished I could join them. "Hail! We request entrance!"

"Who requests entrance?" the guard called down. With the sun glaring over everything, I couldn't even make out his face.

"I'm Green-ranked Plum of Clamsriver, Acting Rowak Ambassador to the Shoreed and the Royal Consort."

The guard paused a long moment, probably taking in our disheveled appearance, but those were titles that one didn't ignore lightly. Another guard came and I showed him my official papers from King Rowak, confirming everything I'd said.

"Are you well?" he asked, even though he could see the answer. He had kind, brown eyes and a graying beard.

I shook my head. "We were attacked by assassins. The guards

King Alder sent with me scattered. We need safe shelter."

The guard signaled to his fellows to open the gate, tsking as he did so—at the ineptitude of my guards, I think. "I can see you to Governor Slate's house immediately," he offered. "Should I call for a cart, or would you rather walk?"

I glanced at the heap of my companions against the city wall. "We'll take the cart."

AT GOVERNOR SLATE'S HOUSE, servants bustled me into a hot bath. By the time I reached the guest room, Dami and Poppy were already asleep in it. I supposed they'd put Bane somewhere else. I thanked the maid and laid down on the other side of Poppy.

We'd made it to Napil. We were under the roof of a man Lady Sulat trusted. I slept as soundly as the dead.

WHEN WE WOKE UP MID-AFTERNOON, Governor Slate graciously had his chef prepare what we needed: hangover food for Poppy, snacks to help with Bane's shallow laceration, and a lovely soup of pickled ginger and grouse in a clear sweet-and-sour broth for everyone. Targeted with endurance and strength, my muscles relaxed, and my pain eased. It wasn't the best broth I'd ever tasted, but it wasn't bad, either.

Our new guards, Governor Slate said, would be ready in two days —when his own men had fetched our carts from the carter station. I spent the rest of the afternoon going over Lady Sulat's notes about negotiating a treaty. It was dry but important information, like how the Shoreed delegate on the border would be responsible for escorting us to the Coral Palace. Governor Slate stayed nearby, helpfully clarifying points as needed, something like pity in his eyes. A bit of coaching from Lady Sulat was precious little preparation.

We ate with his family, then all retired early. Poor Poppy was soon snoring away. Dami and I lay silent on the mattress. She didn't seem tense at all, despite the summer heat thickening the air. But anxiety burned up my throat.

"Dami. Can we talk?"

She rubbed one eye. "I'm *still* not interested in a lecture. Sorry."

"I need to thank you." The words made my jaw ache, but they were true.

"Thank me?"

"For protecting me. At the carter station."

She snorted. "Yeah. Like I was really going to stand by and let some palace flunky run you through."

I chewed my lip and stared up at the ceiling.

Dami propped herself up on an elbow, forehead wrinkling. "You thought I wouldn't fight for you."

"I wasn't sure."

"Of all the..." Dami trailed off, but I could imagine the choice, colorful words she wasn't filling the silence with. "Why do you think I'd want you *dead?*"

I felt like someone had lodged a cherry pit in my throat. "You've never cared before if I'm alive or dead."

"You don't make any sense. I've never been around when someone attacked you."

I studied her face. The genuine confusion. How could she not see? "You've never once apologized for leaving home. That almost killed me."

"No, you almost died because you were an *idiot* and didn't mind your own business and go off with Sorrel."

Idiot? "I'm part of a family, a city, a nation. I couldn't just—"

"Stop right there." Dami held up a hand. "This would be that *lecturing* part I try so hard to avoid."

"Dami—"

"You're infuriating! I never *asked* you to sacrifice your life for me and come to the palace." She said that like an accusation.

"You didn't have to." I couldn't have lived with myself if I'd done anything less—if she'd died, and I could have done something to save her.

"Ugh. Running off to the palace without a thought for yourself, now agreeing to marry Alder. What's wrong with you?"

I peered at her. "Are you trying to lecture me on the virtues of selfishness?"

"Being miserable isn't a virtue, Plum."

"I'm not miserable. I have a chance to end a war, and I have peace of mind knowing I'm doing the right thing."

"Your mind," Dami grumbled, "is ridiculously demanding. You should tell it to shut up."

WE SPENT another blessedly calm day at Governor Slate's house. His men arrived with our carts after lunch and Poppy spent the afternoon repacking them and sending servants out to replace missing supplies. I took advantage of the time to talk with the governor further about treaties. I didn't glance over my shoulder. I didn't stare longingly at Bane. I didn't regret my choice to put the peace negotiations before everything else.

The next morning, our new guards arrived—a dozen men with a rather short, green-ranked officer leading them. Bane had already been on his feet, standing guard, but now he charged forward. I shuffled back. Was something wrong?

Bane embraced the officer like he was a brother. The short man clapped him on the back. "Bane! Personal bodyguard to an ambassador, eh? You've made it further than I thought you would."

"Sergeant Kabrok, I had no idea you were here!"

"Well, it's Lieutenant Kabrok now, thank you. I've seen quite a bit of combat during the past three years." He stepped back, gaze sliding along Bane's arm. "It seems you have, too. You've certainly lost more weight than I have."

Lt. Kabrok held up his right hand. His index finger was missing.

"I'm afraid it was just the one engagement for me, sir," Bane replied.

I raised an eyebrow. "One? The Old Road Ambush and defending us at the carter station don't count?"

Lt. Kabrok smiled. "Your ambassador seems to disagree." He bowed. "Lt. Kabrok, at your service, Ambassador Plum."

"He was my trainer, Plum," Bane said. "The best sergeant—"

"*Lieutenant*," Kabrok said with a satisfied grin.

"—the best, most precise and exacting lieutenant I could have hoped for. We'll keep you safe." Bane grinned, like the worst part of this mission must be over now, with Lt. Kabrok here. "Do you remember that time you accidentally marched us through the raspberry brambles?"

"How could I forget?" Kabrok replied. "My favorite was the time with the duck pens, though."

Bane laughed heartily. I had no idea what they were talking about.

Kabrok sighed. "Well, If I'd known I was meeting an old friend, I would have brought a picnic instead of just a prisoner."

"Prisoner?" Bane asked.

"Lady Sulat's had me interviewing traitors, looking for the person with the most Shoreed contacts and the most motivation to earn a good name in Rowak again. I think he'll be an asset."

"She told me how diligent you were working on finding the right person," I said. "Thank you." We needed all the help we could get in Shoreed, and with this many guards, I doubted the prisoner would have much opportunity to betray us.

Lt. Kabrok gestured at his men. Two in the back walked forward with a man between them I knew all too well. My hands went cold. Bane's shoulders tightened.

Yellow-ranked Fir of Askan-Wod, Violet's co-conspirator, gave a suave bow. "Ah, Plum. How good to see you again. Did you miss me?"

CHAPTER TWENTY

Fir stood casually with all his weight on one foot, like he was merely waiting for lunch. But his cheeks were gaunt and shadows hung under his eyes. An old, yellow bruise spread across his jaw, not quite hidden by the face powder he'd tried to hide it with.

Prison apparently hadn't been kinder to him than it was to anyone else. But Fir still grinned like he owned the world—like he could taunt and threaten me with a handful of words.

Bane stepped in front of me, fingers clenching into a fist.

"I know being around Plum makes you stupid," Fir drawled, "but please remember we're on the same side this time."

I needed to regain control of the situation. I stepped up next to Bane and gestured him to back down. "I've been well, Fir. Thank you for your concern. Now that you're here, we should get going. I welcome you to ride in the passenger cart with me."

I spoke as if there were no awkward past history. His grin soured. He'd expected drama and angst. Fir loved attention. Loved being important. I needed him to feel that way when he was working for me, not when he was goading me.

Fir got into the passenger cart first. Bane moved to follow, teeth grit, but Dami held out a hand to stop him. "I'll keep a watch on Plum," she said. "You should catch up with your sergeant."

That was actually really thoughtful.

Bane frowned and kept his voice low. "Fir is a dangerous, weaseling—"

"—manipulative plotter who lets other people do his dirty work, from what I've been told," Dami said. "I doubt he's going to stain his own pretty hands trying to murder Plum in the passenger cart while surrounded by an entire detachment of guards. I've got this, Bane."

"I agree," I said. "Walk with Lt. Kabrok. Catch up. Brief him on what's happened so far, if he doesn't know."

Bane glanced at the cart again, then nodded. Poppy also opted for fresh air. I headed to the cart with Dami. "Thanks. It's kind of you to—"

"Yeah, yeah, don't ruin it," Dami muttered. We stepped inside, sitting on the bench opposite of Fir. The cart started forward. Dami closed the windows for safety as we rattled down the street. Shadows pooled inside the cart, cut by beams of light from the imperfect shutters.

Fir gave me one annoyed glance, then turned to Dami with a smile that oozed confident charm. "You must be the real Dami. I'd say I've heard so much about you, but I'm afraid the opposite is true. All I know is that you could punch me into a paste with those pretty arms of yours."

"That sounds like fun." Dami leaned forward with a flirtatious smile of her own.

Fir jerked back and swallowed. "I...wasn't suggesting you actually try."

Dami giggled. She elbowed me. "Why didn't you say he was so funny?"

For lack of a better response, I cleared my throat. "We should focus on our mission."

Dami rolled her eyes and echoed me under her breath in an annoyed, sing-song wheeze.

I ignored her and turned to Fir. It would have been so easy to poke at him for the weeks he'd spent in jail. To mock him for his failed, traitorous plans. To point out that, despite his best efforts, I was still breathing.

But none of that would help me secure a treaty. If I wanted to make Fir an asset to this delegation, I needed to make sure there was no taunting. I needed to give him a new place to belong—a new goal through which to pursue his ambitions. "I'm glad you agreed to join us. Your knowledge will prove indispensable."

"What exactly is my role, Acting Ambassador? Am I to be a delegate under you?"

He gave me my real title, well aware that a green-ranked woman couldn't hold the high post of a full ambassador. As a yellow-ranked man, he couldn't hold the post of delegate.

"Let's call you my advisor. Teach me what you know of Shoreed politics."

He looked disappointed that I hadn't insulted his birth and started a fight. "That could take a while."

"We have nearly two weeks before we reach the Coral Palace. We don't have to cover everything today."

I half-expected Fir to say something snide or refuse, but he folded his hands in his lap, stared at the cart floor, and began talking. "King Heron sits on the throne. He's supported by a group of ministers. They're powerful, but they don't have anything as formal as our Purple-Blue Council. His daughter, Lady Oakash, is probably the most influential person besides the king. She's infamously good at gathering information. Chef Palaw regards her highly. And, unfortunately for us, she's a strong supporter of this war."

I studied Fir's face as he talked. Not a wisp of a lie touched his face. But he'd fooled me before.

"What do you know about the Bloodmarrows?" I asked.

Fir laughed nervously. "Are you trying to make fun of me now?"

"Not at all."

Fir shrugged. "They're legends—Vengeful Ghosts controlled by the Shoreed who steal ducks or murder Rowak officers."

I decided to show a little trust in him. "Violet was one of them."

Fir snorted. "I know you disliked her, but she wasn't a ghost."

"No, she wasn't, because the Bloodmarrows aren't ghosts. They're chefs-turned-poisoners who work for Shoreed. Palaw is one as well."

We rattled over a bump in the road. Fir stared thoughtfully at his hands. "I knew Violet when we were kids. She wouldn't eviscerate someone just for fun."

"I didn't say all the stories about Bloodmarrows are true. Only that they themselves exist."

Fir didn't avoid Violet's name the way Sorrel had. He just sounded sad. My insides squirmed, remembering the way she'd died, murdered by an ally to keep her silent and protect a coup that ultimately failed. I wasn't responsible for her death. I'd only gotten her arrested. But the unease still surged through me.

I cracked the window, letting in a sharp wedge of sunlight and the scent of pine trees. "I assume all your contacts in Shoreed are in favor of the war?"

"As far as I know. But even if they know I'm with the ambassador, they'll want to talk to me about you. I'll try to glean as much as I can from them without giving anything valuable away."

I pursed my lips. He spoke so naturally, like he'd been working with me for years. He wasn't agile-of-face, but he controlled his expressions well.

"Don't give me that look," Fir said.

"What look?"

"That disapproving, contemplating, is-he-going-to-stab-me-in-the-back look. It's annoying, and if you do it around company, they'll know you don't trust me."

Dami gave him a gooey smile. "Mm. You are *adorable*. Also, Plum, I agree. You should never make that face again. It's annoying."

"I'm just worried for you," I told Fir, which was true—even if I didn't trust him. "Meeting with your contacts after the coup failed will be tricky."

Fir gave me that self-assured grin, all teeth flashing in the sun. "Before, I miscalculated. This time, I'll be more careful."

To make sure we got our treaty, or to make sure he was on the winning side? He didn't sound the least repentant or ashamed of being a traitor to Rowak. Maybe I ought to remind him that he had a good reason to love our country. "Please do be cautious. I spoke with Lady Egal before we left."

Fir's shoulders tightened.

"She's well," I said. "But she's worried about you."

He instantly relaxed. Fir actually cared for his grandmother as much as she thought he did. That was a pleasant surprise. "I want to return you safely to her as a hero of Rowak."

Fir looked out that thin crack of open window, a pensive frown-line across his forehead. I stopped talking then and let him think. He needed time to envision that future—a reunion with the person he loved best, feeling important and admired for all the right reasons. If he could hold that future clearly in his mind, I could trust him to be loyal to our cause.

WE STOPPED midday for lunch where a small stream curved toward the road. Bane was at the cart door to help me down, every inch of him tense, his lips pursed in an angry line. "We need to talk."

He shot a glare over my shoulder at Fir. Yes, we did need to talk. If Bane antagonized Fir, we'd never get him to feel like he belonged here, helping to secure a treaty.

"All right. Perhaps we can step away from camp?"

"Fine. But we should bring Dami."

Dami glanced between us. "This looks like it might be fun to watch. I'm in."

Bane turned about and marched past the guards unloading lunch. We headed into the forest, opposite the stream. Bane stopped in a small clearing—a redwood circle. A giant, ancestral tree had once stood here. When it died, saplings from its roots sprang up in a ring around where it had once grown. These sacred sites were used by travelers and the poor alike to worship their Ancestors. Bane didn't seem to notice he'd chosen such a place.

"We can't bring Fir to Shoreed with us," he said.

"Bringing Fir poses a risk, but the odds in Shoreed are stacked against us. Lady Sulat thought it was a gamble we should take, and I agree." I kept my voice calm. I didn't want to argue with him here, not where our Ancestors might be listening more closely.

Dami sat on a crumbling log outside the circle and watched us expectantly.

"Fir has *already* caused problems."

I sighed through my nose. "I know. He's a traitor. But I think Lt. Kabrok was right in his assessment. Fir holds no great loyalty to Shoreed. He just wanted to be important. Now, he'll be important helping us. We can give him that. He's good with people and he has friends in Shoreed."

"He's already caused trouble, Plum!"

I stared blankly. Fir had been in the passenger cart all day. He couldn't have done anything

Bane paced in the circle, crushing redwood needles underfoot and sending their dry, spicy scent into the air. "He made that comment. Saying I'm stupid around you. I've spent all morning getting needled by Kabrok's men, Plum. Asking me if that's why I'm your bodyguard. What our history is. I haven't convinced them yet that my regard toward you is purely professional."

I pinched the bridge of my nose. If such rumors got out in Shoreed, it would hurt the credibility of our delegation and give our opponents something to slander us with.

"Lt. Kabrok tried to put a stop to it," Bane said, "but I don't think it helped."

My throat felt dry. "We'll have to be especially distant, then. Perhaps even cold to each other. You shouldn't ride in the cart with me."

THE CORAL PALACE | 165

He shouldn't anyway. I was engaged. How had I thought it was a good idea to bring him? Bane had insisted, but it had been selfish of me to agree.

Dami snorted. "You can't get rid of a scandal by screaming there's nothing interesting to see. You've got to replace it with a *new* scandal."

"Right. That's just what we need," I replied.

"Oooh, was that sarcasm?" Dami rolled off the log onto her feet. "I'm so proud. Bane can cry himself hoarse saying that he doesn't want to share a blanket with the ambassador, and they won't listen. If he tells them Fir was wrong and he's always held affection for *someone else*, they'll have a new story to fixate on."

She sauntered up to Bane, leaned against him, and combed her fingers through his hair. Bane stiffened, eyes wide in shock.

A pit opened in my stomach. I wanted to avert my gaze. And at the same time, I wished I'd be brave enough to touch his hair, to lean against him like that. She inched her mouth toward the side of his face like she was going to kiss his ear. I bit the inside of my lip. I'd never get to do that. Not unless the treaty failed.

Dami abruptly stopped and stomped away from Bane. "Nothing, Plum? Really? I thought you'd at least yell at me. I was hoping you'd throw a punch."

"Of course not," I whispered.

"Cold-blooded monster," Dami muttered.

Bane awkwardly cleared his throat. "Plum, I understand the need to stop these rumors, but I don't think I can convincingly...umm... Dami is a tad intimidating."

When we'd first met, I thought that Dami and Bane would make a lovely couple. Seeing them side-by-side, it was preposterous. "Dami's not our only choice. I can talk to Poppy."

Bane lowered his eyes to the ground and hid his left arm behind his back. "If that's what we need to do."

It was. I hated that it was.

"I'll talk to Fir as well. If he continues to cause trouble, I'll ask Lt.

Kabrok about the best way to send him back to the military prison in Napil." Promising to keep Fir in line was the best apology I could offer Bane.

He gave me a stiff bow and marched back toward the carts.

That left me with Dami. "You know," she glared, "even without your stupid engagement messing up things for you and Bane, I wonder if you'd ever actually get together. Don't you have feelings for him?"

As I watched Bane walk away, a waterfall of emotions crashed through me. Regrets for hurting him. Regrets for bringing him. The stupid, impossible impulse to run up, twine my fingers through his, and go walking through the forest, hand-in-hand. "I do."

"I thought you were the worst sister ever because you were extra fond of making me miserable," Dami snapped. "But apparently, you're horrible to everyone. I used to feel *special*, Plum."

THAT AFTERNOON, I asked to ride in my cart alone after lunch, saying I planned to nap. I smiled pleasantly through our lunch of cold buckwheat branches and salted duck eggs. I made small talk with the soldiers. I refrained from sitting near Bane or sending him longing glances. I didn't make faces at Dami, either.

But when the shutters were closed and the cart rattling away, I cried in the stuffy dimness all alone. I cried until I felt cold inside. Then I promised myself this would be the one and only time I allowed myself such an indulgence.

CHAPTER
TWENTY-ONE

We camped that night in a military palisade near the war front. Dami, Poppy, and I shared a dark tent, with a few of our guards standing watch outside. I kept my voice low to explain the situation to Poppy.

"I know this is awkward," I concluded, "but would you pretend to be in a relationship with Bane?"

Dami groaned and rolled over. It was a hot night, and the tent made it hotter. My hair clung to the sides of my sweat-sticky face.

"When you started with your serious tone, I thought it was going to be something bad," Poppy replied. "This shouldn't be hard at all."

"Oh. Umm. Thank you." I swallowed. This was exactly the kind of response I needed. I should be full of relief. "It won't be a problem?"

"Not at all. I started work in the palace before Bane became a messenger. From his first day onward, he's always done his duty with admirable attention to detail. I'd hoped someone nice would come along and marry him. It shouldn't be too hard to pretend to be that person for him."

"That's perfect." I tried to sound grateful. "Dami makes him uncomfortable."

Poppy laughed. "Bane and Dami? Don't tell me you suggested that first."

Dami rolled back toward us. "I did, actually. I flirted outrageously with him."

Poppy made a small tsking sound in the darkness. "With Bane? He wouldn't like that at all."

"He didn't. You seem to know him well." Dami almost sounded concerned. "Why haven't you gone after him?"

"Romance? Me? My family needs my tax exemption. They're merchants, and a lot of their trade depended on selling Shoreed goods in Askan-Wod. The war hasn't been good for business, to say the least. Maybe when it's over, I'll have time to daydream about such things, but not now."

WHILE THE SOLDIERS restocked our supply cart with more rations, I pulled Fir aside. As I explained the ruckus his comment had stirred, he turned paler and paler.

"I knew you were coming as an ambassador, not a spy. Lt. Kabrok told me that much," Fir said, "but I swear I didn't know about your engagement."

"Please be more careful in the future."

"I promise I will." He had such intense, earnest eyes. He'd been like that from the first day he conned me. He laid a hand on my shoulder. "Are you all right?"

Even if those words were coming from Fir, they were so abominably *kind* that I nearly cried again. "I'm fine."

Fir folded me into a hug. I thought he was going to whisper something biting or tackle me to the ground. But he was gentle. Soft. He stepped back, face still full of concern.

I blinked a few times to clear my eyes. "I appreciate that you're worried about me. I do. But I should probably keep a professional distance from you, too. I don't want to end up in this same situation again."

"Plum, you're charmingly over-focused on Bane. You're marrying my *cousin*. That makes us family. If you need a shoulder to cry on, I'm here."

"Oh."

I'm not sure which was worse: that Fir was my best option for a confidant on this journey, or that I felt like he'd actually listen if I needed to talk.

POPPY WALKED outside the cart with Bane all morning long. Come afternoon, when we were about to cross into Shoreed-held territory, Lt. Kabrok insisted she ride inside, along with Dami and Fir. He wanted no non-military targets out in the open. Just in case.

We stopped at the fort in front of the Quickcurrent River Bridge for Shoreed soldiers to check our papers. They agreed we had the right to peaceably pass through and sent a small squad of soldiers to lead us to Ferndale. In Ferndale, we'd meet with Delegate Ream of Foreign Affairs, who would serve as our escort to the capital city, Pearlfoam.

We rattled over the bridge. Sweat trickled down the back of my neck in the muggy cart. Fir stared down at his hands. Dami peered through a gap in the wooden planks of the shutters. Poppy sewed an armband, nervously sucking on her lower lip.

The Shoreed had asked for us to negotiate a prisoner exchange, I reminded myself. They *wanted* me here. But that didn't make being here feel any safer.

Ferndale was only two miles away; we reached it quickly. We paused at the gates and stayed put while Lt. Kabrok talked with the Shoreed guards. Then we were inside the town.

With the windows closed, the outside sounds were muted. But I could still hear the creaking cart, the footsteps of our guards and our escort, the murmuring of spectators. It didn't sound like Askan-Wod in the slightest. There was no laughter, no merchants calling wares, no women calling after children. This was a city on the war front.

"What do you know about Delegate Ream?" I asked Fir.

"He replaced Delegate Willow a year or two ago, but it's not like we've had a lot of diplomatic contact with Shoreed during that time."

"That's it?"

"I only know that because of reports from inside the Redwood Palace. I'm not acquainted with everyone in this whole country."

"Of course not." I couldn't make up my mind if I was doubting his sincerity, or if I was simply disappointed to know so little about this Delegate Ream. "Thank you."

"You'll do fine, Ambassador Plum." Poppy's voice was tight, but her needle wove up and down through her fabric, just as steadily as if we sat on Lady Sulat's porch. Somehow, that tiny bit of familiarity was a great comfort.

"You don't have to call me by my title, you know."

"But if I do, perhaps you'll begin to wear the title like it belongs to you, Ambassador." Poppy gave me a small, terrified smile.

I returned it with one I hoped looked a little calmer. "Thank you."

I folded my sweating hands demurely in my lap and breathed in and out in time with Poppy's stitches.

"You bested King Alder." Poppy reached the end of her seam and tied off the thread. "You can do this, too."

The cart stopped and Lt. Kabrok opened the door. This had been a Rowak city not a year ago, and the stately home in front of me looked familiar in many ways, with whole-log pillars supporting sloped eaves that shaded a broad, sweeping porch. But a hasty wall of rammed earth surrounded it, and the windows had been partially boarded up, leaving narrow archer slits.

Servants escorted us to a guest house around back where I washed up and Poppy redid my hair. Flanked by Lt. Kabrok and Fir, with five of our soldiers trailing behind, I headed to the front of the house. Guards stood on the porch in sharp green uniforms. They kept their gaze straight ahead.

The door servant, a girl my own age, bowed deeply. "Dinner is ready. Please follow me, Ambassador-Consort."

Her light, lilting accent sounded strange to me—people in Rowak didn't drop sounds at the ends of words like that. She led us to the west side of the building, where the porch faced a garden of trellised morning glory and flower beds crammed with violets. It only made me think of Violet herself. Had she been nervous like this during the coup? I could imagine her being hopeful for her cause and nervous as she navigated the world with smiles and a satchel of poisons.

Maybe the only real difference between us was that I hadn't tried to kill anyone yet.

I shouldn't be morose, I told myself. This was my first chance to connect with a delegate of Shoreed and further the peace treaty. If I did well, I wouldn't have to think about Red Lord Ospren's life and if it should end in the manner Lady Sulat had recommended.

Two tables sat facing the garden—one with a pair of lidded bowls on it, the other with only one. As we approached, servants from around the other corner escorted out a plump, middle-aged man with a severely cut beard—it looked like a triangle pointing at his collarbone. I had no idea if that was fashionable in Shoreed or if he was merely eccentric.

The door servant introduced us. "I bring you Green-ranked Ambassador Plum of Clamsriver, Betrothed Consort of King Alder of Rowak, and her advisor, Yellow-rank Fir of Askan-Wod. Ambassador Plum, I present Second-ranked Officer of Foreign affairs, Third-ranked Ream."

Was he second or third-ranked? I'd have to ask Fir about Shoreed ranks later.

"Thank you for welcoming us." I bowed. "May the Ancestors bless us with many happy gatherings such as these in the future."

"What a quaint prayer." Ream gave me a pitying look. "Please, sit."

What kind of person insulted other people's *prayers?* He had to be against these negotiations.

Delegate Ream gave me a thin, oily smile and clasped his hands behind his back, not indicating which table I ought to sit at.

Fir discreetly nudged me toward the table with only one bowl, then seated himself at the other one. Delegate Ream huffed, smoothed his blue shirt, then sat with Fir. When he took the lid off his bowl, we did likewise.

Buckwheat noodles with dried plums lay piled in a rich broth. I tasted it. The broth was over-salted. Why would Delegate Ream serve a dish that granted perceptive-of-muscles? It wasn't a much-used combination, unless you were practicing archery or calligraphy. Presently, it just made me more aware of my various aches, especially the tightness in my neck.

At least I had enough experience to feel confident it wasn't poisoned.

"Given how long King Alder dithered over whether or not to send anyone, I didn't think I'd be hosting an ambassador at all. *Acting* ambassador, pardon me." He spoke in that lilting Shoreed accent, often dropping the ends of words.

"Then we shall have to make up for lost time. I trust you'll arrange for our escort through Shoreed to the Coral Palace with all haste."

Delegate Ream frowned, jowls sagging beneath his sharply-manicured beard. "If you insist on going, I'll need two weeks to prepare."

Two *weeks?* I wasn't sure how to be indignant and polite at the same time.

Thankfully, Fir stepped in. "What bluster! Delegate Ream, unless there are extenuating circumstances, you're supposed to be ready to depart within two days."

Delegate Ream sighed through his nose. I wanted to cheer out loud for Fir.

"I can't imagine why you're so eager to arrive," Ream said, turning his attention to his supper.

I imagined Lady Sulat at her most gracious and tried to emulate it. "Every day we wait is another day Shoreed and Rowak men rot in prison camps. I'm impatient to help them and impatient to end this war."

"Ocean and moon," he muttered, gathering a spoonful of noodles. "You're even younger than I thought. You think there *can* be a treaty."

I kept my back straight. I wasn't here to be coddled and pitied for my age. "I will always believe in the possibility of peace."

"Oh, we'll have peace—when Shoreed conquers Rowak. It won't end before then. Lady Oakash wants this war to happen. Backed by her vast network of spies and informants, she will push it forward. You can't hold back the tide."

"I will be delighted to meet her, too, when the time comes."

Delegate Ream slurped down his noodles. "I'd be delighted to stay in Ferndale instead of dragging myself all the way to Pearlfoam just to watch you and your cause drown, Ambassador. But, alas, it's rare to get what one wants."

AFTER THREE DAYS of refusing to turn around, Delegate Ream finally relented. We left on the fifth morning. I invited Ream to travel with me in the passenger cart, but he just gave me a look dripping with condescension and pity—like I'd already failed and just didn't know it.

I rode with Dami and Fir instead.

"I think it's good he's keeping his distance," Fir said. "He's only taking us to Pearlfoam; you don't have to convince him that a peace treaty is a good idea. Now we can talk about the Shoreed rank system."

The warm cart made it difficult to focus. Fir droned through the dull facts, and soon Dami's snores accompanied him. The shutters were open, though, giving me a clear view of Bane and Poppy walking down the road next to each other, not ten feet ahead of us.

"I made you something," she said, hands shyly clasped behind her back.

Bane courteously responded. "I'm honored, but you didn't have to do that."

"I've wanted to, for years, actually. But I thought making you a gift would look too forward. And I didn't want to give you the wrong idea."

I could only see the back of Bane's head, but his voice was so warm, I had no trouble imagining the way he'd be smiling at her right now. "I...don't know what to say."

"You really were the best messenger Lady Sulat's ever had. Most everyone else whines when she's not around about how they want a promotion, or they dawdle and waste time. Anyway, it always bothered me that your armband is usually crooked when it ought to be the best-looking."

"Well, here are my faults, Poppy. I'm proud and stubborn. It's hard to get on straight by myself, and I'm not going to ask for help."

She pulled the armband she'd been sewing from her sash. "I know. That's why I made you this. Watch."

Poppy put it around her own arm as they walked. She'd made a slit in part of the fabric, which she passed the end of the band through, cinching it easily into place. To keep it there, she tucked the tail twice around the band where it crossed. "You don't have to use it, of course, but I hope you like it."

Bane took off his armband and graciously accepted hers. It took mere seconds for him to get it neatly and tightly into place.

"I know you can be proud," Poppy said, hands clasped shyly behind her back again. "That's why I thought you might like this. You look as sharp as you ought to now, and you needn't ask anyone for help."

"This is the nicest present anyone has ever given me." Bane's voice was hoarse with emotion; I could hardly hear him. "Thank you, Poppy."

Fir's hand fell on my shoulder. "Plum, I don't think you heard a thing I said."

"Sorry."

He glanced out the window. "I'm the one who should be apologizing. That's my fault. Do you want me to close the shutters?"

I closed them myself. Fir was wrong. I was the one who'd agreed to marry King Alder. I was the reason Bane and Poppy were walking together right now. Bane was a warm, loving person. He could be happy with someone who wasn't me. He *deserved* to be happy with someone else.

When—if—we returned home to Rowak, I'd have to work on securing him some other post, one where he wouldn't have to see me every day. That was the best gift I could give him.

Fir started over. I tried to pay better attention.

WE TRAVELED through forests and meadows, past forts and towns. Some of the architecture had a Rowak look to it, but the farther we traveled, the more stone and mortar buildings we ran across. The fresh food in the local markets changed, too. I rarely saw thimbleberries in Rowak, and I'd never eaten bittercress before.

On our sixth day, halfway to the capital, Delegate Ream requested we take a different road—a detour that would add a day to our travel. His cart was having difficulty with the wheels, and the alternate route avoided steep declines. After a conference with Lt. Kabrok and Fir, we agreed.

I'd continued inviting Delegate Ream to ride with me every day, but that morning he actually agreed. Either he didn't trust his cart, or he appreciated our willingness to change plans.

Just the two of us sat down together, with a few guards keeping near the cart. Outside the window stretched a meadow studded with tiny yellow flowers.

"Will you be staying in Pearlfoam?" I asked. Despite Poppy's best efforts to keep the cart aired-out, it still smelled closely of summer, pollen, and overheated humans.

"Of course not." He leaned back, folding his hands over his ample middle. "After I see you to the palace, I'll have that wheel looked over and come straight back to Ferndale. I could turn around sooner if you're inclined to return home?"

"You're very persistent, Delegate Ream, but nothing is going to dissuade me. Not warnings about Lady Oakash and my impending failure, not even reluctant Shoreed delegates."

"I eventually came to that conclusion. A nation that uses Bloodmarrows would, of course, have neither sense nor scruples."

The cart hit a bump, and my stomach jumped up into my throat. He couldn't know about the men I'd poisoned. He didn't know. "The Bloodmarrows are Shoreed's agents. I'm afraid you're mistaken. Perhaps it's the summer heat."

"Mistaken! How petty of you, to blame us for the crimes of your nation."

"I know a variety of stories circulate about them, but I have it on good authority that the Bloodmarrows were involved in the attempt on King Alder's life. They tried to give his throne to Shoreed."

"Internal Rowak politics," he spluttered, the tip of his beard quivering. "How *dare* you accuse the ocean-washed land of Shoreed of encouraging such horrors?"

"I assure you—"

"Your assurances mean nothing," he snapped. "I've seen what's left of soldiers that the Bloodmarrows get a hold of. Sentries, messengers—picked off and then gutted open, their insides scooped out."

I frowned. That didn't sound like anything Violet or her father would do. "Sometimes bears—"

"Those clean cut marks weren't made by a bear. They were made by human *monsters*. I praise Lady Oakash for pushing this war forward. Shoreed blood cries out for vengeance."

Whatever had happened to his men, Delegate Ream believed Rowak had wronged him. Badly. I could empathize with that instead of arguing my point. "I am sorry for the deaths of your soldiers."

"Not sorry enough to surrender. Not sorry enough to turn around instead of prancing on to the capital, pretending our nations are equals. Instead, you keep praying to your abominable Ancestors and harboring Bloodmarrows. I hope King Heron breaks you in pieces."

I exhaled and tried to push aside the insult to my nana. "Delegate Ream. I'm not sure why you agreed to ride with me today. Rudeness will not convince me to abandon these negotiations."

"Oh, I know. But I was hoping what we'd see on this road *would* get you to turn around."

My blood turned to ice. "Halt!"

We lurched to a stop. My guards rallied around my cart and waited.

"You sabotaged your own wheel." It wasn't a question.

He smirked. "Of course. Don't get so upset. I've planned nothing to harm you or your men."

"You will tell me now what this is about."

"I'd be happy to. Walk with me, ambassador. I think we're just about there."

Cautiously, I followed him out of the cart. My guards pressed close to him, but I waved them back. Delegate Ream did likewise with his men. It would do the negotiations no good for us to get in a fight before we'd even arrived.

We'd walked a good twenty paces away from the group before Bane's voice cut through the air. "Ambassador Plum, as your bodyguard, I request permission to follow you."

"Permission granted."

We paused there for a moment while Bane jogged up behind us. I didn't turn around. I couldn't see him. Or smell him. But I still felt safer just knowing he was there.

And I hated myself for still wanting him to be close to me.

Delegate Ream continued down the road a quarter mile. On our left, the meadow gave way to a sheer drop, maybe thirty feet high. He strolled over to the edge. I stayed a safe distance back.

"I'm not going to push you," he said. "But I suppose you can see from there."

He gestured to the land below the drop. A pit gaped open in the earth. I frowned and took two steps forward. Hundreds of emaciated men sweated under the sun down there. Their joints stuck out like knobs, and their hair hung in patches on their heads. Some limped. Some were covered in boils. Shoreed soldiers in green moved between them, occasionally yelling, sometimes kicking or beating a man to the ground. They were mining something. Salt? Obsidian? I couldn't tell.

But the workers were half-dead on their feet. I stared, unable to look away.

How could Delegate Ream summon such righteous indignation against Rowak while his own country harbored this open sore?

Bane went rigid next to me, the color draining from his face.

"There are the Rowak prisoners of war," Delegate Ream gestured broadly at the men. "Do you still want them?"

CHAPTER
TWENTY-TWO

I ached for a kitchen twice as expansive as the one in the Redwood Palace, with two dozen hearths and long, granite counters to prepare and spread out food for those laboring and dying below. Whole-duck stock—that's what they'd need at first. Something gentle and warm that their shriveled stomachs could handle.

"You can trade your many fit prisoners for these corpses if you must," Delegate Ream mocked, "but would you really trade all those hale Shoreed soldiers for these?"

I wanted them *more* than I had before. I wanted to save them, to feed them, to nurture them until they were strong again—in both body and spirit.

How could human beings do this to each other? Bane's fist quivered at his side.

"There are no men worth saving here. And there is no hope of a treaty in Pearlfoam. Rowak and Shoreed will fight until the battlefield proves which of our nations is superior," Delegate Ream said. "So? Shall we stop wasting everyone's time and turn around?"

"Did you bribe someone to get your position?" I demanded.

Delegate Ream's smug expression slid off his face. "Excuse me?"

"You are easily the *least* diplomatic person I've ever met. We are continuing on. You may do so in your own cart or on foot." I headed back to my cart. I couldn't stand to look at Delegate Ream for another moment. Even if I wasn't strong-of-arm like Dami, I felt in real danger of breaking his nose.

Bane followed a step behind me. I could feel the tension radiating off his skin, the heavy thump of his sandals on the road.

Endurance-of-soul. That's what I'd cook for him tonight. I wished we had hazelnuts, but I'd make do with the old beets in the supply cart. I couldn't turn and embrace him. But I could still make him a comforting meal.

Poppy ran up, skirts fluttering behind her, stopping just short of both of us. She worried her lip with her teeth, like she didn't quite dare interrupt.

"Fir," I said.

He slipped out from among the guards. "Yes, Ambassador?"

"Ride with me."

The two of us climbed in and the whole delegation started off again. Poppy stayed by Bane's side, gently touching his arm, speaking softly. They were far enough away that I couldn't hear them. I could just watch.

Bane didn't get any better, though. His posture only seemed to get heavier. His footsteps slower.

After a half mile or more, Fir broke our silence. "I'm not the one you want to be riding with."

"You're the one I should be riding with."

He gave me a mischievous, suave grin—the kind of smile he'd worn when he was about to cleverly trick me. "Everyone believes Bane has eyes for only Poppy now. Don't you think always avoiding him is just as suspicious as being too close?"

Without giving me time to protest, he opened the carriage door and hopped down with a surprising amount of grace. "Bane! The ambassador wants to discuss her security with you!"

Bane turned. He looked ashen and his hand was quivering. A number of our soldiers gave me appreciative nods or flicked a nervous glance at Bane. No one would assume anything untoward; I was merely giving him some privacy and rest in a way that didn't insult him.

The guards pulling the cart paused long enough for him to climb inside. I closed the shutters. Bane rubbed his hand over and over on the knee of his pants, like there was something on his palm he couldn't scrape off.

"What do you need, Bane?"

He looked up at me, his gaze somehow hollow and brimming with memories at the same time. "That's where they held me."

"I know," I whispered.

"If they'd just cleaned the wound on my arm. If they'd been willing to give me a *bandage*..."

I wanted to hold him close. I wanted to run my hands through his hair until the memories faded. Instead, I sat on the bench, his grief soaking through me like water wicking up old cloth. I couldn't change what had happened. But I could sorrow with him. "Your wardens shouldn't have been so apathetic."

"Apathetic?" Bane's face twitched. I couldn't tell if he was about to cry or laugh. "Plum, they held me down and rubbed refuse into my already-infected wound, grinning the entire time."

Delegate Ream was right to call me naive. I couldn't imagine that kind of senseless cruelty.

Bane wiped his bloodless face with his hand. "It's the way the world is, Plum. I lost my arm simply because they could hurt me, and I wasn't strong enough to stop them. It's my fault as much as it is theirs."

His fault? "That's not true."

Bane hung his head. "Poppy argued the same thing. That whatever that camp means to me, I shouldn't feel ashamed. But it's not true. You can blame the wardens for being strong, or blame me for being weak, but it's the same thing in the end. I couldn't protect myself."

The air grew thick and stuffy in the summer heat, but I didn't open the windows.

"They shouldn't have done that."

"Power turns men into monsters. It was practically inevitable," Bane replied.

"The most helpless person I've ever seen was a premature infant. He couldn't even survive without Lady Sulat's body warmth. But that power didn't turn her into a tyrant."

"It's not the same."

"Isn't it? Those men didn't have to hurt you just because they could. They did it because they thought hurting someone, controlling someone, would make them feel powerful and strong. They *chose*. I have to believe that."

Bane turned in his seat, hiding his left arm from view. "I don't need pity."

"Maybe not, but I do need to believe it's Sorrel's fault he beat me. Not mine for being too weak to stop him."

Bane froze. "Plum. That's not...I wasn't trying to imply..."

How I wanted to reach out and wrap my hand around his. "I know you weren't. You're holding yourself to a double standard. I do think you're remarkable, Bane, but even I don't think you're quite so special that you, and you alone, are guilty for the horrible things other people have done to you."

Bane smiled softly at me, looking as exhausted as if he'd just run a circuit around Askan-Wod. "Thank you, Plum."

"For what?"

"For loving me."

Those quiet words filled the muggy air around us. I swallowed. "Bane...I...we can't..."

I couldn't lie to Bane. I wouldn't. But perhaps it would have been kinder to lie, to crush his heart quickly and let him move on.

He knew my fumbled words for what they were, and his smile deepened.

"Bane, my engagement to another man ought to fill you with doubts." There. That was true.

"Plum, when I talked about the prisoner exchange and why it

mattered to me, you saw me. You heard me. And in a very Plum-like fashion, you jumped in headfirst and didn't look back. Your determination—that's the first thing I loved about you."

He loved me. As if I'd gulped my tea too fast, warmth rushed though me. And just as quickly, it cooled into guilt. "I can't return your feelings. I'm sorry, Bane. I hope, one day, you find happiness elsewhere."

He leaned toward me, all those familiar juniper-and-smoke smells mixing with worn wood and the scent of summer-drenched meadows. "I'm going to spend the rest of my life protecting the woman I love. As far as lives go, there are plenty of men who don't do half so well."

I couldn't even pretend that I wanted to run away with him. Saving the prisoners, ending the fighting—*that's* what I wanted the most. "You should want more than that."

"I do. I want a peace treaty, just like you. That's enough."

It wasn't. I wanted more. I wanted Bane. But it seemed incredibly greedy to hope that my Ancestors would help me save so many lives, then grant me a life of my own afterward as well.

"I'm sorry—"

"You don't have to apologize, Plum. I'm exactly where I want to be."

CHAPTER
TWENTY-THREE

Another week of travel passed. Sometimes we stayed in carter stations. Often, we camped on the road. I suspected Delegate Ream could have brought us into any number of towns to be hosted by local mayors and governors but chose not to.

I smelled the ocean long before we reached the capital city. A sharp, briny scent blanketed the usual smells of the foothills. The redwoods seemed to grow thicker here in the humid air and ferns covered everything, encroaching on the road.

We stopped for lunch at the top of a rise and I caught my first glimpse of the ocean. It rolled all the way out to the horizon, sparkling like fine blue chalcedony, decorated with white froth. I breathed deeply. The city of Pearlfoam spread next to it, all slate-gray tiles and sloped roofs running together, like frozen, tumultuous waves on an overcast afternoon.

Dami, Bane, Poppy, and Fir joined me to look at the vista.

"It's gorgeous," Poppy exhaled.

Fir waved a hand. "It's a giant puddle. Maybe we should spend our last hours before arriving at the Rowak embassy thinking about how Chef Palaw is probably still down there. Am I the only one wondering if he'll arrange for a bunch of Bloodmarrows to murder us all when we show up?"

"All of us? I doubt it," Dami scoffed. "They'll want someone to return as a messenger."

Fir nodded. "Good. I volunteer to take the news of your demise back to King Alder."

Dami laughed, but Bane glared at him. "No one is going to die."

"Protesting doesn't make it so." Fir ran his fingers through his hair. "Somebody probably will. I'm just hoping it's not me."

Bane's fingers twitched. "If you're planning on betraying us—"

"Oh, please. Can't a man have a healthy sense of self-preservation without being accused of treason?"

"I've *seen* your sense of self-preservation before," Bane rumbled.

Now I remembered why it was a good idea to keep the two of them separated. Before I could say anything, Poppy deftly interlaced her fingers with Bane's and pulled him to the side to examine a wildflower we didn't have in Rowak.

She held his hand so comfortably. He didn't flinch or stiffen at her touch. They bent to smell the pink blooms at the same time and bumped their heads together. Bane laughed and Poppy blushed, looking as radiant as the flowers themselves.

I turned and stared at the ocean. "Fir. I have a few more questions about the Shoreed rank system. Posts, as well as people, are assigned ranks, correct?"

"Ugh," Dami groaned. "I'm not listening to that again. You're making me wish the Bloodmarrows would attack us now."

"Plum, I'm afraid your sister might be the tiniest bit unhinged," Fir said, looking at Dami.

She giggled and punched him in the shoulder, like he'd just said the sweetest thing. Fir winced and clutched his arm.

As WE HEADED toward the long-empty Rowak Embassy inside Pearlfoam, we kept the cart's windows shut for safety. Outside, merchants called and children played—the familiar sounds of a city, and yet so different than Askan-Wod. Everyone's accent was sing-song and foreign. Sea birds called and squawked. The aroma of grilled street food wafted into the cart, but unnervingly, I couldn't name what was being cooked.

When we stopped, muted arguing rattled outside—Delegate Ream and Lt. Kabrok if I wasn't mistaken. One of Kabrok's men cut in.

"Sir, I was stationed at the embassy before the war broke out. This is it. Well, *was* it."

Bane and Dami shifted closer to the two doors, ready for trouble.

"You're sure, Feden?" Lt. Kabrok asked.

"Yes, sir."

Lt. Kabrok sighed, then ordered four of his men inside to make sure no ambush awaited us. I sat without moving or speaking in the stuffy cart, letting him do his job. At last he opened the door and we all stepped out.

I gaped. Parts of the embassy's eight-foot cobblestone wall had been smashed in, seemingly at random. There was an arch for a gate, but not a scrap of wood or strip of leather hinges remained. I ducked under the arch and stepped into the garden. Weeds nearly covered the stumps dotting the ground.

But the house was worst of all. The doors, the shutters, even the roof tiles were gone. Someone had smashed the porch steps in. I waded through the thistles and bindweed to the shell of a building. It reeked of rot. Small wonder, with no roof. Frilly mushrooms bloomed along the floor and up the corners of the walls.

Delegate Ream offered to take us back to the border one last time, then left. Poppy inspected the building. She assured me it needed to be burned and rebuilt, not just repaired—and that we didn't have enough funds for either.

I consulted with Lt. Kabrok and Fir, but we really had little choice but to ask for King Heron to shelter us for the time being. It wasn't ideal. Being inside the palace limited our autonomy to hold meetings and gather others to our cause.

Maybe that's just where King Heron wanted us—under his roof, where he could watch us carefully.

Lt. Kabrok and a handful of his men went to request lodging in the Coral Palace. They returned with grim faces.

"King Heron left yesterday for a two week sabbatical," Kabrok muttered. "He put his daughter, Lady Oakash, in command of the palace. She refused to admit us for any reason."

Fantastic. I kept my face calm and swatted away the midges trying to crawl up my neck. They seemed to like the weeds here. "Fir, take a pair of guards to the marketplace. Buy some appropriate gifts— candied nuts or jugs of wine—and go visit your contacts. Try to learn where King Heron is. If his location is no great secret, we can petition him directly."

"Huh." Fir swatted bugs away from his face. "That might work."

"I'll go," Dami volunteered.

She'd been slouched in a shady corner; I'd half-forgotten she was here. "With Fir?"

"He can't take uniformed guards to visit people. It's conspicuous. I'd just look like some girl he's interested in." She winked at him.

I hated that she was right. "Take one other guard with you anyway, in regular clothes. And be safe."

WHILE THEY WERE GONE, the rest of us stomped down the weeds in the courtyard and set up camp like we were still on the road, including tents and a pit fire for cooking. The embassy had a stone hearth, but it was covered it rat droppings and I didn't have anything to scrub it clean.

Fir, Dami, and Feden returned that evening, just as I dished up the first bowl of venison jerky hot pot. Dami swept it from my hands before I could give it to Lt. Kabrok. "Perfect! I'm starved!"

She plopped down on the ground, not caring how her skirt

bunched, and began devouring it. I silently sighed and turned to Fir. "You don't look especially happy."

"Well, I didn't find King Heron. And I couldn't learn anything about the Bloodmarrows or if Chef Palaw is still in Pearlfoam or not. But it's not all bad news."

I dished up Lt. Kabrok, myself, and Fir, then the three of us sat on the creaking, questionably-stable porch.

"So?" I prompted.

"I *did* find us a new place to stay. And I have the names of six people who might become our allies, given a chance to talk."

Trepidation fluttered in my chest. Was the new location he'd found a trap? I glanced at Dami, but she was face-down, slurping her bowl like an enemy army was likely to interrupt supper any second. "Someplace where we're not likely to die?" I asked.

Fir grinned and leaned closer. "Well, if we do, we'll be in good hands."

I was hot, sweaty, and exhausted. "More information, less cryptic messages, please."

Lt. Kabrok, mouth full, nodded his agreement.

Fir's smile dropped, put-out. "Fine, fine. One of my contacts started lobbing insults at me, saying the only people daft enough to support a treaty were the sages. So Dami and I visited their compound. They'd be happy to shelter us for as long as we need to stay."

I frowned. "Pearlfoam's *sages* have an opinion about the war?"

At least in Rowak, sages stayed out of politics. Their job was to care for the bodies of the dead, prepare the heads of Ancestors for veneration, and to instruct their communities in the interconnected nature of human life. Not squabble over who got which post.

"They don't want to kill us, and they have an *unbroken* ten-foot wall around their compound. We could do worse." Fir gestured at the crumbling embassy.

"How soon could they take us?" I asked.

"Tonight."

I turned to Lt Kabrok. "Your professional opinion on which locale is better for our safety?"

Kabrok slurped down the last of his hotpot. "Let's pack up."

A COBBLESTONE WALL encircled the sage's compound, topped by curved clay shingles. Inside, the setting sun filled the courtyard with long, wavering shadows. But it was still easy to see that this was nothing like the sage's compound back in Meadowind. Where was the mound where they burned wood into charcoal? The crematorium lined with refractory bricks? The cylindrical ball mill that had to be turned with chunks of flint inside to pulverize the deceased's remains into ashes? The giant crock used to boil the skulls over and over into a pearly white? This place didn't smell like charcoal and burning flesh —it smelled like city roads and the flowers that grew between the houses.

I did see a pit for clay, covered to keep it moist. Sages sculpted faces onto the skulls of the deceased so they could be enshrined for generations to come. Nana's beloved head rested back in my family's home in Clamsriver, her gray hair elaborately braided, her eyes replaced with two smooth stones that Dami and I had selected.

"You're sure this is the sage's compound?" I whispered to Fir. In appearance, it could have belonged to some potters.

"Positive."

An ancient woman hobbled from one of the houses. Her eyes were clouded like an unskimmed broth, and the flesh on her hands sunk between the bones. She smiled at us, showing more gums than teeth. "Welcome, travelers from Rowak. Welcome, ambassador. We're happy that we can share our home with you. I'm Sage Raven."

She wore the traditional garb of the sages—a long, rectangular dress of simple white, belted with leather embossed with words from the First Sages.

"We are most grateful for your kindness, Sage Raven," I replied, bowing.

"You may use the house on the far left." She gestured with a wizened hand. "I am afraid you will be cramped. Some of your men will have to sleep on the porch, but in this fair weather, that is not such a horrid thing. Rest. In the morning, we will talk more."

CHAPTER
TWENTY-FOUR

Inside that building, the first thing I did was search out the kitchen. It was small, and the otherwise-clean hearth had a thin layer of dust on it, like it hadn't been used for ages. There was no wood, cutting boards, or knives, but we had our own. I'd be able to make breakfast.

Then I slept. In the morning, I talked our situation over with Lt. Kabrok and Fir while I cooked. The first order of business seemed to be writing notes to the six prominent people Fir had learned about who were likely to support our work toward a treaty. Since Poppy had the nicest writing, she copied out letters proposing that we meet. Lt. Kabrok handed them over to one of his men, a lanky fellow named Sonall, who jogged off to make the deliveries.

Hopefully, some of them would want to meet. Hopefully, some of them would know something useful—like where to find King Heron.

"I should probably spend the rest of the morning getting to know our hosts," I said, pushing aside my empty bowl of porridge on the low table we all sat around. "But I'm not happy that we don't know where Chef Palaw or Red Lord Ospren are. I feel like we need to be better guarded."

"I can try to find out," Fir offered. "I thought that Dami, Feden, and I made a great team yesterday."

I reluctantly nodded. They had made a great team. Lt. Kabrok had done well to pick Fir to come on this mission. And yet, I *still* didn't like the idea of Dami out there with him. Admittedly, I didn't like the idea of her at large in Pearlfoam, regardless of who was with her.

"Should we go now?" Fir asked.

I had a nagging feeling in the back of my mind. "I think Violet mentioned someone else important we might want to keep an eye on. Let me check my notes."

Fir followed me to my room. He leaned against the doorway, casually watching as I searched through my papers. It was hard to remember that those inquisitive, bright eyes belonged to a traitor. Fir had never attacked me head-on. Not like Sorrel. He'd always smiled and manipulated events.

Maybe that's why I didn't feel nervous when he was nearby, but the thought of sending him out into Pearlfoam with Dami made my stomach churn.

"Let's see. Ospren. Lady Sulat. There's someone named Murrelet. And bother—LOA. That's who I was thinking of. But whoever she is, she's probably inside the palace according to this."

"LOA?" Fir asked.

I read Palaw's letter again. And I groaned. A woman inside the Coral Palace with an amazing information network—I knew who that was. "It's Lady Oakash."

"Well, I do know where to find her," Fir said. "Mission accomplished."

I shook my head, panic welling in my throat. "No, it's worse than that. Palaw thought she had ghostly powers. What if she does? What if she's spying on us right now, or what if—"

"Plum." He crossed the room, gently took my papers from me, and tapped them into a neat stack. "She's a person, just like you or me. In two weeks, King Heron will be back, and we won't have to deal with her."

Fir was wrong. Even after King Heron returned, Lady Oakash

would still be in the palace, she'd still be King Heron's daughter, and we'd still have to figure out how to push against her warmongering. But his smooth voice calmed me. I took a deep breath. Palaw had at least proved she wasn't a Hungry Ghost, I reminded myself. And if she was omniscient, the coup wouldn't have failed.

"We should still be careful," I said. "You especially, out in the city."

Fir scoffed and gave me one of his disarming grins. "I'm taking your sister with me. Of course I'll be careful."

I FOUND Sage Raven in the compound's garden, harvesting sprigs of chervil, coriander, and parsley. She offered to sit with me on the porch and talk, but I joined her instead and started weeding. I'd had plenty of opportunities to cook since I left home, but I hadn't gotten my hands muddy in months. Weeding herbs was particularly nice; just from brushing up against the fragrant plants, the air soon smelled grassy and sweet. I let Sage Raven ask her questions first—how the sages in Rowak fared, how well the shrines were maintained. My answers seemed to please her.

"I hope I'm not trying your patience," she said. She reminded me of Nana, though I couldn't say why. Sage Raven was taller, paler, and she smelled like clay and ground paint, not honey. Maybe it was the kindness in her rheumy eyes.

"Not at all." This was far nicer than discussing how things stood in Shoreed—though I eventually needed to bring the conversation around to such things.

Raven shuffled down to the perennial beds of thyme and chives and gathered some of them, too. "I don't usually meet people as pious as you. I can feel that the souls of the deceased have spent much time around you."

"Are you perceptive-of-soul?" I asked. It was a common birthgift among sages, one that helped connect them to their Ancestors.

"Yes. You must pray often!"

I did. But she was probably sensing all that time I spent around a Hungry Ghost. Somehow, that didn't seem like the right thing to say. I yanked out more of the thin grasses trying to overtake the thyme. "My grandmother died less than a year ago. I think of her often."

"Ah. That explains it. The dead need a year to reach the Realm of the Ancestors. It's good you remember her. That will help her reach her destination safely instead of turning into a ghost."

She said *ghost* so casually, I was sure she'd never actually seen one. Other sages in the compound walked by, but none of them interrupted us. There were, perhaps, another half-dozen adults and eight or so children about, preparing food, cleaning clothes, and tending to the clay pits.

"Now that I've pelted you with questions," Sage Raven said, "you must have some for me, young ambassador."

She was right. But it seemed crass to start with politics right away. "I have to admit I'm curious. This is a sage's compound, yet I see no crematorium."

Sage Raven shook her head. "I'm afraid Rowak clings to the old ways better than we do. The Toksang Empire influences us too much —with our ports on the coast, we're more connected to them than you are. There, most people bury their dead."

"And the Shoreed imitate them? Does no one here preserve the heads of their Ancestors anymore?"

Raven gave me a wry smile. "Oh, we aren't *that* bad. After someone has been buried for a year or two, their descendants dig up their skulls and bring them to us to layer with clay. The hair's lost, of course. And the poor Ancestor spends their first year without the best prayers."

"But that's when they need them the most."

"I know. You'd think Shoreed would be covered in ghosts, but we only ever hear the odd rumor." She sighed, her smile gone. "Burying is cheaper than burning and boiling. And those who worship the ocean frown on fire touching the body, anyway."

"Worship the ocean?"

"The Toksang Emperor claims to be chosen by him. Only the common people in that land still worship their Ancestors. I don't understand it either. The sea is powerful, but it's not your father or your mother. Why would you worship mere power, when you could appeal to your Ancestors, who love you?"

I could understand it. The ocean was beautiful. Awe-inspiring. But I felt as Raven did—I'd rather pray to my nana than some uncaring, inhuman force. "I...think it's entirely possible that the delegate who escorted us here was an ocean-worshipper. He didn't speak kindly of anyone's Ancestors."

"Too many these days feel similarly." She gestured at their mostly-empty compound. "You see now why we hope you succeed? Only in Rowak are Ancestors venerated as the First Sages prescribe. If Shoreed conquers you, they'll bring their ocean-worship and impious practices with them and destroy our ways."

I hadn't known that was a risk of this war, too. I felt ill. It was time for the political questions. "We're concerned about the safety of our delegation. Do you know if the Bloodmarrows are active in Pearlfoam?"

"Did some follow you from Rowak? I don't think I've heard stories about the Bloodmarrows coming this far into Shoreed—they stay by the front lines."

I'd scoffed at Delegate Ream's insistence that the Bloodmarrows were a Rowak organization, but Sage Raven seemed to hold the same belief. "I think I've heard different rumors than you. Who are the Bloodmarrows, in the stories you know?"

"Oh. They're an evil cult from Rowak that worships Death itself."

I'd read all of Violet's notes. All of Palaw's letters. There'd been no mention of religious rites. Sage Raven was wrong.

But she still agreed with Delegate Ream that the Bloodmarrows came from Rowak, and that alone filled me with unease. I wanted to believe so badly that the Bloodmarrows originated in Shoreed and that Palaw and Violet had joined their ranks merely to support Red Lord Ospren. I asked Sage Raven about Chef Palaw, but she'd never heard of him.

From there, I asked her who might support a peace treaty. She named all six people Fir had found out, plus another half dozen. We'd have to write more letters to them.

"Do you know much about Red Lord Ospren?" I asked.

She frowned. "Who?"

Apparently, his presence here was not common knowledge in Shoreed, either. "Never mind. It's not—"

A scream pierced the air. Frantic shouting following, from near the gate. I ran toward it, brushing off my dirty hands on my skirt as I went. But I didn't get far before Bane stepped out in front of me. I hadn't seen him leaning against the building there. I hadn't even realized he was the one assigned to guard me this morning.

"Plum," he said softly, urgently, "we need to get you inside until we know what the situation is."

Poppy's voice cut clear over the rest of the shouting. "A chef! We need a chef! Plum, where are you?"

Bane didn't step aside.

"Please," I said. "I have to help."

"And I have to keep you safe."

I bit my lip and reluctantly followed him. Once I was inside, Bane shouted out at the nearest guard to figure out what was going on and to report back. My hands turned clammy. I couldn't smell anything except my own salty fear. Fir had betrayed us. Dami was hurt—or worse. The Bloodmarrows were here to destroy us all. I couldn't stop my thoughts from racing. My bones itched and ached like I'd stood there for hours, but it was probably only a few minutes before Lt. Kabrok came and cleared me to leave the shelter of the building.

I followed Bane around the porch to the courtyard in front of the gate. Poppy knelt next to Sonall, the messenger Lt. Kabrok had sent out with our letters. I didn't need to get any closer to see that I wouldn't be of any help.

His arms were limp, his pallor ashen, and a spear stuck out of the middle of his chest. Blood was drying on his shirt, but nothing fresh flowed out of him. He was long dead.

CHAPTER
TWENTY-FIVE

My first thought was a prayer of relief. It wasn't Dami. My sister wasn't dead.

I hated myself for thinking that first. For being grateful before I was horrified at the awful way he'd died. Poppy shook, her face ashen.

I vaguely heard Bane asking Lt. Kabrok to take over guarding me. Then he crossed the courtyard, put an arm around Poppy, and gently led her away from the carnage while I stood there uselessly staring.

I walked up to the body and knelt where Poppy had been. Six pieces of paper had been skewered onto the spear. They were pulpy with blood, but I still recognized Poppy's handwriting. Rashes ringed Sonall's wrists and ankles—he'd been bound before he was killed. No trail of blood on the ground outside. He'd bled out somewhere else.

Beneath the blood, I smelled something else herbal, bitter, and unnervingly familiar. Gently, I opened his mouth. Yes, definitely bittersleep leaf. He'd probably been poisoned first, slowing him. Then bound. Possibly interrogated. And lastly murdered.

"Someone left him at the gate like this, didn't they?"

"Yes." Lt. Kabrok's voice was ice. "Pushed him off the back of a cart and rushed off. We didn't think it safe to give chase and split up our force, so I'm afraid we don't know who to blame."

"Bloodmarrows."

202 | M. K. HUTCHINS

Lt. Kabrok shifted uncomfortably. "Possibly. Ambassador, I don't think you're in any immediate danger, but I'd feel much better if you went inside now."

That was probably prudent. I gravitated toward the small kitchen in the building the sages had loaned us. Hazelnut praline. Everyone would need endurance-of-soul. I could do that. I could help in some small way. Even though it wouldn't be enough.

Dami had mocked me for always cooking when I was stressed, but I knew what to do in a kitchen. I knew how to heat a crock and clean knives and oil cutting boards. It was a world I understood, a world I could control.

"We should ask the sages if they can prepare a proper funeral for Sonall," I said, moving through the hallway.

"I already have. It will cost quite a bit more than it would in Rowak. They'll need more fuel for an open pyre."

"Pay them whatever they require from the delegation funds."

Lt. Kabrok bowed his head. "Thank you."

One of his men was dead because I'd carelessly sent him alone to deliver those letters. Kabrok shouldn't be thanking me for anything.

Before I reached the kitchen, I heard Bane's voice. "—or maybe some kind of tea. I don't know. But Plum's always taken good care of me. She'll take care of you, too."

"Food can't fix this," Poppy replied.

I pushed open the door. Poppy shook, her legs bouncing as she sat on a stool, eyes squeezed shut. She hugged her arms tight to her chest.

"You're right. Food can't fix this," I said. "But I'm going to make you something anyway."

Poppy looked like she might rattle the stool to pieces. "I wrote those letters. I wrote them. And they killed him."

"Trying to transform your horror into guilt won't make it better, either," I said.

I started up a crock of water for an infusion. The motions were familiar, easy, even with my blood pumping too fast through my body. One of my men, dead. The shock of it was fading, replacing itself with imagined scenes of what his last moments had probably been like. I tried not to picture Dami, out in the city, getting captured just as Sonall had been. Bound, poisoned, murdered.

I was grateful Poppy needed me. Grateful for something to do. I made tea. I made praline. I gave Poppy some of each.

"Thank you," she said, "for not trying to tell me everything will be fine."

"Nothing about this is fine."

Bane took praline out to our other soldiers. I sat down, sweaty from being near the hearth, my hair plastered to my face and neck. I followed my own advice and popped a piece of candy in my mouth. It didn't seem to be doing anything.

The door opened. I expected Bane with an empty tray, but Dami swaggered in with a huge grin, Fir and Feden trailing behind her. "You're about to have a fantastic day."

I sprinted across the room and crushed her in a hug.

Dami peeled away from me. "I expected you to be excited, but not quite that excited." She glanced around the room. "You all look like someone else ate the last buckwheat branch."

Lt. Kabrok's cold voice cut through the room. "It was worse than that."

I briefly explained, including what I'd found out about Sonall's poisoning. Fir and Dami went solemn and still. Lt. Kabrok bitterly shook his head. "We should retreat. We're not prepared to defend ourselves against these threats."

I swallowed. We couldn't abandon the treaty. More lives than our own were at stake.

"Surrender?" Fir asked. "No. We should take more precautions. Only send men out in groups of three or more."

Kabrok's jaw tensed. "If we stay and Plum gets her throat slit, King Alder will, more likely than not, kill all his prisoners of war in retribution. Then nothing will stop this war from rolling on."

"If we leave," I said, "King Alder might try to use Sonall's death to the same end."

"He'll have less support, less outrage, over the death of a guard than over the death of his beloved consort and ambassador."

I hated that Kabrok was right. Sonall was just as human as I was.

He continued, "If we go home now, another delegation with a real ambassador and real advisors, prepared for our lack of an embassy, can return in the spring. This ragtag group never should have come."

The words stung—probably because they were true. I wasn't the master diplomat that Rowak needed. I was a chef. Not all problems could be solved with cooking, however much I wished otherwise.

"I don't think whoever did this wants to kill Plum," Fir said. "They're sending a message with Sonall. They're trying to frighten us away."

"Or they don't have the resources to attack Plum directly. Maybe they only need more time to plan her assassination," Kabrok said. "There are few of us. We have no allies. We have far too many enemies. We can't win this."

"Then we should at least do some good while we're here," Fir retorted. "Dami, Feden, and I found Red Lord Ospren. He's not five blocks away, settling in for a *picnic*. One well-placed poisoned arrow loosed from a nearby tree, and he'd never bother Rowak again." Fir turned to me. "Before you became the ambassador, that's why Lady Sulat wanted to send you, wasn't it? It's the only reason to send a chef as a spy—to poison someone. And he's the most obvious target."

It hadn't been obvious to me, not even when Lady Sulat was trying to tell me her intentions. I didn't want to kill anyone.

"Can you do that?" Lt. Kabrok asked. "Poison an arrow to kill Red Lord Ospren with one shot?"

I'd told myself in Rowak that I'd find a clever way to end this war, without poisons. But was my peace of mind worth the fate of Rowak? I hated that I'd poisoned King Alder's men into a deep sleep at the carter station, but I couldn't regret it, either. It had been the right decision. Using poisons to actually kill someone would make me just like Violet. But it would preserve my homeland. And the worship of our Ancestors.

I hadn't lied in front of Bane since I'd told him my real name. But there was no easy way to make him leave while I spouted untruths, and he belonged with Poppy now, anyway. "I'll need to be there to personally mix the poison. It's delicate, and it loses its potency quickly."

If Ospren was going to die because of me, I shouldn't send someone else off to do it and rest comfortably here. I should be there to witness his death.

Lt. Kabrok swore.

"Then Plum comes," Fir said. "It's not like we won't all be in danger after we do this. I need to be there to point out which man is Red Lord Ospren. Who's your best archer?"

"Feden," Lt. Kabrok said. "You three go. We'll make ready for a quick, quiet retreat out of the city. I think we should strike south, into the Toksang Empire. The border is only three days away, and with ambassador's papers, we should be able to get safe travel on their roads back to Rowak."

Bane frowned at all of us. "King Heron will be back in two weeks. Surely it's better to hole up here and wait for him than it is to send our ambassador out on an assassination mission."

Kabrok's calm finally cracked. "Do you think we'll make it two weeks? We haven't been here a full day yet, and Sonall is dead. We should at least grant him a little justice before we retreat."

Arguments wouldn't put Bane at ease; he needed a job to keep him busy. "Will you help Poppy pack?" I asked. "We may need to leave here quickly."

"I should accompany you," Bane protested.

Yes, I wanted him with me. But it would be selfish to bring him. Just as it had been selfish to accept him as part of this delegation in the first place. "Poppy will know what's most important to pack. As shaken as she is, she needs you to steady her."

I WALKED out into the streets of Pearlfoam with Fir and only one guard. Part of me still expected Fir to draw a knife and gut me, but he didn't. He led Feden and me to a sprawling mulberry tree full of leaves. We only had to climb up a few branches to see into the courtyards of the nearby houses.

Feden strung his bow.

"That's him," Fir whispered. He pointed down into one of the courtyards. Two men sat on the porch, eating lunch, while a trio of young children chased a ball on the lawn.

"The one with the beard?" Feden asked.

"The other one," I said. He had King Alder's strong chin, Valerian's boyish smile, and the intelligence in his eyes reminded me of Lady Sulat. His clothing was of the finest brocade, glittering with amber beads. But the long sleeves had been slit to the shoulders, leaving the fabric to drape at his side, almost like folded-down butterfly wings.

Lady Sulat had spent years doubting this man. Maybe exile had changed him, and he'd personally ordered Sonall's death without remorse. Maybe he was still the man she'd known before—thoughtful and open to discussion.

I'd spent weeks doubting Lady Sulat. I didn't want to spend the rest of my life wondering if Ospren's death was necessary and just.

I passed Feden a small ceramic jar. "If things go poorly—if I'm captured or killed—dip your arrow tip in this, finish Ospren, and flee back to Lt. Kabrok."

He frowned. "I thought you had to mix it in some special way."

"I thought the plan was to kill Ospren," Fir said.

I grabbed the branch in front of me and swung to the ground. "If there's no other option for saving Rowak, killing Ospren is exactly what Feden is going to do. But first, I'm going to try talking to him."

I strode to the main gates of the residence. Feden followed his orders and stayed in position. Fir dropped out of the tree and ran after me. He grabbed my wrist and turned me around. "Plum, this is idiocy. That man in your *enemy*."

"That man is *probably* my enemy. But I'm supposed to be an ambassador, Fir. Not an assassin."

It's what I wanted to be, at least. Not the mirror of Violet. I yanked my hand back from an astonished Fir, stepped up to the gate, and pounded on the worn wood.

The door opened and a middle-aged woman—a servant, I think— peered out at Fir and myself.

I put on my best smile. "Will you please tell Red Lord Ospren that Green-ranked Ambassador Plum of Clamsriver, Betrothed Consort of King Alder of Rowak and her advisor, Yellow-ranked Fir of Askan-Wod are here to see him?"

CHAPTER
TWENTY-SIX

We waited for some time at the gate. By the time the woman escorted us inside, the other man and the children were gone. Red Lord Ospren alone stood on the porch, his slit sleeves twisting in the sulky summer breeze.

Sour panic bubbled in the back of my throat. I wasn't ready for this meeting. Could he see my pulse pounding in my throat? He was perceptive-of-eye, just like Lady Sulat.

I wasn't sure if it was proper etiquette to bow to this man or not, but I did it anyway. "It's a pleasure to meet you."

"And you. You're truly the ambassador? And you're engaged to be my brother's consort?" Ospren's deep voice had a pleasant, sleepy quality to it.

"Yes."

"It seems harsh of him, to send his beloved away to Shoreed."

"It's a long story."

Lord Ospren nodded and turned to Fir. "I haven't seen you in years, cousin."

Fir mumbled something no one could hear, staring off into the bushes.

Ospren cleared his throat. "Would you both join me?"

I didn't glance up into the tree where Feden was watching us, but I did choose a spot on the porch that wouldn't block Feden's line-of-sight to Ospren. The lunch we'd seen before had been replaced with tea and a bowl of fresh fruit.

"Please, eat. I came here today to ask Minister Tidal if he knew where you were. Lady Oakash has heartily denied the arrival of any delegation, which is how I knew you must be somewhere in Pearlfoam. I only managed to sneak out of the palace because she's so busy in her father's absence."

My head throbbed. I'm not sure what I expected—the monster Lady Sulat feared he'd become, or the brother she'd loved—but I certainly hadn't imagined a polite, dignified man who had to sneak out of the palace to make visits. "Do you know where King Heron is?"

"He usually travels to the Windswept Surf Shrine this time of year. I fear Lady Oakash somehow knew you were coming and moved the timing of his travels to coincide with your arrival."

"Can you tell us how to reach him?"

Red Lord Ospren frowned. "The road's not hard to follow, but the devotees of the ocean guard it diligently. They might, ah, attack you for trespassing."

That would hardly help our diplomatic efforts.

"Why did you want to find us?" Fir demanded, far blunter than I would have been.

The corners of Ospren's eyes crinkled with kind concern. "I wanted to warn you. I don't think it's safe for you to be in Shoreed."

It was a little late for such sentiments. Or was that a veiled threat, expertly delivered with a face of innocence? I sipped my tea and refrained from making accusations.

Fir was not quite so reserved. "I'm surprised you'd be generous enough to offer a warning."

"I don't want to see more people get hurt," Ospren mumbled, running his finger up and down the side of his cup.

"A fine sentiment for a man who covets the Rowak throne! Or are you just happy to sit back and let people like me do the hard work for you?" Fir demanded.

Ospren flinched. "It's...complicated."

"Well, we have plenty of time to talk," I said calmly. I set my mug down and folded my hands in my lap. "Fir and I would both be happy to listen."

Fir's jaw was still tight, but he exhaled and nodded, accepting my chastisement.

Ospren kept running his fingers nervously up and down his cup. "You see, I didn't mind my exile. Not that much. I had plenty to read. But Mother arranged for me to slip away. She brought me to the Coral Palace. I thought we were merely going to start new lives here. Maybe if I'd paid better attention...but I was busy enjoying the archive, reading about Shoreed law structure."

He smiled faintly when he mentioned the archive, and in that moment, he looked so much like the scholarly, idealistic Heir Valerian that my chest ached.

"I didn't understand Mother's maneuverings at first. She urged me into a closet marriage—I know we don't do such things in Rowak, but they're not uncommon here among the elite. Only after the birth of my first daughter did I understand that she wanted to use Shoreed to put me on the Rowak throne. Shoreed wouldn't help without the marriage, but my old allies in Rowak would shun me if they knew of it. Hence the secrecy."

"You have a *daughter?*" Fir gaped at him.

"Two, actually." A small, proud smile touched his mouth.

Two of the girls playing on the lawn had been his, then.

"And you didn't think to tell anyone?"

Ospren sighed. "How often did anyone in Rowak actually get a letter from me, personally?"

Fir frowned, like he desperately wanted to shout out a crushing response but didn't have one.

"After your daughter was born, what happened then?" I prompted, trying to get back to his story.

"Well, a lot of people, including my mother and Lady Oakash, started pushing for this war. I spoke against it, but I wasn't very effective. You must think me a horrible politician. Mother always tried to get me to think of the good I could do as king, but in truth, I'd rather live in a quiet cottage writing essays and let someone else implement grand changes. Being a king is rather demanding."

And there was a hint of his father's laziness, in the tilt of his mouth. Still, I could easily imagine him and Valerian sitting on the porch of the House of Reflected Learning with the pond stretching before them, reading manuscripts and philosophizing together. I wondered if he knew how much his nephew was like him—Valerian would have been four when he was exiled.

Lady Sulat had been wrong to prepare me to poison this man. She shouldn't have doubted her own opinion of him.

"It's too late to bring back the lives of those who are lost," I said, "but you can help us prevent further bloodshed."

He laughed bitterly, then drained the last of his tea. "Weren't you listening? I'm not any good at politics. I barely made it out of the Redwood Palace alive."

Fir's voice was as hard as chert. "You could have sent a letter. You could have said—done—something."

"No. I couldn't have." Ospren shook his head. "You don't understand."

I cut in before Fir could respond. "Help me understand, then."

Ospren glumly hung his head. "There are two reasons, really. But to start, the Bloodmarrows have Mother."

"They kidnapped Queen Laurel?" With everything else they'd done, I shouldn't be surprised.

"Well, no. She asked Chef Palaw—he's one of them—to take her hostage and kill her if I stepped out of line. She's in one of their hideouts. The Obsidian Palace, Palaw called it once. Mother's always been, well, very focused on her goals. She felt it was the only way to keep me in check."

I shivered. Lady Sulat had warned me that her mother had been ambitious. This war wasn't about getting Ospren his rightful place back. It was about putting an easily-manipulated son on the throne, so she could rule Rowak through him.

"After that, I stopped trying to write to anyone in Rowak, or speak against the war." Ospren shrank down into his shoulders. "I'm not...I think I said I'm not much of a politician."

"Who *are* the Bloodmarrows?" I asked.

"I fear they're Lady Oakash's personal spy network."

"You don't know?" Of all people, I'd thought Lord Ospren could give me a straight answer.

"She always seems to know what they're up to. She used to be close to Chef Palaw, but for the past year or two, she's tried to kick him out of the palace. I think perhaps they're fighting over Bloodmarrow leadership."

"Palaw is here?" I asked.

Ospren nodded. "At the palace. But maybe not for much longer. King Heron trusted him when he said he could end this war quickly with a coup inside the Redwood Palace, but Palaw's plans ended in disaster. His Majesty is eager to get his captured soldiers back."

I could only pray that he was also eager to end the war now, after all our nations had suffered.

Fir peered hard at Ospren. "Queen Laurel's captivity is the first reason you said you can't help us. What's the second?"

Ospren fiddled with his cup. "Lady Oakash is my wife."

I stared at him. I'd doubt my hearing, except Fir looked just as startled.

"Did you think Shoreed fought to give me my position back for the sake of justice?" Ospren asked. "They want to make her Rowak's queen. But if anyone knew that King Heron's daughter was coming with me..."

"We wouldn't have helped you," Fir finished, his voice dead. "How can you have such a bloodthirsty tyrant as a wife?" Fir demanded.

Ospren flinched. "I don't know for sure if she's behind the Bloodmarrows. I could be wrong."

So many thoughts swirled in my mind. I had to focus on what mattered. "Ospren. If we can rescue your mother from this Obsidian Palace, will you flee Shoreed? Without you, Shoreed loses any internal support in Rowak, leaving us in a much better position to defend ourselves or negotiate a treaty."

"Abandon my wife?" Ospren asked, shocked. He tried to drink from his cup again but found it empty.

Fir yanked the cup away from him and tossed it onto the lawn. "Yes. You abandon your warmongering, manipulative, Bloodmarrow-wielding wife. That shouldn't be *hard*, Ospren."

Fir was years younger than Ospren, but he sounded like a parent lecturing a spoiled child.

"She's not all bad. I rather like her."

"Not all—!" Fir fumed. "You're an idiot! No wonder Queen Laurel wants you on the throne. She'd control you."

I'd already reasoned that last bit out, but calling Ospren an idiot seemed a touch harsh.

"Don't talk about my mother like that! She's your great aunt, in case you've forgotten."

I placed a hand on Fir's shoulder. He turned, his usually mischievous eyes filled with open hurt and betrayal. He stilled under my touch. I let my hand fall. I fetched Ospren's thankfully unbroken mug from the grass and poured him another cup of tea. "Why don't you tell me more about your wife?"

We needed to know all we could about her to defeat her.

Ospren's face turned dreamy. "She'll read anything I give her. She's the only person in the palace I can actually talk to about ideas. And she dotes on our children. She's a good mother."

His pinched tone at the end implied she was the kind of mother he did not have.

Fir muttered, "She's probably training all your brats to be harbingers of war and destruction, just like her."

"Fir," I warned.

Red Lord Ospren stood. "I should be getting back to the palace.

But please don't think you can succeed here. Lady Oakash won't let the negotiations open, I promise. She was livid when her father sent the offer for a prisoner exchange in the first place."

That meant she didn't control her father. That meant there was hope. I stood and bowed again. "Thank you for meeting with us."

He clasped both my hands in his long, delicate ones. "Flee, while you can. And welcome to the family, Plum. May our Ancestors protect you."

WHEN FEDEN, Fir, and I returned to the sage's compound and explained what had happened, Lt. Kabrok gave me more than an earful about what a rash idiot I'd been. I was only saved by Sage Raven informing us that they were ready to begin the skull-cleaning and cremation process for Sonall. Usually, outsiders weren't allowed on the premises during such times, but since we had nowhere else to go, they permitted us to remain inside with the windows closed.

"I think we should kill the sorry sod." Fir sat slumped against the wall in the kitchen, arms crossed. Sweat beaded on his forehead. It wasn't a particularly warm summer day, but with smoldering coals on the hearth and the windows blocked, the room was already unforgivingly hot.

Bane stood guard at the door. Lt. Kabrok and Dami had come in as well.

"Isn't he your cousin?" Lt. Kabrok asked.

"First cousin once removed. We could remove him a lot more, though." Fir grumbled. "What a spineless, useless slug. If Dami had come with us, she could have broken both his kneecaps with one punch."

Dami beamed like he'd just complimented the color of her eyes. Fir left off brooding just long enough to grin back at her.

"We're not attacking him," I said firmly. "Yes, he lacks political skills. That doesn't make him spineless. Everyone in this room has a different expertise, and that makes us stronger."

"Yay, sunshine and happy thoughts." Dami rolled her eyes at me. "Maybe he's not evil. But his existence makes it easy for the Shoreed to wage war against us."

I exhaled. "I know. First thing first, we need to send word to Lady Sulat about everything we've learned. She can announce Ospren's marriage. If his supporters learn they're also working to bring Lady Oakash in as their next queen, their loyalty will falter."

Lt. Kabrok's mustache twitched. "Lady Sulat gave me instructions for safely sending her a message if need be. But a rumor is going to be too little help, too late."

Fir flopped his head back. "And we've returned to the topic of assassinating my cousin."

He said it so flippantly, it *almost* sounded like joking.

The smell of smoke and flesh from Sonall's cremation crept into the room, mingling with our own sweat. No one else seemed to notice the smell yet, but I was choking on it.

"I'm not killing anyone," I said.

"Which means we retreat without achieving anything," Lt. Kabrok replied icily.

"We can send word through Ospren's friend that we want to meet again, then we can finish what we started," Fir suggested.

"No."

Dami shrugged. Lt. Kabrok grit his teeth. Fir groaned. Only Bane looked at me approvingly. Was I wrong? My head pounded. Even though Ospren meant well, maybe this situation was still just like the one at the carter station, where a little poison prevented much harm. Was sacrificing one life worth stopping a war?

I'd asked myself that before. And I'd answered yes. I'd given up my future for the chance at a treaty. But that had been *my* future to give. "For the last time. We're not killing anyone."

"Then what *are* we going to do?" Lt. Kabrok demanded.

The heat felt slick against my skin, and the smell of charcoal was making me nauseous. "I...need a day to think."

Kabrok's nose twitched. He could smell Sonall's cremation now, too. His expression hardened, and his tone turned harsh. "A day, then. I'll hold you to that. If you haven't come up with another plan by this time tomorrow, I will assume control of this delegation, send you out of the country, and remain behind with Fir and a few of our men to finish Red Lord Ospren and clean up your mess."

FOR ONCE IN MY LIFE, I didn't want to cook. One of the guards took over that duty while I paced my small room. Poppy sat in the corner mending and not commenting on how frantic I was. The sun had gone down, bringing a modicum of relief from the heat, but the reek of charcoal clung to the air.

I still had no answers. And I wasn't going to find them pacing in this room. I needed someone to talk to. Someone steady. Someone with kind brown eyes and a firm voice. I needed Bane.

"Poppy." My mouth was so dry from the heat, I had to pause and swallow. "I have to think clearly right now, and Bane helps me think. Would you mind terribly? If I went and talked with just him and me? It would strictly be about the future of the delegation."

She looked up, a quirk of a smile on her face. "I'm not sure why you're asking me permission. Bane's his own person."

"I know, but I don't want to have misunderstandings between us. I'm happy for both of you. Really. I'm not trying to ruin that." I sounded like a rambling mess.

"Plum, being around Bane is probably the nicest assignment I've ever been given since I started work at the palace. But it's still just an assignment."

I stopped pacing. "But...the two of you..."

"I'm afraid it would never work out."

Suddenly, I was defensive. "I don't see why not!"

Poppy laughed and my stomach twisted. She was going to blame his arm. Ancestors, I didn't want to hear her reject him because of that. The two of them ought to be happy together.

"Well, to start, I might admire him for his dedication to his job, but I've worked for five years at the palace now. And if I ever marry and leave, I don't want to be tied to the palace anymore. I want a husband who can enjoy long, lazy mornings or stay out late stargazing. Even if he isn't on duty, Bane isn't like that."

No, he wasn't.

Poppy lowered her voice. "Besides, he has the obnoxious habit of talking about you far, far too often. It gets rather grating after a while."

My cheeks burned. I hoped Poppy couldn't see it. "Oh."

FEDEN HAD BEEN STANDING guard at the door, but it was quick work to find Bane and ask him to take a shift. "Is something the matter?"

So many things were wrong. My delegation was failing. Sonall was dead. If I didn't come up with another plan, Lt. Kabrok was set on sending me away and murdering Lord Ospren. And Bane hadn't moved on to imagining a life for himself without me.

"I was hoping you'd mull things over with me." I headed down the hallway.

"In the kitchen?" Bane guessed—my room was the other way.

"Mull things over a cup of tea, then." I pushed the door open. The hearth was out, but someone had left a candle burning there. It gave precious little light, sending flickering shadows everywhere.

It took me more than a moment to realize the shadows in the corner weren't just shadows. They were moving. Someone had left that candle there—someone who was still in the room.

Bane's reflexes were faster than mine. He stepped in front of me and yanked the short spear off his back. But no assailant emerged.

Now that my eyes were adjusting, it seemed like there were far too many elbows over there, all moving with no attempt at stealth.

Even when my eyes could see what was happening, it took my mind an extra moment to digest the image: Dami and Fir, their hands tangled in each other's hair, their mouths locked together.

CHAPTER
TWENTY-SEVEN

"By our Ancestors!" I cried. I knew Dami wasn't a barefoot little girl anymore but panic and disbelief kneaded themselves together in my gut.

Fir jumped like someone had jammed a white-hot coal against his back. "Umm, ahh..."

Dami casually wiped her mouth with the back of her hand. "Hey Plum." She glanced at Bane. "I see you had the same idea."

"The same—!" My face burned. No—I wouldn't let her put me on the defensive this time. "This isn't about me."

"Yeah, I know. Because all your problems are always *my* fault."

My head pounded and I wanted to grind my teeth together. Everything else aside, this put our delegation at risk. "Why can't you ever think things through?"

Fir stepped forward. "Your concern for your sister's good name is admirable, but I assure you—"

"What if a sage had found you, objected, and kicked us all out onto the street?" I demanded. "What if we actually figure out a way to *stay*, and then the entire delegation gets undermined by rumors of scandalous behavior? We've worked so hard to avoid rumors."

Fir had the decency to look down at his toes in shame. Dami pursed her lips, as if seeking some kind of retort. Bane stood silent next to me, as sturdy and immovable as a whole-log pillar. I felt steadier with him there, even if I was doing all the talking.

"Our enemies don't need *more* weapons. Our behavior has to be irreproachable. This can't happen again," I said.

"Of course," Fir muttered.

Dami stared at me long and hard. I braced for a sharp retort. But her shoulders slumped, and she sighed expressively. "Fine. If you think who I swap saliva with is a matter of national importance, I'll stop."

"Thank you." I'd fulfilled my obligation to Rowak as ambassador. Without our parents here, as her older sister, I also had a responsibility to Dami. But Dami didn't want me telling her what to do, and I couldn't think of anything wise to say anyway.

I just kept staring at the two of them. My sister had been kissing a man who'd once tried to kill me.

"Why are you looking at me like that?" Dami demanded. "I swear I'm not kissing anyone else. Gah. Plum, you know you're no fun, right?"

"Absolutely none," I agreed. Dami was exciting enough for both of us.

She mumbled, "I'm sure Bane can attest to that," as she slunk out of the room.

Fir watched her go, then stepped closer to me, his face shifting from blue to orange as he entered the ring of candlelight. He glanced once at Bane, then held my gaze. "Might I speak to you privately?"

"I'm not sending away my bodyguard. This is as private as it gets."

Fir nodded, like he'd expected that. "I want you to know that I wasn't just..." He paused, pursed his lips, and started over. "Once we're finished here and we're all safely back home, I'd like to become your brother-in-law."

I gaped at him. The feeling wasn't mutual. He looked so contrite, with his ruffled hair hanging over his eyes and his hands clasped before him.

This wasn't the calculating Fir that I knew.

"I care for Dami deeply," he said. "She's quite unique."

Unique or beautiful? Dami had broken the nose of more than one admirer back in Clamsriver. A bad military haircut didn't hide her even features and flawless skin. But Fir was careful and shrewd—he didn't seem like the kind of man who'd fall for a pretty face. Did he actually care for her personally, then? Everyone else in the delegation, myself included, treated him with caution. But Dami didn't look at him with judgment, and she wasn't afraid of him.

"Thank you for letting me know your intents. You may go now."

"I hope this hasn't poisoned you against me," Fir said.

I didn't answer that. "Go. Now."

He fled the room.

I groaned, dropping my head into my hands. I'd expected Fir to stab me in the back like an honest man—not kiss my sister. Had I been too harsh on Dami? Should I have pretended to approve of their relationship to cement Fir's loyalty?

"Dami always accuses me of lectures, and there I was. Lecturing."

"She's your younger sister and your servant, Plum," Bane said. "You weren't out-of-bounds."

That didn't mean I'd done the right thing. I doubted Dami would see it the way Bane did. Though she *had* backed down when I spoke of protecting our mission. I bit my lip. I wanted to stay in the kitchen. The candlelight softened Bane's face and left our surroundings blurry, making me feel like I wasn't in Shoreed or Rowak, but someplace else entirely. Some other world without wars, royal engagements, or a treaty to navigate.

But I needed to go face Dami. "I should head back to my room."

"No tea, then."

I'd come here with him to brainstorm ideas for saving the delegation and preserving Ospren's life, but I wouldn't be able to focus properly on that until after I spoke to my sister. "Would you join me for breakfast instead?"

Bane nodded and escorted me back to my room.

Poppy snored softly in the corner. I laid down on my mattress next to Dami. Neither of us bothered with a coverlet in this thick, sticky heat. "Are you upset?"

"I didn't mean to endanger the delegation," Dami muttered. She stared up at the ceiling. I was trying to ask forgiveness for scolding her, but she was apologizing instead.

Well. This was probably better than yelling at each other. "I know. And I didn't mean to sound so...harsh."

"I've just been bored, you know? Not a lot of stuff to punch. And Fir's been flirting with me since Napil."

I blinked. "Really?"

"You're kinda dense, Plum."

"When it comes to you, yes I am."

Dami snorted. "And you're horrible at flirting. Let's not leave that off the list."

I sighed. I didn't want to talk about me and Bane again. And I had an uncomfortable voice in the back of my mind—it sounded like my mother—telling me that I still had more things I needed to say as Dami's older sister. "I...don't know how to talk about this without making you upset. But Fir, well, he could be dangerous. I'm worried about you. And kissing a man in a dark place, all alone, well, you see—"

"Plum. Mother gave me that whole talk a *long* time ago. I'm not an idiot. The army gave me quite an education, too. I was just having a little fun. Passing time."

I frowned. "No one in the army knew you were a girl."

"Yeah. Exactly." She propped herself up on an elbow. "They didn't censor themselves around me. I heard about *all* their exploits. It would have burned your ears off, Plum."

I squirmed on my mattress. "I'm sorry you had to listen to that."

Dami shrugged. "I didn't have to live it. No one was trying to win me over. That was kinda nice. Not that I would have been that desirable, with so many red-ranked women in town."

"I...don't follow." Red was the lowest rank, dishonored citizens unable to hold any government office. "You're two ranks above red."

Dami patted my arm. "You're sweet, you know that? Sweet, and a little stupid. At every town we stopped at, there were always red-ranked women who'd do anything for a soldier who said he'd come back after the war to marry her. It's one way to leave the slums—if you can find someone who will actually keep his promises. For a man who only wants a little company, they're a better bet than a higher-ranked woman with prospects."

"Oh, those poor women," I exhaled.

"Says the girl who engaged herself to a man she hates," Dami grumbled.

I shook my head. Dami would never understand why I'd done what I'd done. "Please tell me most of Rowak's soldiers didn't behave like that."

Dami shrugged. "There were plenty of sticks-in-the-mud like you. All honor and duty and Ancestors. But there were lots who were happy to be away from the watchful eyes of their parents or wives. Maybe a third of the soldiers bragged about running around town? Though I'm sure that with some of them, their mouths were bigger than their—"

"Please don't finish that," I cut her off, feeling queasy. "They *bragged* about it?"

"Uh. Yeah." Her tone alone made me feel foolish.

"They disrespect themselves and their Ancestors," I murmured.

"Got that lecture from my sergeant all the time. You would have liked him. Boring. Dry. He got mad at us for gambling our wages, too."

"*Gambling?* Dami, tell me you didn't."

"You're impossible," she groaned. "Can we go back to talking about what whoremongers some soldiers are?"

"I wasn't trying to lecture," I apologized.

"And yet..." Dami trailed off. "Anyway. I'm sorry I nearly caused a national incident with my tongue. Really, I'm just bored."

"Maybe you need a new hobby. You could ask Poppy to teach you embroidery."

Dami laughed and slugged me lightly in the arm. From her, it still felt like a hammer-blow. I winced.

"Embroidery? That's a good one, Plum. Next you'll suggest I clean something. Or do laundry."

"Isn't there anything you like doing?"

She paused. "Punching people. Gambling. But I won't do that here—promise. Wouldn't reflect well on Rowak. And I liked kissing Fir. He's charmingly bad at it. I think he's been locked up in the palace, focused on killing you for too long, or whatever scheming thing he did before that. Hmm. Punching, gambling, kissing. I think that's everything."

"You liked springball, once."

I could hear the smile in her voice. "Yeah. That was fun. Bane said you play now?"

"With him." Then I realized what I'd just said. "I mean, I've played several times with him. It's a nice game."

Dami laughed, causing Poppy to grunt and roll over in her sleep. "You can't tell me that you were headed to the kitchen with Bane for a game of springball, though."

She sounded hopeful—like she wanted me to admit I'd had something salacious in mind.

"I just wanted to talk. You heard Lt. Kabrok's ultimatum. I'd like to think I just insist that we stay..."

"But the soldiers are all loyal to him." Dami flopped her limbs every which way on the mattress. "You didn't even have the least intention of kissing Bane first? Holding hands?"

"No, Dami. I'm engaged."

She groaned. "No one would have to know. You could pretend it didn't happen."

"I'd know. Bane would know. And it wouldn't be fair to Bane, to string him along. If pretending could solve everything, I'd just pretend that Ospren was dead."

"You'd have to get everyone else to pretend along with you on that last one," Dami said.

"I suppose I would."

Dami fell asleep not too long after that, but I stared at the ceiling, listening to the hum of summer insects outside. I chewed over her words. Perhaps there was a way to get everyone else to pretend, without hurting Ospren at all.

CHAPTER
TWENTY-EIGHT

That morning, I sat down to breakfast with Lt. Kabrok, Bane, Fir, and Dami.

"We don't need Red Lord Ospren dead," I said, laying out bowls of porridge for everyone. "We just need him out of Shoreed."

Fir plopped his spoon into his bowl. "He won't come willingly."

"I know."

"You're proposing we kidnap him, then?" Lt. Kabrok shook his head. "I don't have the manpower to quietly get him across the border without anyone noticing."

"And we've returned to killing him." Fir leaned back on his elbow. "It's simple. It's clean. It's easy."

"*No.*" I exhaled. I wouldn't become as calloused as my enemies to accomplish my goals. There would be no more bodies on pyres because of me. "We're not killing anyone. But we might pretend to."

That got even Dami's attention. No one was eating; the porridge sat, steaming, untouched.

"I'm going to poison Red Lord Ospren." The words tasted foul in my mouth, but I knew in my gut that this was my best option.

"So, you did come around to killing him," Fir said grimly. I couldn't tell if he was pleased or disappointed.

"No. We're going to ask him to poison himself."

Dami blinked at me. "I know you're new to this and all, but I think poisoning people usually involves being a lot more secret about it than that, Plum."

"First, we send notice to the palace that we're preparing to leave Shoreed. Hopefully that keeps the Bloodmarrows from lashing out again. They don't need to attack us if we're already on our way out."

Lt. Kabrok nodded. Finally, I was talking sense to him.

"Then we give a note to Minister Tidal to deliver to Ospren. We ask simply to meet with him again."

Lt. Kabrok's face sagged back into a disapproving frown, but everyone else stared at me, waiting for the whole plan.

"I craft a poison that grants agility-of-spirit, with a touch of endurance-of-soul. If I do it just right, Ospren's soul will leave his body, but stay nearby. He'll appear to be dead. Before he takes it, he'll need to act like he's coming down with something and make it clear that he would like to be brought to the sages here, should the worst happen. When he arrives, I'll give him an antidote full of endurance-of-soul, and he'll wake up. We leave as previously announced, smuggling him out with us."

"You think the sages will cooperate?" Lt. Kabrok asked doubtfully.

"I'll talk to Sage Raven. She's the only one who needs to know. But yes, I think she would."

"What if his wife wants to keep his skull?" Fir asked.

"Unfortunately, the sages have one of those to give to her."

Silence followed—a moment of respect for Sonall.

"His family deserves to have it," Kabrok protested, voice low.

"And they will. When that second envoy you talked about comes back, prepared for the situation here. But Lady Oakash might not request it at all."

Kabrok still wasn't satisfied. "It puts all of us in danger, trying to smuggle him out. He won't be safe in Rowak, anyway."

"Then we take him to the Toksang Empire."

Fir was nodding slowly. Dami actually looked excited. Bane seemed thoughtful. By now, everyone's porridge had to be lukewarm.

Only Kabrok still scowled. "You think Ospren will do this willingly?"

I had no idea—but I also didn't have a better plan. Despite my doubts, I tried to project confidence. "Ospren's only against running outright because the Bloodmarrows are holding his mother against him. They'll likely release her if they believe he's dead. Once she's safe and a treaty has been signed, he can come out of hiding and reunite with his wife."

"Sounds convoluted to me," Lt. Kabrok muttered.

Fir shrugged. "If he feigns an illness and then collapses, we're much less likely to be blamed than if an archer takes him out, or if he's poisoned while he's here."

Maybe Fir didn't really want Ospren dead. I hoped so.

AFTER BREAKFAST, I talked with Sage Raven. I left our plans vague, but she assured me she'd be happy to help us fake as many funerary rites as we needed. I thanked her, then dictated three letters to Poppy —one to the messenger Lady Sulat recommended, to inform her of Ospren's marriage; one to the palace to tell them we were leaving; and one for Minister Tidal to pass along to Red Lord Ospren, asking for a meeting. Lt. Kabrok sent four men out together to deliver them.

Then I headed to the kitchen. I usually enjoyed all kitchen tasks, from oiling cutting boards to putting the final garnishes on a bowl of noodles. But I did not enjoy hand-crafting poisons. I had to take natural foods and concentrate them down into one edible tidbit. I spent hours making hazelnut oil, laboriously grinding the nuts with a bit of warm water until they formed a paste. I covered that with a towel and left it in a corner to separate. Then I grated beets and radishes, salted them, and collected the juice.

Thank their Ancestors, all our men returned safely. They reported that Minister Tidal had agreed to deliver our message the next day.

None of us slept well, but no Bloodmarrows attacked us that night.

In the morning, I had Poppy bring me the box with Violet's vials. Violet had never made something like this before, but I re-read every similar poison recipe to gauge the ratios before I mixed the oil and juices and bound them together with powdered helproot—something Violet had in her kit. The stuff amplified the effects of multiple ingredients that all targeted the same thing. With hazelnut oil, beet juice, and radish juice, I should have something very potent indeed. The juice was already perfectly salty, so I added a touch of honey, the barest bit of sweetness to grant—I hoped—enough endurance to keep the soul nearby.

I rolled the poisonous dough into two pumpkin-seed sized balls, dried them by the fire, then stuck them in a pouch and tied them under my skirt. I didn't want anyone eating one on accident.

Then I began work on an antidote.

DAMI WOKE me in the dead of night. "Ospren is here."

Poppy was up before even I was. She lit a candle, helped me right my hair, and tied on my skirt. "You're presentable, now."

"Thank you."

Together, we rolled up the mattresses. Then Poppy and Dami left and Lord Ospren entered. The pouch with the poison hung heavy inside my skirt. The one burning candle created a puddle of light in the dark.

"I take it you need help safely leaving the country? I can't come like this again," Ospren said, "but I do have some friends here who can aide you."

As an ambassador, as the betrothed of the king, I could have silently whispered a prayer to any of the great kings and queens of Rowak. But the most familiar prayer blossomed in my heart: *Nana, please watch over me.*

"You don't want this war," I said.

Ospren rubbed the back of his neck. "We've talked about this. I can't do anything to stop it."

"I think you can."

And then I explained what I wanted him to do—fake a sudden illness. Make it known, loudly, that if anything should happen to him, he wanted the sages to care for his body. Take my poison, appear dead, get delivered here where I'd give him the antidote, then smuggle him out of Shoreed.

He stared at me, wide-eyed, irises shimmering in the candlelight. "My wife, my children, they'll think—"

"Only for a short time," I assured him. "Six months. Maybe a year. Without you here, negotiations can begin in earnest. What does Lady Oakash have to gain from this war if she won't become Queen of Rowak? Who in Rowak will continue to secretly support Shoreed with you gone?"

A studious line creased between his brows—it reminded me immensely of Valerian. "How do I know your poison won't just kill me? That's a much simpler solution for you than all this subterfuge."

"I don't want to kill anyone." Least of all Lady Sulat's beloved brother. I hoped she'd get to see, one day, that he was still the man she'd hoped and doubted him to be. "But I do have to warn you. This is an untested poison. It *shouldn't* kill you. But there's always a chance. And if you don't get the antidote in three days, your body will die of thirst anyway."

"You're not being terribly persuasive."

I pulled out the pouch. This was the part I hadn't mentioned to anyone else. That I shouldn't be offering now. "I made two identical doses of poison. Choose which one you want me to take, and I'll try it first. The antidote is right there." I nodded to a jar by the door. "Leave me for as long as you want but see that I get a spoonful of that sometime."

"That's a horrible plan. If you die here and now, there *will* be war. You can't be the one to try it out."

"Of course I can. All I have to do is swallow." I clutched the top of the pouch, twisting my fingers up in the strings. I braced myself for a fight. He'd probably suggest one of my soldiers try it—that was the pragmatic thing to do—but I wasn't about to sit through another cremation. If he was willing to take it if it worked, I was willing to test it.

"I'll do it. No need to risk yourself."

I blinked, my mind digesting his words slowly.

"Give one to me." He stretched out his hand. "If I die tomorrow, at least some good will come of it."

I handed over one of the small balls. He wrapped it in a handkerchief. This man was braver than Fir—or I—had given him credit for.

"If...if I don't make it, promise me that one day, long after this war is over, you'll tell my daughters the truth. I want them to remember me as a man of learning and peace."

"I promise."

I tied the pouch with the remaining poison back inside my skirt for safekeeping, my heart pounding in my throat. I hoped my plan worked.

More than that, I hoped I hadn't just made myself a murderer.

CHAPTER
TWENTY-NINE

We made preparations to leave the next day, as we'd told the palace we would. In the afternoon, a man named Delegate Gull visited and informed us he'd act as our escort out of Shoreed. His narrowed eyes seemed to flit everywhere, soaking in details. He was sure to be difficult, and Lt. Kabrok was already grumbling and asking if I had a poison that caused blindness.

I did, but I wasn't about to tell Lt. Kabrok that.

The rest of the day passed slowly as we packed our things and stocked up on rations from the marketplace. At least it went slowly for me—Poppy was a whirlwind of activity, but she assured me I'd just get in the way if I tried to help with the bags. I cooked and I prayed to my nana, but my thoughts were with Red Lord Ospren and the poison I'd given him. Would he really take it tonight? We all ate dinner quietly together. I retired to my room, feeling as listless as the warm, muggy air.

I didn't remember falling asleep that evening, but I must have. A commotion woke me. I jerked upright, skin clammy. Ospren had done it. And now for the antidote—to see if it worked.

I tied on my skirt, not waiting for Poppy. The pouch with the remaining poison still hung there. I needed to find a safe way to get rid of it.

Thuds. Grunts. I opened my door. Someone screamed outside and I froze. That didn't sound like a body being brought to the sages.

Bane stood guard by my door. He waved me back into the room. When I didn't move right away, he stepped inside himself, closed the door, and took up a defensive stance with his spear.

From somewhere nearby, Lt. Kabrok shouted, "This is a diplomatic envoy of Rowak, here with the permission of King Heron! You can't—"

A series of sickening cracks followed, then a low groan. Nothing more.

The door ripped open. A flood of Shoreed soldiers—two with torches—stood on the other side. Soldiers. Not Bloodmarrows or a funerary procession. Bane shifted lower into his stance.

"Acting Ambassador Plum of Rowak. You are under arrest for the attempted murder of Red Lord Ospren."

Attempted? Something had gone wrong. Very wrong. They shouldn't have been able to trace it back to me, in any case.

My stomach sank. Maybe Fir had been right. Maybe we should have quietly assassinated him instead with some clever, natural-looking poison. Thanks to Violet, I knew a dozen of those now. One man's death could have ended a war.

My plan had been too complicated.

"Bane, you can't fight that many," I said softly. "Stand down."

At least I wouldn't make it back to Rowak to tell Lady Sulat how badly I'd failed. Lady Oakash would see me convicted, and would-be-murderers tended to hang.

But even now, most of me was glad I hadn't assassinated Ospren —that I knew I was still a chef. Was keeping my conscience worth the consequences? I wasn't sure, and it didn't matter anymore. All I could do was give myself up and try to smooth this incident over. Claim Rowak had nothing to do with it. Perhaps I could say that Lady Oakash's Bloodmarrows had recruited me. Yes. That would do nicely. Testify, blame the warmongers. They'd asked me for a poison that would *look* like an assassination attempt but leave the man alive.

How could I know they'd planned to use it on Ospren purely to incriminate me? I was just a greedy girl with dark skills, happy to sell them.

It wouldn't save me, but I could cast that seed of doubt, just like King Alder had made me doubt Lady Sulat. Perhaps that seed, that question, would be enough to protect the war prisoners and give Rowak and Lady Sulat one last chance to sue for peace. This whole incident, after all, might be the fault of an amber-hungry chef and the war-hungry daughter of the Shoreed king—nothing more. I just had to testify. To tell a story.

"Get yourself and the others home safe," I told Bane. "That's an order."

A protest hung unspoken on his lovely mouth. I put my hands on his shoulders, soaking in the warmth of him, the tenseness of his muscles. I inhaled his juniper scent. I'd likely never see him again.

"Would you say all attempts at a treaty have failed?" I asked.

His eyebrows quirked together, confused. "Yes."

"Good. Then I'm not engaged anymore."

I kissed him. Bane tasted like smoked trout—firm, smooth, and luscious. Sweetness and salt swirled across my palate. He kissed me back until the Shoreed guards yanked me away. My fingers trailed down his arm and into open air.

"Go home," I said. "And make a happy life for yourself."

"*Plum.*"

That was the last thing I heard him say—a whisper, a prayer, a plea, a farewell.

THE SOLDIERS LED me through the city. I couldn't see much more than a blur of torches, starlight, and shadows.

I'd been so furious at Lady Sulat for arranging Osem's engagement. Now, it seemed like such a kindness to put two people together and ask them to enjoy a long life in each other's company. I hoped Lady Sulat would arrange such a marriage for Bane when he returned. I knew she'd take care of him.

She was far better at taking care of her people than I was.

We didn't head to the palace but to a walled compound with more uniformed men. We passed a nicely-kept building, probably administrative, and continued to a low prison with no porch, just rows of wood-barred cells that reeked of urine and musty hay. Torches jammed into the ground burned at regular intervals around it.

But the guards didn't stop there. Next to the prison stood a small shed with *Solitary Confinement* scribbled on it. They tossed me inside and barred the door shut.

It was dark and dank and foul—like a corpse left to stew in the sun in a puddle of its own loosed bowels. I tugged the front of my dress over my mouth and breathed shallowly. It was probably the exhaustion, or a delirium brought on by failure, but part of me wanted to laugh.

King Alder might be a murderer, but he did keep a rather nicer prison than this.

I EXPECTED them to let me fester, but early the next morning, guards yanked me into the sunlight and dragged me into a small building behind the administrative one. It had no windows, just the tang of blood in the air. The guards shoved me down onto a chair and bound my wrists to it with lengths of stiff, reddish-brown fabric. A middle-aged man stood in the corner next to a table full of obsidian knives, watching. His sleeves came down to the elbows like mine, but the fabric was expertly woven, shimmering with fancifully embroidered chive flowers and finches. He looked like he belonged in a palace, not a prison.

When the guards left, he stepped in front of me. Apart from his clothes and his flat, dead glare, he was perfectly average—average height, average build, average features. "Green-ranked Plum of Clamsriver," he drawled. "Daughter of Yellow-ranked Chef Linak."

I flinched at my father's name. His identity wasn't a secret, but it still wasn't information most in Shoreed would know. He spoke with a dry, Rowak accent, too. "You're not from here."

A smile curdled up his face. "You don't know who I am."

"Should I?"

He didn't respond to that. "Your plan failed. Did you really think you could get away with assassinating Red Lord Ospren?"

He didn't know what the actual plan had been. I refrained from grinning back at him, keeping my face politely neutral instead. "When is my trial?"

"Trial?" He laughed. "You'll be publicly hanged in an hour. Lady Oakash revoked all your diplomatic rights. She's not exactly concerned about fostering good relations with Rowak."

He smelled like parsley and coriander—he definitely wasn't a soldier.

"This will send us straight back to war."

"Says the would-be assassin." He sounded almost amused. "Shoreed's troops are readying as we speak. Preparing for a direct assault on Napil." He leaned against the table, drawing my eyes back to the gleaming ripples and whorls of those obsidian knives. The man examined his nails.

I wished I had dozens of people to spin a story to, but this man in courtly garb might be my only chance to sow doubt against Lady Oakash's warmongering.

"I joined the Bloodmarrows to make extra amber for my family. Lady Oakash is part of their organization. She told me to make a poison that would incapacitate someone, not kill them. She paid well. I didn't realize she just wanted to frame me so she could continue this war."

His laughter rang out cold and bitter. "Inventive little thing, aren't you?"

"I abused my talents for ill. But it was under her direction."

He put his hands over my bound wrists and leaned into my face. "*I* am at the heart of the Bloodmarrows. And I never recruited you. If we'd needed a poison, I would have made it myself."

My stomach quavered. Ancestors preserve me. Chef Palaw stood in front of me.

"Lady Oakash has sent for King Heron to approve the deployment of soldiers. He should arrive in Pearlfoam tomorrow, long after you're already a corpse. King Alder was a fool to send you. You're no match for Lady Oakash—or me."

Seeing as King Alder wanted me to die and the prisoner exchange to fail, no, he wasn't particularly foolish. He was getting exactly what he wanted.

"You cost me one of my best poisoners," Palaw said.

Violet. I ought to apologize and grovel for understanding. But I was already strapped to a chair. I was already a dead woman. Indignation bubbled up my throat. "She deserved a better father than you."

"You'd rather she'd grown up under the tutelage of a third-rate chef like your father? We worked together in the royal kitchens. He was so formulaic. So tied to traditional recipes—and with only acceptable execution. Why do you think he got assigned to a backwater like Clamsriver?"

I wouldn't let him make this about me. "My father nurtured me, encouraged me, and let me make my own choices. You raised Violet to be your tool—to murder and lie for you, to marry a man just to advance her mission. I don't care how well you cook, Palaw. You sent her to die for your schemes."

He whipped a knife against my throat. Maybe I wouldn't make it to that hanging after all. "I've heard from my people in Shoreed how you and Lady Sulat had her tortured to death. You've no right to talk like your hands are clean."

"Your contacts lied. The interrogator—General Behon, one of *your* men—cracked her skull open to keep her quiet. I exposed her, yes, but I expected her to have a fair trial."

I didn't feel it when that impossibly sharp obsidian slipped into my skin. I smelled the tang of blood, then felt a bead of it meander down my throat.

"I already know you like spinning stories, but you're not very good at it. General Behon wouldn't betray me like that. I have some questions. You will answer them. *Truthfully.*"

"Why? Are you going to delay my sentence?"

"No, but I will let you hang instead of finishing you here." He leaned closer, smothering me in his herby smell. "Do you know that you don't actually need a stomach for the food you swallow to affect your body? I can keep you alive long enough to show you how it works."

He pulled the knife back from my throat, then trailed the tip of it to my midsection. No, I did not want to die slowly at the hands of this Bloodmarrow. In the dimly lit room, Palaw's fine features looked almost skeletal.

I hoped Bane was already out of Pearlfoam. I was glad he wasn't here to see this. In his last memory of me, I'd be alive and well and loving him.

"After he stabilized," Palaw said, "I persuaded Ospren to tell me about his recent activities—including the fact that he'd visited you. I'd appreciate it if you stop the false pretenses."

So Ospren hadn't told Palaw he'd taken the poison willingly.

"I came here for one purpose, and one purpose only," Palaw continued. "Tell me about the poison. It wasn't like anything I'd seen before. Ospren was melancholy all day and overly affected by the heat. He was so despondent that the palace's Master Chef made candied hazelnuts for him with his own hands. Not long after, he collapsed to the floor, convulsing. I can't imagine how endurance-of-soul could trigger a poison's effects."

I squeezed my eyes shut and exhaled through my nose. The treat hadn't triggered anything. Ospren had been depressed about the whole matter, ate the snack, then took my poison. Candied hazelnuts. Endurance-of-soul. I silently swore. I hadn't made the poison poorly

—Ospren had destroyed its balance by eating soul-targeting food just before taking it. Instead of appearing dead, his soul had fluttered between his body and the outside world.

I'd learned something new about poisoning people. But it didn't matter. The realization had come too late.

Palaw nuzzled the knife tip against my belly. "I'll know how you made it before you die, Plum, one way or another."

My thoughts raced. If I revealed the truth, he'd know that Ospren had taken it voluntarily. I didn't care much about protecting Ospren's mother, but it would probably put Ospren in danger, too. What else could have produced those effects? "I mixed helproot with powdered celeriac and strawberries, to target the heart, and made a salted tea with it."

Violet's notes called this poison The Quiet Demise. It had an aftertaste and it wasn't foolproof, but it did cause strange, erratic heartbeats that had a fair chance of killing someone.

"That should have acted faster."

"I...I don't know why it didn't." I didn't need to fake the fear in my voice. "This was my first time poisoning someone. I had Violet's notes—I thought I'd followed the recipe exactly."

"Hmm. What kind of tea did you hide it in?"

"Mint."

He asked a dozen more questions—about how I'd ground the celeriac, how old the helproot was, and how long I'd steeped the tea.

With every fabricated answer, his brow furrowed deeper. "Trying to duplicate this is going to take an age."

Duplicate it? My stomach roiled.

"Don't worry," he said. "Not on *you*. You're going to hang very publicly instead. I'll keep my word."

He stood to leave. My pulse raced. This man was my only link to the outside world. I had to try something to save myself and stop this war from avalanching forward. "If you take me with you, I'll make the poison again. You can watch. Surely your trained eye would catch something mine didn't."

"Tempting, and a valiant effort at saving your neck. But I'd hate to rob Lady Oakash of this execution she's planned. You're a walking corpse, ambassador, and you have precious little time to come to peace with that."

Former Master Chef Palaw, infamous Bloodmarrow, turned and left.

The guards returned and dragged me out. For a brief moment, the sun blinded me, then the men stuffed me back in that small, rank shed.

The sheer quiet of that place pressed on my ears. Clogged my nose. Less than an hour until I hung.

My palms sweated. I didn't have days to hope and plan and think. I didn't have a Hungry Ghost to help me escape. I wasn't getting a last meal.

I knelt in the moldering straw and wished that I could be in my family shrine, with Nana's smooth clay face staring lovingly down at me.

"Ancestors, please watch over Rowak. Don't let my death be the catalyst that launches us back into war. And watch over Dami. And Poppy. And Lt. Kabrok and his men. I know Bane isn't yours, either, but..." But he should have been. He should have been their son-in-law. "You would have liked him, Nana. I'm sure of it. Please watch over him like he was your own. And if you have any brilliant ideas for me, I wouldn't mind that, either."

What assets did I still have? Palaw would be of no help to me. Could I bribe a guard? Unlikely—I couldn't even set up a secret meeting with one of them. I had no time.

You're a walking corpse.

Maybe if I'd been strong-of-leg, I could have sprinted away. Maybe if I'd been strong-of-arm, I could have punched through the prison door. A thousand more *maybes* ran through my mind.

But I was a chef with no food before me and no hungry person waiting for a meal. Once again, I wondered if Fir had been right with all his talk of assassination.

Ancestors, I hated that nagging doubt. I'd miscalculated, and now thousands would die. Uncounted more would be wounded, like Bane. And lose their families and homes like Osem. I couldn't do anything more to stop it.

You're a walking corpse.

When I died, would they deliver my body to the sages? To my envoy? Slowly, I pulled that small pouch out from its place beneath my skirt. I untied it. Maybe I needed to die sooner rather than later. The last thing I'd eaten was poached egg hot pot. Not candied hazelnuts.

I rolled the bead of poison between my fingers. Would Dami be alert enough to give me the antidote? Had I even made the poison correctly? Or the antidote, for that matter?

Footsteps neared my door.

No more time for deliberation.

I swallowed my own poison whole.

The last thing I saw was a pair of green-uniformed guards rushing toward me and a blur of wall and ceiling as my soul jerked free of my body.

CHAPTER
THIRTY

S ouls don't have eyes. Or ears. Or noses. For the first time in my life, I couldn't smell *anything*.

I expected acidic bile rushing up my throat and a knot in my gut, but I didn't have any of those things, either. I couldn't feel my own panic. I couldn't scream.

Shouldn't I be happily walking toward the Ancestor's Realm? Or hovering over my own body? I felt like I was as vast as the night sky, opaque and incomprehensible—that, or so small that I could not be seen. Or see.

Was I actually dead? Worse—was I a ghost, holding myself back from the Ancestor's Realm with my own regrets and failed ambitions?

I couldn't pinch the bridge of my nose. I couldn't stretch my arms. There were no arms.

So, I did about the only thing I could do. I prayed.

Nana, if I'm dead, you can still hear me, right? Nana, I'm lost and scared and...dead. I think.

Would I never smell wood-oil again or buckwheat branches as they toasted over brilliant maple coals? Would I never admire the jewel-tones of beets and carrots or feel the grit between my fingers as I cleaned a parsnip? Hear the burble of a hot-pot?

It felt like all the wanting should leave my gut hurting, but I couldn't physically *hurt*. Instead, thoughts rushed through my mind with the vengeance of a river swollen with the spring thaw. I'd left Bane alone. I still hadn't reconciled with Dami. I hadn't stopped this war, either. I'd accelerated it.

Nana, are you there? I begged, drowning in my own nothingness.

Even if she couldn't hear me, she had to have some way to understand me. She'd answered my silent prayers before.

Someone answered softly. *Peace and calm to you.*

They weren't words, not spoken ones. It was more like staring at the insides of my eyelids and watching patterns of black overlapped with black. Fuzzy. Hard to focus on.

Nana? I asked.

I'm sorry. I'm not her. But you'll see her soon. Be patient. Remember, it usually takes the deceased a year to reach the Realm of the Ancestors.

I paused to take a deep, reassuring breath, but my lungs didn't budge. My lungs were gone. *How do I move? Which way do I go?*

It's not about moving. It's about becoming. Already, the words felt more distinct in my mind, less slurred. *The Ancestors' Realm is here. When you've gained mastery of your soul as your form of existence— when you can see and smell and run again—you'll emerge into that place of spiritual being.*

Again, I expected my stomach to drop. And it didn't. *I'm not broken, then?*

No. Calm, calm. Have you never wondered why the souls the Ancestors weave for their descendants come to be born into bodies instead of lingering with the Ancestors?

No, I hadn't. But I supposed it was a good question—if we all end up back there, why leave?

Bodies are strong and powerful. They can hear, run, speak, touch, taste, and watch. Souls don't have hands, or ears, or eyes. But with the memory of a body, you will eventually learn how to observe the world as a soul. I can't take you to the Realm of the Ancestors. You must master yourself to see it. You're like a baby right now. But you don't need to be afraid. You will learn how to walk again.

Poor Nana. Had this terrified her, too? I'd spent so much time asking for her help and guidance and all the while she'd been busy with her own journey.

Do you help all those who die? I asked, hoping she'd been there for Nana, too.

I help those that I can. Tell me about yourself. How did you pass away?

Somehow, telling a benevolent spirit sage that I'd consumed poison and was hoping to wake back up seemed like a bad plan. Or maybe her presence meant I wasn't waking up? I tried to swallow and didn't. *I'm not ready to talk about it.*

Then tell me about something else. This conversation is already helping you control your soul. You're still quite amorphous in shape —and will be for several months—but your voice is a little clearer.

She was right. The words she sent at me were easier to understand, and I felt almost as if I could hear an echo of a voice—a real, spoken voice in them. Soft and musical.

I had a wise, ancient spirit to talk to. I doubted she knew much about stopping wars, and I might never wake up. But maybe she could give me advice about something else. Something I still hadn't been able to figure out on my own. *I miss my sister.*

One day, you'll see her again. Is she living or dead?

Living. And I know we'll be reunited someday, one way or another. That's not the problem. I lost her a long time ago. She changed. Or maybe I did. We used to be close. Now, I don't understand her.

But you want to.

Yes. This kind spirit was probably hundreds, if not thousands, of years old. Surely, she'd have some good advice for me.

Tell me more about her.

So, I did. All about growing up with Nana and how wild Dami had always been. How she'd started hiding in the woods and then ran off to join the army. I explained that I went to the palace in her place. A bit about how I met Bane. But not much—I already knew exactly how I felt about him. Our problems were all rooted in the mortal world, and I doubted unearthly guides to the Realm of the Ancestors had much to say on the subject of politics, treaties, and state marriages.

The particulars aren't important, but I helped stop a coup so now I can talk to my sister again. But it's no different than before I left. I paused and failed to sigh. *Lately, she's not seemed so abrasive, but I'm not sure why. What can I do? What should I have done?*

Whether I reconciled with Dami when I—hopefully—woke up, or if I had to wait for her in the Ancestors' Realm, I wanted us to be sisters again.

For a moment, the silence made me fear that I was alone once more, a tumble of thoughts trapped in a void.

Then that musical voice resonated again, somehow both softer and more audible than ever. *You're Ambassador Plum, aren't you?*

I froze. I didn't have arms or legs or a face, but whatever my substance was made of—it all went rigid. Like someone had breathed frost up me. *Who are you?*

The voice grew even more clear—was that a Shoreed accent?— but it also turned hard. *You're an abomination. Ospren almost died.*

I wasn't trying to kill him!

No words followed, just anger—like boiling water crawling up my flesh, engulfing me...except I didn't have flesh.

I should have asked Palaw to perform one of his horrible experiments on you. The voice cut through me. I could hear it perfectly now, both inside and as something auditory. Definitely a Shoreed accent. My soul was learning how to sense the world around it. *I hope you fester in your crimes, turn into a ghost, and never reach your Ancestors.*

That voice left me to the void of myself. To darkness and vastness and nothingness. To a lack-of-smell, a lack-of-sound. A lack of everything.

I hung in the emptiness. I couldn't even keep time with my own heartbeat. It felt like seconds had passed. It felt like eons had passed. I was alone.

And then a new voice rippled through the nothingness, softer than a whisper.

I love you, Plum. Come back to us.

This voice didn't have a lilting Shoreed accent. It sounded so familiar. It almost sounded like Dami.

My eyelids cracked open. They felt as heavy and real as granite boulders. I swallowed, my mouth full of something sweet and hazelnutty. The antidote.

I blinked. Dami's moon-rounded, flawless face stared down at me, her cropped hair swinging on one side and tucked behind her ear on the other. "Plum! You're alive!"

"And I did something bad, right before I woke up." The words creaked out, like air pushed between stones. I tried to sit up but couldn't. How had I never noticed how *heavy* a body was?

"Bad?" Dami peered at me. "Is your brain okay? You were dead. You couldn't have done *anything*."

I wished she was right about that, but I was nearly certain I hadn't imagined pouring out my soul to an angry, belligerent spirit.

"Is King Heron back in Pearlfoam?" I asked.

"Only for an hour longer. He's marching his troops to the border so he can personally oversee the war. Plum, you were out for nearly *three days*. I thought you weren't going to come back. Ever. Poppy and I dripped antidote and broths down your mouth every hour and rubbed your limbs to keep them from getting sore. I even *prayed*."

She didn't usually? "You watched over me? For that long?"

"Of course I did, you idiot."

"I love you, too." Smiling made every ounce of my face hurt, but I did it anyway.

I wanted to just lay there and talk, but if we didn't stop King Heron and his army, our chance for peace was over. It sounded like we might already be too late. "Is Poppy nearby? I'll need her help to get dressed." I could move my toes now, though it felt like they were buried in mud. "And I'll need Lt. Kabrok to put an escort together. Quickly."

"Oh Plum. Plum." Dami gently squeezed my hand and laid her other one on my cheek.

She hadn't shown me this much affection since she was six. I began to tremble, terror seizing up along my too-heavy muscles. "What happened?"

"They're...they're gone. Bane, too. It's just me and Poppy here."

I tried to sit up again and faltered. Dami supported me. We were in the front room of the building in the sage's compound. The door was ajar, letting in fresh air, but no guard stood there. No Bane. No Bane anywhere. Just empty space.

My throat squeezed itself shut. "Dami. Tell me."

She gave me a pitying look. That was more frightening than anything she'd said.

"When they arrested you, they arrested everyone else but Poppy and me—the maids. I guess we weren't worth bothering with. We're not soldiers or diplomats. They took everyone else...away."

The way she said *away* made my skin crawl. "Tell me," I demanded again.

"They were declared war prisoners. They took all of them back... back to the prisoner camp."

"They took *Bane* there?" I remembered the way he stiffened just looking at the place. The hollowness in his eyes. He couldn't go back to that camp.

"That's what *all* means, Plum. He's gone."

CHAPTER
THIRTY-ONE

I shouldn't have asked Bane to become my bodyguard. I should have left him in Askan-Wod, with a decent, safe post as a messenger.

"You can mourn later," Dami said. "Over Bane, over the other soldiers, over the utter failure this envoy is. We'll be lucky if the three of us can sneak back across the border and give Lady Sulat a report. Poppy's filling packs for us in the kitchen. We were going to leave tonight if you didn't make it."

I stared at the open door where Bane should have been standing. I'd let this war devour him again.

"Can you walk? I'll carry you if I have to, but it'll look odd and draw attention."

No one appeared to fill the doorway, no matter how long I stared at it. "Does everyone know I'm dead?"

"Lady Oakash waited two days for King Heron to return and see your body himself before shipping you over here. There are posters in the market mocking you for committing suicide in your cell and dishonoring your Ancestors. All of Shoreed probably knows by now."

King Heron had seen me himself. "Good."

Dami tugged me to my feet. "Are your limbs all stiff?"

Just heavy. But that didn't matter right now. "You and Poppy should head out as you planned—once Poppy dresses me one last time."

"What are you up to?" Dami peered at me, her concerned face looking uncannily like Mother's.

My palms were sweating, and my pulse raced, but I managed a dry laugh. "*Now* you care that I'm planning something dangerous? You didn't before."

"Of course I cared! I still care. You're going to do something all stupid and noble and likely fatal."

"Well, I hope it's not actually fatal. Again." I rubbed the side of my head. "I'm going to talk to King Heron before he leaves Pearlfoam."

Dami stared at me expectantly. "That's it? Stroll up in front of his army and ask him to execute you properly this time?"

"He saw my dead body," I replied. "Miraculous resurrection seems like a good starting point for opening peace negotiations."

"Gah! You've never even met him! You'd gamble your life that he's a peace-loving, idealistic idiot like you?"

I was gambling for my nation. For Bane. Standing in front of his army was my only chance to stop the war. "Yes."

Dami balled her hands into angry fists.

"It's not a senseless gamble. If he was against a prisoner exchange, he wouldn't have asked for one. If he didn't want an ambassador, Lady Oakash wouldn't have timed his trip to the Windswept Surf Shrine to coincide with my arrival. She wouldn't have made him examine my corpse. She started the mobilization of the army. He might only be marching because—with my supposed assassination attempt and then suicide—his hands are tied."

"Sometimes I really hate you, Plum." Dami stomped out into the hallway, then called, "Poppy! She's awake! And she's definitely still herself—I owe you three amber beads! We need to get her dressed up nice!"

"Coming!" Poppy called from somewhere near the kitchen.

"When she's done," I said, "you and Poppy should leave."

Dami folded her arms and leaned against the doorframe. "I know you haven't caught on yet, but I *hate* it when people tell me what to do. Go serve at the palace. Be polite. Don't punch that. Feel guilty about running away to join the army. Eat your pickled celery." She wrinkled her nose. "Pickles. Ugh. And now this—run away nicely back home."

"Dami..." I began. She didn't need to stay. For all my brave talk, this could easily end up with King Heron issuing orders to hang us from the city wall.

"Yeah. Shut up, Plum. I'm coming with you. You can't make me do otherwise."

"Umm." Poppy gave me a look-over. "We don't have time for a real bath, but if you walk up to the army smelling like a prison, they'll skewer you before you even reach King Heron."

I got a bucket of water over my head, a quick rebraid of my hair, and a fresh set of clothes. Poppy knew how to move; it only took a few minutes. "You look like a bumpkin who stole a nice dress, but it's better than the mangy mess you were before."

"Er, thanks Poppy. Can you make it safely back to Lady Sulat by yourself?"

She blinked at me. "I'm staying with you. An ambassador needs some kind of a retinue."

"And we need to get information back to Lady Sulat."

"We already sent her word about Ospren's marriage," Poppy said. "That's good enough. I'm seeing this through."

I didn't protest anymore. There wasn't time to argue.

Dami supported me on one side, Poppy on the other. We made our way into the city.

As we neared the main road, the streets of Pearlfoam came alive with crowds waiting for the army to march by. Children ran and shrieked, waving streamers behind them. Women sold sweet dumplings and roasted nuts. Jugglers and dancers performed for amber chips.

"Turn left here," Poppy whispered. "Now straight."

We followed her directions, stepping out onto the main thoroughfare in front of the palace. Not three blocks away, the army filled up the entire breadth of the road, marching toward us. Banners whipped in the wind. Obsidian spears glittered in the sun.

Hundreds of armed men. Thousands of armed men. All headed east, to start the killing all over again.

Dami, Poppy, and I were like pebbles standing before a stream. But we had to turn this tide.

Or, I supposed, die trying.

"Umm, Plum?" Dami said. "I know I'm always telling you to put me in a position to punch things...but I can't punch that many things."

Drummers beat out a march tempo in a deep, relentless boom that reverberated in my lungs. Ranks of archers and spearmen marched forward, the tips of the weapons like a mobile forest.

Between all the fighting men, I glanced a handful of colorful, covered passenger carts. One of those would hold King Heron.

"Are you sure you want to stay?" I asked, one last time. Dami and Poppy both nodded grimly.

I exhaled and strode forward. I straightened my back. I schooled my face. I found myself walking in time to that drum. Smooth. Confident. As unintimidated as if I had my own army behind me. We neared the flag bearers.

"Move aside!" One of them shouted.

I planted my feet. I imagined roots stretching and twisting down into the ground. I imagined myself as tall as a redwood, piercing the sky. I imagined my voice to be as loud as a waterfall.

"I am Green-ranked Acting Ambassador Plum of Rowak! I am the betrothed consort of Purple-ranked King Alder of Rowak! And I demand to speak with First-ranked King Heron of Shoreed!"

The flagbearers' eyes widened. They fumbled. They took small, mincing steps as if doing so would allow them to keep walking forever without running into us. Eventually, they halted—staring at me. Was I a madwoman? Or had I come back from the dead?

I kept my chin parallel to the ground, my face cold and regal. I did not stare at them, I stared through them. Let them see an ambassador. Let them not dare shove me aside.

Poppy's hasty work and my expression were convincing enough. The flagbearer who had yelled at me sent one of his fellows as a messenger. On either side of the street, the crowd murmured and whispered, sounding like angry mosquitos.

The sun baked into my skin. My still-wet hair made the back of my neck humid and itchy. But I remained where I was. I didn't look around. I didn't flinch.

The flagbearer returned. "You are to come with me."

The ranks of the army parted for me, Dami, and Poppy—spearmen and archers, short men, tall men, lanky men, and men roped in muscles. They smelled of wood polish and leather and sweat.

Near the center of the army, next to an elegant passenger cart, someone had laid out a rug.

Guards ringed the place, each wearing an armband decorated with a pair of embroidered wings. I supposed these were the king's personal guards. The man himself stepped out of the cart.

He was older than King Alder. Maybe sixty, with gray all through his neatly-squared beard. His clothes flowed like water over his arms, covering all but his fingertips in shimmering emerald fabric. The belt at his waist was a handspan thick and densely beaded with amber that glowed like fire under the summer morning sun. A fortune. His leggings were a rich, dark brown, complementing the amber.

He looked every inch a king. I stepped onto the rug and bowed deeply. "King Heron. It is a pleasure to meet you. Or should I say to meet you again? I am told that you examined my corpse and proclaimed me dead."

I straightened. King Heron peered at me, examining every nook and cranny of my face. "Turn around."

I did so, slow and dignified. Behind me, Dami and Poppy stood formally next to each other, backs straight. Faces proud. I was terrified to have them here. And at the same time, seeing them filled me with fierce determination. I turned until I looked at King Heron again. "Are you satisfied?"

"No." He paused, his sharp eyes flickering over me. "Who officiated at your trial?"

"There was no trial."

He tilted his head to one side and then the other, as if changing his perspective would change the way I looked. "Who interrogated you?"

"Green-ranked Palaw, a former Master Chef of Rowak."

His mouth twitched. My answers unsettled him.

"You saw me yourself, and yet you doubt who I am?" I asked.

He shook his head. Did he think I had an identical twin?

"I have one last question for you." Still, he didn't call me Ambassador. "What did you see when you were dead?"

"Nothing. The dead can't see. At least not at first."

He swallowed hard. How did he know that was true? The sages taught no such thing. "You *are* come back from the dead."

"Yes. I am." By antidote, but it didn't make the statement any less true.

"Sit with me, Ambassador Plum."

I obeyed as gracefully as I could with my aching limbs. He sat in the river of the precious fabric he wore. I folded my hands in my lap and tried not to squeeze them together. I was calm, calm and still as a mountain lake. We kept our voices low—I doubted anyone but Dami, Poppy, and the nearest guards could hear us.

"Why did you come back?" he asked.

"I want to negotiate peace."

"Yet you tried to kill Red Lord Ospren." He stated it as a simple fact, not an accusation.

I waited two heartbeats before answering. I breathed. I tried to ignore the fact that my mouth had dried, turning my saliva into a thick slime. "Tell me, King Heron. Which is more likely? That the young ambassador before you came this far with nothing but a badly thought-out plan to kill her own brother-in-law? Or that Chef Palaw wanted to frame me to get his vengeance? You probably know that his daughter Violet secretly poisoned people in Rowak. I was responsible for her capture."

King Heron tilted his head to the side, looking thoughtful.

Now I needed to step carefully. I couldn't directly attack his daughter and make him defensive. "Is it not possible that Lady Oakash, overzealous in her affection for Lord Ospren, assigned blame too quickly?"

I sat silently, watching him think. Watching him tumble those words around in his mind, chew them, and swallow them.

Yes, my story made sense. But he still didn't trust me.

Time to press him. To see if I was right about him. "But I didn't come here to make accusations. I came to sue for peace. We can negotiate a prisoner exchange. We can negotiate an end to this war, even."

In that moment, he looked older. Sadder. Worn down by death. Concerned for his people.

I glanced about at his personal guards, drawing his eye to them as well. "I would rather not see any more soldiers die—Rowak or Shoreed. I've been given a second life. We can give these negotiations a second chance."

His shoulders relaxed. Yes, that's what he'd wanted to hear. "If death itself sent you back, who am I to argue?" There was a tinge of fear in those eyes. Fear that I wanted to betray him, that this was a trick. "I know the state of the embassy is poor. And your guards have been arrested."

"Yes. My men should be returned to me at once."

Bane. I'd see Bane again. I needed to apologize that he'd even spent one moment headed back toward those abominable camps.

"No," King Heron said.

I stilled.

"They're prisoners of war. They resisted my guards."

I paused. I needed a logical argument. "If you leave me unprotected, I'll be assassinated by those who favor this war. You won't have any peace."

"I'm glad we agree. You'll be my guest in the Coral Palace. My own men will see to your safety."

And watch my every move, no doubt. Surrounded by his army, I didn't have much leeway to negotiate.

But that army had stopped marching. Our countries were not headed back to war right now. Instead, we were opening peace negotiations. "I'll have my maids pack our things, then."

Implicitly, I was demanding to keep Dami and Poppy. King Heron looked at them for a long moment, then nodded. "Very well." He turned to one of his guards. "Send General Chert to me. We need to cancel the march. Then tell Anok to make arrangements for the Ambassador's lodgings in the Coral Palace."

The young man bowed and ran off.

"Dead and alive again," King Heron said softly, still peering at my face. Even now, he didn't know what to make of me.

An elaborately carved and lacquered sedan chair approached. None of the guards stopped it, but the bearers glistened with sweat. They'd been running. They lowered the chair and folded back the front of it.

A woman sat inside, with King Heron's aquiline nose and the poise of a fox. Her sleeves flowed down to her wrists and her skirt billowed so far over her feet I wasn't even sure where they were. Every inch of her dress was red—as red as blood, as red as her painted lips.

"Ah. Ambassador Plum. I don't believe you've met my daughter, Lady Oakash."

I stood and bowed. "I'm honored to make your acquaintance."

She didn't move from her seat. "I didn't think we would meet again."

I froze. That voice—that lilting, Shoreed accent. I tried not to show the panic jolting through me, but the ghost of a smile on her face told me I'd already betrayed myself.

Lady Oakash. She'd been that voice, that spirit. I'd confided my fears and hopes to my one true enemy.

She turned to King Heron. "You can't honestly consider opening the negotiations after what happened."

"She was dead and lives. I can only believe that it was for a purpose," King Heron replied. "We'll discuss it at the palace."

She pursed those scarlet lips but nodded. Lady Oakash was apparently too cautious to throw a tantrum when her king had already spoken. Her eyes were as cold and pitiless as the obsidian spearheads all around us. "I look forward to spending more time with you, Acting Ambassador Plum."

Despite her polite tone, her eyes promised to destroy me. She gestured for her porters to lift her up. Then she directed them to pass right by me. She leaned outward, close enough to set a hand on my shoulder, and whispered too soft for anyone else to hear, "The next time you are dead, I will take precautions to ensure that you stay that way."

She closed the front of her sedan chair, and her porters took her away.

"Shall I send for a chair for you as well, or would you rather walk?" King Heron asked.

Lt. Kabrok would tell me to ride—a wooden box gave some protection from arrows. "A sedan chair, please."

CHAPTER
THIRTY-TWO

The Coral Palace was not much like the Redwood Palace. Instead of dozens of freestanding buildings half-hidden by gardens, a few broad lawns spread between six huge, two-story sprawling edifices. The broad pillars that supported the porch roof were painted white and pale green, like seafoam. The carved eaves depicted waves and shells. And inside, instead of fabric-backed lattices, the doors were all solid wood.

We were given a set of rooms on the first floor of one of those buildings. They were lovely and well-furnished—easily big enough for fifteen people to live in. The large sitting room felt hollow with just me standing in it.

So long as King Heron wanted peace, I should be safe here, shouldn't I?

The door burst open. Poppy and Dami rushed in and dropped the bags they were carrying, then smothered me in hugs.

"You did it!" Dami beamed. "You're not dead!"

I exhaled. I'd lost all my soldiers. I'd lost Bane. I'd even lost my life for nearly three days. I'd lost my autonomous housing. But Dami was right. We'd finally reached King Heron. We had a chance for peace.

And we had formidable opponents in Lady Oakash and Chef Palaw.

"Thank you for staying." Those four words weren't enough, but I think they both understood we needed a team to succeed here. Even if our team was drastically smaller than we'd all planned on.

"Now that we've seen you, I've got to go find the Matron of the Household and negotiate some things," Poppy said. "I should be the one washing our clothes. And if you have time, you should cook our food to protect against poisoning. I want to make us as independent as I possibly can and give everyone else as little chance as possible to stab us in the back."

Poppy was brilliant at what she did. "Do whatever you see fit."

"Thank you." She bowed and hurried out.

Dami plopped ungraciously onto a cushion. "For someone who got peace negotiations open, you don't look as happy as you should. We'll get Bane back. Promise."

Bane, Lt. Kabrok, his men, all the captured sons of Rowak in that prisoner camp. I swallowed hard. Was Bane surviving? How could he cope, going back to that place? "I hope we do."

"How hard can negotiating a treaty be?" Dami asked.

"You can't *punch* a treaty into existence."

"Oh. Right."

I sat next to her. "Lady Oakash is against us. And all the Bloodmarrows."

"I could punch *her*."

Pummel the king's beloved daughter? No, that wouldn't help at all. "Lady Sulat told me once that knowledge is a powerful weapon. And Lady Oakash? She knows everything about me."

"Calm down. You just met her today." Dami picked at the fringe on the rug. I resisted the urge to chide her for it.

I breathed in all the scents of this place—ocean salt and cloth and thick wooden walls. "Lady Oakash was there. When I died."

"She's some kind of ghost?"

"I'm not sure."

Dami raised an eyebrow. "You didn't know who she was, so you sat down and told her all your secrets?"

That made me sound like a fool. "I thought she was some kind of guide to the Realm of the Ancestors."

"Again: why did that make you think it was a good idea to tell her all about yourself?"

"I wanted advice." Now I was fiddling with my sleeves.

Dami raised her other eyebrow, making a confused triangle on her forehead.

"About you. I...I wanted to be like real sisters again."

"Real—?" she peered at me. "Did you come back to life with half a brain? Of course you're my sister."

I paused. Was this just another conversation that would lead to fighting? I wished we had some sweet salmonberry tea. I was so tired of fighting. "Do you remember when we were little? When we actually acted like we loved each other?"

I left unspoken the rest—before she abandoned her family. Before she abandoned *me*. Before she left me to cover her mistakes. Before I almost died for her. Before she shrugged off my near-fatality with persistent indifference.

"Yeah. You should work on that whole loving thing."

"What?" That's not what I meant at all. I'd never stopped loving her.

Dami rolled her eyes. "You're always lecturing me. Always telling me what I should and shouldn't do. Should and shouldn't feel guilty for. Yeah. You're a horrible sister. Get over it. I already have."

For a moment, I almost blurted out everything she'd done to me. All the ways she'd hurt me. Instead, I asked a question. "Do you hate me?"

"Of course not! How many times do I have to tell you that?" Dami shook her head. "When have I ever told you what to do? I mean, I do think you're a bit of an idiot sometimes. I don't think you're actually choosing what you *want* to do. But I've never stopped you from doing it. I've always let you be free."

Her words percolated through me. I *wanted* Dami to worry and fret over me. I *wanted* her to apologize for the pain she'd caused me because if I were her, that's what I'd do. That's how I loved people.

Dami never told me what to do because that's how she loved people. She craved freedom, so she gave others freedom. It just also happened to look a lot like apathy.

"We're not very well-matched as sisters, are we?"

"Yeah. Well, I wouldn't get to be all sulky if someone wasn't trying to drag me around for my own good." She gestured vaguely at the room. "Who knows. Maybe this whole duty and responsibility stint will be fun. I liked the army, and it was full of that."

"Are you sure you want to stay? You could still leave."

A real smile blossomed over her face. "I'm staying. But thanks for asking."

I leaned back on my hands. "A soldier, a chef, and a maid. Up against all of Shoreed."

"All of Shoreed and the weird, undead daughter of a king. Don't forget her."

No, I wasn't about to forget Lady Oakash. "This isn't going to be easy."

"It wouldn't be fun if it were easy." Dami laughed and punched me in the shoulder. That'd leave a bruise.

"Well, then," I said. "Let's see what we can do."

ACKNOWLEDGMENTS

It is a delight to be able to release another Plum book. It would not have been possible without the help of many fantastic readers. Thank you Matt Brown, Ailsa Lillywhite, Carolyn Duede, John Hutchins, and Michelle Cowart. You are all amazing.

Once again, I've had a great team at Immortal Works. Beth Buck, thank you for pushing me to write it better. Natalie Brianne, this manuscript is so much cleaner thanks to your sharp eye. Holli Anderson, Staci Olsen, Ashley Literski, Rachel Huffmire, everyone—thank you for your work on this series.

I'm also grateful for a supportive family who value my writing time simply because it brings me joy. Extra thanks is due to my husband for also listening to me ramble over book problems until the answers appeared. Love you.

ABOUT THE AUTHOR

 M.K. Hutchins regularly draws on her background in archaeology when writing fiction. She's the author of the YA fantasy novels *The Redwood Palace* and *Drift*, which was a Junior Library Guild Selection and a VOYA Topshelf honoree. She's written over thirty short stories, appearing in Analog, Podcastle, Strange Horizons, and elsewhere. A long-time Idahoan, she now lives in Utah with her husband and four children, where they endeavor to grow bushels of delicious food, play heaps of board games, and read mountains of books. Find her at www.mkhutchins.com.

This has been an
Immortal Production